Praise for Raven Hart's
Savannah Vampire series

"Raven Hart's *The Vampire's Seduction* and its sequel, *The Vampire's Secret,* held me captive from the very first page! I love the world she's created and the incredible characters who live there. I can't wait for the next installment!"

—ALEXIS MORGAN,
author of the Paladins of Darkness series

"Suspenseful . . . Sexy . . . This foray into fangoria is atmospheric and occasionally funny."

—*Publishers Weekly*

"An excellent treat . . . An excellent read!"

—Fresh Fiction

"An exotic, exciting thriller."

—Futures MYSTERY Anthology Magazine

"One can almost feel the heat rising from the pages . . . A stimulating read."

—Curled Up with a Good Book

"Dark, seductive, disturbingly erotic, Raven Hart drives a stake in this masterful tale."

—L. A. BANKS,
author of the Vampire Huntress Legend series

Also by Raven Hart

THE VAMPIRE'S SEDUCTION
THE VAMPIRE'S SECRET
THE VAMPIRE'S KISS

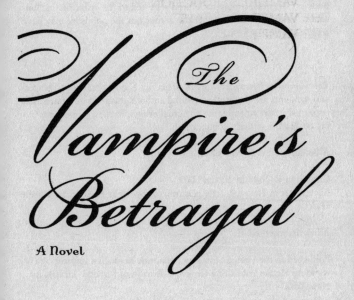

The Vampire's Betrayal

A Novel

RAVEN HART

BALLANTINE BOOKS • NEW YORK

The Vampire's Betrayal is a work of fiction. Names, characters, places, and incidents are the products of the author's imagination or are used fictitiously. Any resemblance to actual events, locales, or persons, living or dead, is entirely coincidental.

A Ballantine Books Mass Market Original

Published in the United States by Ballantine Books, an imprint of The Random House Publishing Group, a division of Random House, Inc., New York.

BALLANTINE and colophon are registered trademarks of Random House, Inc.

This book contains an excerpt from Raven Hart's forthcoming novel. This excerpt has been set for this edition only and may not reflect the final content of the forthcoming edition.

ISBN 978-0-345-49857-3

Cover illustration: Kathleen Lynch based on photographs © Oleksiy Maksymenko/Alamy (canal) and © Superstock (woman)

Printed in the United States of America

www.ballantinebooks.com

OPM   9 8 7 6 5 4 3 2 1

I dedicate this book to everyone in Georgia Romance Writers. Thank you all for your advice, support, and friendship.

Letter from Jack, a Vampire

My name is Jack McShane, and I am a vampire in a world of hurt. First, I hear that the love of my life, a lady cop named Connie Jones, is a vampire slayer. And if that's not enough of a kick in the fangs, next I find out that she's talked a voodoo queen into opening the door to the underworld so she can dole out some vigilante justice to the ex-husband from hell. Or rather, the ex-husband *in* hell.

Now, you might think that a person in hell was suffering enough. But that's not the way Connie sees it. She's out to personally kick his ass. Sounds like overkill to me, if you'll pardon the expression, but whatever cranks your tractor.

Problem is, once you get to the underworld, whether you belong there or not, it's a little bit tricky to get yourself back out. Vampires like me can travel to there, but since we did a U-turn out the first time around, our cosmic get-out-of-hell-free ticket's already been punched. If the man in charge down there catches me, he might just decide to keep me forever.

See, my sire, William, once voluntarily went to hell to save somebody he loved, and he almost didn't make it back. Now I've gone and done the same thing, and it seems like I might be stuck down here. I aim to bring Connie back if it's the last thing I do. But I don't know whether I'll be able to find my way home again like William did. He has a lot more experience dealing with hellish dilemmas than I do.

My friend Melaphia—that's the voodoo queen—says that if I don't let Connie go, my Latin lovely will slay me someday. There will be no escape for me. All I can say is: if my destiny on this earth is to be staked by a vampire slayer named Connie Jones, so be it.

For now, all I'm going to think about is getting my woman and flying out of here like a vampire bat out of hell. As far as the Slayer business is concerned, I'll think about that tomorrow, as Scarlett O'Hara used to say.

One problem at a time.

Letter from William, a Vampire

I, William Cuyler Thorne, am already dead, a blood drinker for some five hundred years. I have suffered losses that would make most mortals beg for death. They say that whatever doesn't kill you makes you stronger, but I will not be blessed with more strength. My strength arose from an infernal source, not from the supreme being who gives both suffering and salvation to the living. I am a vampire. I'm on my own.

My comfortable world, carefully built over many human lifetimes, is falling apart like the proverbial house of straw. My loved ones are in the deepest peril. In order to save the child of my heart, Melaphia's daughter, I was forced to slay one of my own. I had made my offspring Eleanor for myself, thinking that she would be my loving mate through all eternity. To kill her felt as if I'd had my soul ripped from me all over again.

I loved her. Contrary to popular belief, vampires can love. Passionately. I hungered for her, and her absence cuts me like cold steel. The whisper of her final breath as I drained the last of her blood will haunt me until I am returned to dust.

Now my first offspring, Jack—more a son to me than the male child of my own flesh—is in mortal danger. As I did, he has gone to save the woman he loves—a woman whose very nature is poison to him, and to me as well.

If I have to, I will descend into hell to get him back. Only the devil knows if either of us can return.

Even if we do make it back to our Savannah home, our problems will have only just begun. For powers vastly greater than those wielded by my little Savannah family are bearing down on us like hellhounds unleashed by Satan himself.

One

William

I stood in the basement vault of my home and stared at the lifeless bodies of Jack McShane and Connie Jones. They were lying peacefully. Little altars surrounded them, bearing flickering candles and strewn with fragrant herbs.

Melaphia, the foremost voodoo *mambo* in this hemisphere and my adopted daughter, teetered on the brink of madness. The confusion in her eyes made me want to take her in my arms and comfort her, but first I had to find out what had happened to Jack and his lady friend. Jack still had his corporeal form, so he might not be truly lost, and Connie had the blush of life on her cheeks. Whatever was wrong, it might not be too late for them, but I knew I must act quickly.

I had just arrived home with Melaphia's nine-year-old daughter, Renee, after rescuing her from kidnappers. When Renee was stolen Melaphia had gone catatonic. I had hoped that the child's return would restore Melaphia's sanity, but I could see now that I'd been foolish in thinking it would be that simple. Whatever had happened in this room only served to further traumatize her. The only thing she'd said since we'd reached the vault was *Everything is fine. I have much to tell you.* Clearly, whatever she had to tell me, everything was not fine.

"What has happened here?" I asked, willing the panic from my voice. "Tell me all of it. Focus, my dear. You must, for Jack's sake."

Melaphia licked her lips and squinted at me. "She wanted to see her son."

I glanced at Connie, who was dressed in a flowing white gown. "Connie has a son? Where is he?"

"Dead," Melaphia whispered.

My heart sank. "The underworld?"

"Yes."

My mind raced ahead of Melaphia's explanation, and I didn't like where it was going. I knew Jack had discovered that Connie possessed some extrahuman powers and Melaphia had been helping to investigate the specifics. No matter what Connie turned out to be, I found it hard to believe she could have crossed over from the world of the living to the world of the dead by herself.

Melaphia, on the other hand . . . She was a voodoo practitioner of the highest order, and the ways of the dead and the land they inhabited was her birthright.

"Melaphia, did you help Connie cross over?" I put my hands gently on her shoulders and turned her to face me when she tried to turn away. She met my gaze again and nodded. "Why?" I demanded.

"Because I know what it is like to lose a child," she said. "My baby was gone. I would have done anything to be at Renee's side, even if she'd been in hell. Connie begged me, William."

There was more she wasn't telling me. Much more. "You have to tell me everything."

"Uncle Jack . . ." Melaphia said, kneeling to touch his alabaster cheek. He was as still as a statue. Indeed, the pallor of his skin and his exquisite masculine bone structure made him look as if he had been rendered in marble by some master sculptor. The only thing that looked lifelike about him now was the blue-black sheen of his wavy hair.

I felt as if my emotions were being whipped this way and that by an epic storm. No sooner had I gotten Renee to safety than I'd discovered Jack, my first-born and best-loved offspring, in this gruesome tableau à la the ending of Romeo and Juliet. It grieved me to see this powerful bear of a man so helpless.

Jack had remained more in touch with his own humanity than any other blood drinker I had ever known. He moved in and out of the human world effortlessly and maintained a bevy of human friendships. He had risked his immortal well-being for his mortal friends more than once.

Hanging on to his erstwhile humanity was a trait I had unconsciously encouraged, never objecting to his relationships beyond a casual warning to be careful. Not that I could have stopped him from doing as he damned well pleased anyway. I couldn't help but think that my inattention to his dalliances with humans might now have contributed to his destruction.

"Help me," I said. "Help me to help Jack. We have to get him back before he wanders too far for us to reach."

Melaphia straightened up and appeared to be making an earnest effort to focus her attention on me. "Yes. We have to get him back. But not her. She must stay."

Jack

Damn, it was dark. And worse, I didn't sense Connie anywhere. While I waited for my super-duper vamp vision to adjust to the unnatural blackness, I breathed in deeply, hoping to catch the scent she always wore. She smelled like lilacs. My sense of smell, as sharp as my vision, didn't pick up anything as sweet as flowers. Instead, it smelled like . . . hell. The stench of decay, and nastiness I couldn't even identify, made my nose twitch.

I tried to remind myself that there were good places to be in this land of the dead as well. *Heaven,* if you want to put it like that. I remember William telling me about helping Shari—a poor girl who wanted to be a vampire but didn't make it—into one of those better places. That's where Connie was headed. She wanted to see that her little boy was fine. That his soul was at peace, you might say. How in the world would she find her way? And how was I going to find her so I could make sure she got back home?

It occurred to me that I should have thought of these questions before I'd gone off half-cocked and used voodoo to get myself into this pit. These souls in eternal torment produced noises that ranged from piteous whining to ferocious snarling. It was enough to make my hair stand on end. There's not much that scares a vampire. I'm pretty much the scariest dude you could ever run across topside. Hey, if it's true it ain't bragging, as they say. But I had a feeling that here there was a whole slew of creatures that could kick my behind.

My eyes were as accustomed to this infernal darkness as they were going to get, but I could still only make out shapes. The slithering, scaly, slimy sliding sounds of ghoulies in motion made me almost glad I couldn't see. If I was scared and grossed out, how must Connie feel? My first instinct was to call out for her, but I hesitated because I didn't think many of the denizens of this dark place had noticed me yet, so they might not have noticed her either. If I started yelling, they might figure out that we were both down here.

But what if something else found her first? Connie is a tough lady. That's one of the zillion or so things that makes her so awesome, but for all her experience catching bad guys, nothing in her background would help her with what she now faced.

As I stood and wondered which way to go and what to do, it struck me how great things had been just a few hours ago. Connie and I had just had sex for the first time. The earthmoving, toe-curling, eyes-rolling-back-in-your-head variety of sex as a matter of fact. And I was as close as a bloodsucker can come to cloud nine. Then I'd realized that the lovemaking was Connie's way of saying good-bye. By the time I figured out what she'd done and where she'd gone, it was almost too late to follow.

Oh, hell. If I was going to find Connie before she got too far away from me in this darkness there was no way around making enough noise to let her know where I was—and wake the dead at the same time, no doubt. "Connie," I called. Immediately I sensed that I had the full attention of the other citizens of the underworld. They thought I was calling *them*. To *me*.

Oh. My. God.

I suddenly remembered my little gift, as William liked to call it. I was so focused on getting to Connie I'd forgotten the effect I have on dead people. Dead people other than myself, that is. Ghosts, zombies, and everything in between. It's like they're attracted to me. Hell, they love me. Jack McShane, corpse whisperer.

Savannah's full of dead people, and not just in the cemeteries. The city's history is full of wars, piracy, great fires, epidemics, you name it. In battle, people were buried where they fell. In the fires and yellow fever epidemics, their bodies were burned and their ashes scattered to the four winds. Brigands and cutthroats robbed and killed men unlucky enough to cross their paths and the bodies were stashed in the tunnels under the city and in hidey holes along the riverbanks.

Those spirits reach out to me as I go about my business by night. They reach out for solace, for confession, for someone to talk to. This doesn't happen to other vampires, and I don't know why it happens to me. What can I say? I'm a popular guy.

Now the dead were coming toward me from all sides. Something bony grasped my shoulder, and I shook it off. Something wispy and filthy-smelling brushed my hip, and I stepped away. I was being surrounded, and I wasn't going to hang around to see what they would do to me when they got me completely hemmed in. I sensed that this bunch wanted more than conversation.

Since I couldn't locate Connie anywhere around, I did what any sensible guy would do. I ran.

I ran blindly, bouncing off demons so fast I felt like I was a ball bearing in the devil's pinball machine. Once in a while, something howled in pain and rage or something else made a grab for some part of me, but I kept going. Right until a solid form landed on my back and rode me to the ground like it was fixin' to calf-rope me.

Whatever it was had a familiar scent. A good scent, but not Connie's. This was someone freshly dead. I decided it was lavender I smelled. The thing eased up on me just enough to flip me over to face her.

"Eleanor?" I gasped. "What in hell are you doing . . . in hell?" In response, she hauled off and punched me on the chin with every bit of her vampiric strength. The last thing I remember thinking was that old saying about how there's nothing like a woman scorned.

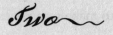

Two

William

"What are you talking about?" I tried to keep the emotion from my voice. "Why must Connie stay in the underworld?"

"She has unfinished business. A few years ago her ex-husband murdered their child in front of her and then turned the gun on himself."

In my bloodthirsty days as a fledgling vampire, I visited enough cruelty on humanity to burn in hell for a thousand lifetimes. But as hardened as I was to mortal suffering it still filled me with horror to think of what Connie had gone through.

Melaphia continued, "When Connie realized at Sullivan's funeral that Jack can communicate with the dead, she wanted him to help her—but not just to serve as a medium like he did for Iban."

"She wanted Jack to take her to see her dead child?"

"Yes. She demanded that he take her to the underworld. Not only to make sure that her child was in a good place, but to make sure her ex-husband was in a bad place."

The more she talked, the more lucid Melaphia sounded, but I had no time to appreciate it. "But he didn't agree to it," I said, remembering Mel's earlier admission of culpability. "Tell me what happened."

"He refused her. That's when she came to me. By that time, I had performed some rituals to try to figure out what she is and what she was put here to do. I told her about the first revelation, that she is a goddess of the Maya."

"The *first* revelation?" Something tingled along my spine.

"For the rest I had to consult the most sacred of texts. It took me weeks, but I finally connected the dots. William, Connie is the vampire slayer who was prophesied by both my people and the Maya thousands of years ago. When two or more different cultures as mighty as these have the same prophecy, that which is prophesied is a virtual certainty."

"How can you be sure it's Connie?" My mind raced with the implications.

"There's too much to go into right now. But the clincher was the birthmark. Connie has a sun birthmark that matches the ancient drawings exactly. I've seen it with my own eyes."

I thought back to the conversation I overheard between Diana and Ulrich. *For all we know, the Slayer may already be among us.* Even the dark lords didn't know for sure. But Melaphia did. "I take it you didn't tell her that she's the Slayer."

"Of course not. She doesn't even know what a

slayer is, as far as I know. But she's bound to discover it at some point. That's why I agreed to help her reach the underworld, and that's why she has to stay there. Her kind are sworn to kill you and Jack. I hate for her to be trapped in that place, but I had to protect my fathers. I never meant for Jack to follow her. He wasn't even supposed to find out where she'd gone. But he found us just as I'd finished the ritual and Connie crossed over."

"How did he manage to follow her? Jack doesn't know how to cross that boundary by himself."

"He didn't do it himself. He called on Loa Legba." Melaphia broke down in sobs. She obviously blamed herself for teaching Jack enough about voodoo to summon the god to whom Maman Lalee had assigned him. "I taught him just enough to be dangerous," Melaphia said.

Maman Lalee was a voodoo queen so powerful that she could hasten the souls of the dead on the way to the underworld. She had been my ally from the time I'd first arrived on these shores, and Melaphia was her descendant. When it became clear that the peaceable New World vampires were headed for battle with the most evil of ancient blood drinkers, Melaphia had agreed that we should increase our powers by appealing to the gods of her religion. Channeling Lalee, Melaphia had directed each of my family to pray to a specific god or goddess of the voodoo pantheon. Jack, with his gift of communication with other dead beings, was assigned to appeal to Loa Legba, the god of the portal to the underworld, among other things.

I put my arms around Melaphia and comforted her

as I had when she was a child. "That's our Jack," I said. "As resourceful as always, and just as pig-headed." And as brave, I thought. Like the mythic Orpheus, he had gone to rescue his Eurydice.

"The portal opened for him," Melaphia said and sobbed. "And then he was gone." She looked up at me with pleading eyes and called me by the title she hadn't used since she was a child. "What are we going to do, Father? How are we going to get him back?"

"I'll go get him myself. I went to the underworld and made it back safely once. I can do it again." I tried to imbue my voice with more confidence than I felt, but Melaphia's look of horror let me know that I wasn't convincing.

"No! What if you both got stuck there? Who would protect Renee and me and all the other people who depend on you?"

As much as I hated to admit it, I knew that she was right: Jack and I both being trapped in another dimension was a strong possibility. Even if Melaphia was able to manifest Lalee, they might not be powerful enough to release us both from the grip of the underworld.

"You're right," I said, "I wasn't thinking."

Melaphia released a pent-up breath, but the furrow of worry still creased her forehead. "Do you think that if all of us who practice the religion were to come together to entreat Loa Legba, he would send Jack back to us? We don't have Jack's bond to him, but maybe he would hear us if we banded together."

"It's worth a try. My only worry is that opening the

portal would allow other entities through to our world."

"Bad entities, you mean?"

"Yes. But it's the best idea we have. As a precaution, why don't you consult your sacred books to see if you can find any information on how to banish the unwanted back to the underworld? I'll go and find Werm."

"Can't you summon him through your bond between sire and offspring?"

"Unfortunately, Jack has cleverly taught Werm how to block my thoughts," I explained with slight bemusement. "That young man must enjoy his privacy because I haven't been able to reach his mind since shortly after I made him . . . unless he expressly wished it."

Melaphia stepped back and smoothed her hair, done up in the style she called dreadlocks. I could see that she was gathering her mental strength for the work ahead. I was glad to see her acting more like herself. I just hoped it lasted. I needed her knowledge and power as never before.

"Werm has his own business now," she said. "It's a bar. A goth bar." Melaphia told me the address and I turned to leave.

"I'm sorry," she said.

I turned to face her. "For what?"

"For letting this happen."

"Don't blame yourself. Even if I had been here, I don't believe I could have stopped Jack from following Connie."

As I went back out into the night, I thought about the way the events of the last few weeks had spiraled out of control faster than I could repair them. For the first time in ten human lifetimes I was beginning to fear for my humans and my kind.

As for myself and my own safety, I cared no more than I ever had. Especially now that I had lost my Eleanor forever. Whatever essence of her might be left in some far-off dimension, I wished her as much peace as could be had there.

Jack

When I came to, Eleanor had her hands clamped around my throat, squeezing for dear life. When you've been a vampire only a short time, you forget what it takes to hurt one of your own kind. If she meant to kill me, this wouldn't do the trick.

I brought my forearms upward and broke her hold on my neck. "Seriously," I rasped. "What are you doing here, and why are you trying to choke me? Aren't you supposed to be in England?"

In the dimness I saw a fiendish glow in her dark eyes that had never been there before. This thing hovering over me might look like her, but it wasn't the Eleanor I knew.

"Do I look like I'm in England?" She drew back a fist to hit me again, but I rolled off to the side and scrambled to my feet. The other creatures had drawn back, as if they were giving this one a wide berth. "William destroyed me," she hissed.

She crouched and circled me like a lady wrestler waiting to pounce on her opponent. She was naked and I saw to my revulsion that her formerly beautiful skin had turned scaly. It was like she was morphing into a snake to match the tattoo on her torso.

As I looked her up and down she followed the direction of my gaze. "How do you like what's happening to me?" she asked. She touched her belly lightly with her hand as if she could hardly stand the texture of her own skin. "It's Satan's little prank. The girl turns into her own tattoo."

"I can't believe William destroyed you. He was crazy about you. He made you for himself."

"Like God made Eve for Adam," she said bitterly. "What *I* can't believe is that I *sold my soul* for that bastard." She lunged, connecting with my midsection and sending me sprawling back. She was on top of me again before I could get on my feet. I put my hands against her shoulders and pushed her, and she landed on her still-shapely bottom a few feet away.

"I take it he staked you for double-crossing him and helping to kidnap Renee."

She lunged again, and I sidestepped her. "He drank my blood. All of it."

"Is—is this what happens when a vampire gets killed, um, again, I mean?"

"Yeah, Jack. This is what's in store for you. Take a good look at me."

It's not easy for anybody to face down their own mortality, especially vampires, since we're extra hard to kill. But there's a trade-off for potentially eternal life. If somebody does manage to kill you, it's go directly to hell. Do not pass go. Do not collect two hundred dollars. So we vampires don't talk much about death unless we've been gravely threatened, no pun intended.

"As vampires we've lost our souls to begin with," Eleanor spat. "When we are destroyed for the final time, we're considered to be the most doomed of the damned."

"What about Shari? She didn't turn into—whatever it is that you are."

"She never made it to being a vampire, thanks to you and whatever curse to women is on you."

Her words stung. My failure to make Shari a vampire had doomed her to this demonic realm until William—with Lalee's help—had sent her on her way to a better place. "So you're the worst of the damned. Is that why all these other . . . things . . . are afraid of you?"

"Yeah. And it's why you should be, too. I'm a *real* demon now."

She flew at me like she had wings. I ducked and struck upward with both fists, catching her in the stomach and causing her to somersault into the gathering crowd of ghouls behind me. Collectively, they didn't seem as afraid of her. They grasped her with bony, clawed fingers and raked at her flesh.

While they were all distracted, I took off running again, Eleanor's screams echoing behind me. I began to feel a little better as I opened the distance between me and the demons. Then, very quickly, I felt worse. The darkness was giving way to a thick mist. I still couldn't see where I was going, but now I sensed an oppressiveness that hadn't been there before. I started to feel like I was a deep-sea diver without a pressure suit. My surroundings were squeezing out what life there was in me. I dropped to my knees and my body started to cramp like an athlete whose muscles have run out of oxygen.

There was a reason those demons hadn't followed me in this direction. It wasn't safe for them here.

Not safe for *us*, that is.

Three

William

I entered Werm's drinking establishment in the wee hours of the morning, as he and his employees were preparing to close for the night. I was surprised to see that his staff consisted almost solely of Eleanor's prostitutes, or perhaps I should say former prostitutes, since they now all seemed to be cocktail waitresses. But I was even more surprised to see my old friend Seth Walker washing glasses behind the bar.

The young ladies greeted me warmly and inquired after their former madam. Out of necessity, none of them had been told why Eleanor had left town. In fact, before my own departure to rescue Renee, I had lied and told them that she had gone on a European vacation. My evil sire, Reedrek, had just burned down the residence of Eleanor and her "ladies" in Savannah, which doubled as their place of business, so it was only natural that she would want to get away for a while. I'd put Jack in charge of the young whores, who'd lost not only their homes but their livelihoods. It was clever of him to have found them legitimate work. Except for a few misunderstandings, Jack never let me down.

As I was preparing for my journey, I noticed that Ginger had now assumed a leadership position. She stepped forward and asked, "Where is Eleanor? You brought her back with you, didn't you?"

A fresh pang of anguish made me wince. I'd known the moment was coming in which I must tell them their mentor wasn't returning. But now was not that time. "She stayed behind," I said. "I'll tell you more about it later."

Werm came over to greet me and dismissed the girls for the night. I was thankful when they said their good-byes and departed.

"William! Did you get Renee back?" Werm asked excitedly.

"Yes," I said, and submitted to an eager hug from the fledgling vampire.

"Thank goodness. Melaphia must feel like a new woman. Hey, how do you like my place?" He made a grand, sweeping gesture with his hand—as grand as one of his stature could, I supposed. Werm was a slightly built youngster of twenty or so years with hair dyed black in classic goth style. His pale flesh was so riddled with piercings that he jingled when he walked, and he always decked himself out in black leather from head to toe.

Werm was the only human in recent memory to discover that vampires were real. He had pestered Jack to make him a blood drinker, but Jack refused. Then Reedrek came to town and forced me to do the job, despite the fact that Werm seemed a miserable candidate. Recently Jack had come to the conclusion that Werm might become a respectable vampire after all. I was still reserving judgment.

I looked around at the gaudy wallpaper, tacky color scheme, and other unusual aspects of the decor. "It's very distinctive," I told him. "I congratulate you."

By that time, Seth had come over to shake hands. "It's good to see you," he said. "It's been a while."

"Indeed it has. I trust things are well in your . . . community." Seth came into town on vacation at least once a year for hunting—and drinking—excursions with Jack. Other than that, he came on business. Either law enforcement business—he was the police chief of a small town in north Georgia—or werewolf business. Seth was also a werewolf.

Seth and I had similar philosophies about our species, and we helped each other to keep them in force. I felt that vampires should keep our problems within our own ranks. Seth felt the same about were-wolf business. Jack and I kept the vampires in these parts under control, dealing out vigilante justice to those blood drinkers who would bring trouble to our community. *Trouble* being any kind of criminal mis-behavior that might attract the attention of the human world, particularly law enforcement. Seth performed the same function among the shape shifter population.

"Things are fine now," he said. "We had a little trouble on the furry side of town while you were gone, but Jack—and Werm here—helped me handle it." He clapped Werm on the back, causing the little fellow to wince, but with a grin. "I still have some local pack business to take care of, so I'm in town for a while longer. My assistant chief is handling things back home while I'm gone, and he's an experienced guy, so I'm in no hurry to get back. I thought I'd help Werm with the bartending while I'm not knocking heads together down at pack headquarters."

I was glad that Seth was in Savannah. Not that he could do anything to help rescue Jack, but having allies close by never hurt. Besides that, I felt Werm needed all the positive male role models he could get. Seth was a big man—as tall as I and as darkly handsome and burly as Jack. He moved as easily in Savannah society as he did roaming the territory of his own kind in wolf form.

"Hey, William, where is Jack? I haven't seen him all night, and the last time I talked to him he said he was coming by. They haven't seen him at the garage either."

I'd forgotten all about Jack's garage, the all-night auto repair business he owned. I'd have to call his partner Rennie and make up some excuse for Jack's absence. "That's why I came. Jack's in trouble. Werm, I need you to work with Melaphia and me to help him."

Seth looked concerned. He and Jack had gotten along famously since the first time Seth had come to town years ago to assist us with some shape shifter trouble. I would go so far as to call them kindred spirits.

"Is there anything I can do?" Seth asked.

I shook my head and explained briefly where Jack was, why he had gone there, and the plan to get him back. As a fledgling, Werm had no knowledge of the underworld. His eyes became wide and frightened when I described my recent foray there and the dangers Jack faced.

"Wait here," Werm said. "I'm going to the cellar and get the sacrificial stuff I use when I do my own voodoo rituals."

"Hurry," I called after him. "It's almost daylight." Werm waved his understanding over his shoulder and scurried toward the cellar door.

"Oh my God," Seth said gravely. "Him and Connie both. I don't know any voodoo, so I can't help you with the religious stuff. Are you sure there isn't anything else I can do?"

"I don't believe so. Perhaps you can run this place for Werm tomorrow night if he's still working with us by that time. Meanwhile, if I can think of anything else you can help with, I'll send for you."

Seth nodded and ran a hand through his short dark hair. "I was afraid something like this was going to happen."

"What do you mean?"

"I'm the one who told Jack about Connie's past. The murder-suicide she witnessed. I imagine he confronted her about it."

"How did you know?"

"Connie and I dated when she lived in Atlanta," Seth admitted.

Something told me I had missed much more than werewolf trouble while I was away. With Jack's intense feelings for Connie, I was loathe to think of his reaction when he found out one of his best friends had dated her. Jack is rather emotional, in a southern male way. For example, any mention of a late motor sportsman—

Dale Earnhardt, I believe was his name—could make Jack stop whatever he was doing for a moment of silent reflection.

"It doesn't matter," I explained. "Connie evidently demanded that he lead her to the underworld to see her son. When he refused, she took her case to Melaphia. That still would have happened whether you gave him advance warning or not."

"I guess you're right," Seth muttered, and looked at the floor.

"Is there something else?"

"Yes. But I'm not sure it's related to this thing with Jack and Connie in the underworld."

"What is it?"

"It's only a feeling, really. I'm sensing that something is on its way. An event of some kind. Damn, this is hard to explain. It's a shape shifter thing, you know?"

"Yes, I think so."

Shape shifters have their own unique gifts, including the ability to draw on collective animal memories and instincts. Any feeling of unease on the part of a shape shifter should always be taken seriously. Especially if it was felt by more than one. I made a mental note to consult some of the other shape shifters of my acquaintance, that is, when the current trouble was behind me. "This event that you anticipate—I take it that danger is involved?"

"Yes. Definitely."

"To us or to the human population?"

"Both."

"It sounds serious. When we have this crisis with Jack under control, perhaps Melaphia with her magic can help us explore this further. Until then, continue to keep your consciousness open to any intuitions of approaching trouble you may have. We'll talk about it again as soon as possible."

Seth nodded. Werm appeared with a plastic bag stamped WAL-MART. ALWAYS LOW PRICES. ALWAYS. This was the store Jack favored because it was open by night.

"I'm ready," Werm said. "I've got the special herbs."

"I'll bet you have," Seth said, narrowing his gold-green eyes. It was Seth the law enforcement officer speaking, not Seth the werewolf.

Werm shrugged. "For sacrificial purposes only," he said, following me out the door. As we climbed into my vehicle, Werm said, "I want to own a Jag some-day."

"You're a man of taste," I said, noticing the new piercing in his lower lip. "Good luck with that acquisition."

Werm must have detected a note of sarcasm in my voice. "I'll have the money someday, you'll see. I think the bar is going to be very successful. I'm positioning it in the marketplace very carefully."

"Do tell."

"I see it as a hangout for the goth crowd, of course, but not just them. I think it could become a meeting place for people like us, nonhumans of all kinds."

"That could be a volatile mixture," I warned. "Jack has explained to you, has he not, that vampires don't always mix well with shape shifters and other nonhuman entities?"

"But Jack's got lots of shifter friends," Werm insisted. "Like Seth and Jerry."

"Those friendships are the exception. Jack makes friends with everyone. It's one of his gifts. And the concept of bringing vampires together with goths, so many of whom are vampire . . . how is it you and Jack put it? Wannabes? That could prove disastrous. Look at your situation. You're a case in point."

Werm looked hurt. "Are you saying I'm a disaster as a vampire?"

"No. I'm concerned that more intelligent young people like yourself, with open minds, shall we say, will figure out that the nonhuman world really exists. That, as you have been warned many times, could be a recipe for catastrophe."

"I promise that I'll keep a close eye on things. I think I'll be able to tell if someone starts to get ideas. I'll be behind the bar most of the time, and you know how people love to gossip to bartenders. If somebody starts asking the wrong kinds of questions, I can warn you and Jack. I'll have my ear to the ground for all kinds of information. If there's any buzz in the nonhuman community, I'll be the first to know."

I considered this. There was something to be said for good informants. I maintained several in the city's various walks of life, from society matrons to the lowest criminal element. "All right then," I said. "I won't give you grief if you promise to come to me with any information, no matter how small, that might be of significance. Not many vampires unknown to me come through Savannah, but extra eyes and ears can never hurt."

Werm snapped his fingers, which must have been

difficult as laden as they were with silver rings shaped like skulls and dragons. I occasionally suspected that the motive behind Werm's adornments was the same as his motive for wanting to be a vampire. He feared the world at large so much that he wished it to fear him back.

"I nearly forgot to tell you," he said. "There's a new vampire in town right now. He came into the bar earlier tonight."

I was tempted to box his ears. Werm was under strict orders to alert Jack or me to any blood drinker he encountered who he had reason to believe was unknown to us. "Oh?" I said calmly. "Who is he then?"

"His name is Freddy Blackstone, and he says he's a friend of Tobey's. He said to tell you that specifically, because Tobey told him how wary you are of strange vampires in Savannah."

Tobey was an indigenous North American vampire, descended from an ancient clan out west. He was made in the heyday of the transcontinental railroad. "And how did he know how to find you?"

"He didn't know anything about me before he wandered into the bar. When he sensed I was a vampire he introduced himself. He figured I must know you since Tobey told him there are so few vampires in Savannah. When I told him you were my sire, he said you could talk to Tobey and check him out if you wanted."

"I'll do that," I assured him.

By that time we'd arrived back at the house. When he opened the car door, I laid a hand on his arm. "There's something you should know. Eleanor is dead."

Werm went even paler than usual. "I'm . . . I'm sorry." He opened his mouth and I sensed he was about to ask what happened but thought better of it. He was not completely insensitive to his psychic bond to me, after all.

"Most members of my household do not know as of yet. Keep it that way until you hear otherwise."

"I will. I promise."

"All right. Let us hurry. The sun is almost up."

We entered the house to utter silence. Renee would be in bed, and my companions Deylaud and Reyha, the mystical Egyptian sighthounds who guard my rest in the daylight hours and take human form at night, would be wherever they went when they made their change at sunup.

I took the steps to the basement two at a time with Werm on my heels. When we reached the vault, he pulled up short in horror to see the bodies of Jack and Connie prostrate on the floor.

"Courage, young one," I said. "Keep your wits about you for their sake." Werm nodded solemnly and backed into the corner of the room, clutching his plastic bag of sacrificial items and awaiting instructions.

Melaphia was at my desk, carefully turning the pages of an ancient book while wearing a pair of white cotton gloves. She didn't look up when Werm and I entered. But then she said simply, "I need more time. I haven't seen any information on . . . what you wanted to know."

There was no use alarming Werm about the danger of bringing back uninvited demons from the underworld. He needed all the concentration he could muster.

"Very well," I said. "Werm, you wait there and do whatever Melaphia tells you. I recommend that you feed. You'll need all the strength you can get, so use the human variety from the blood bank. It's in the refrigerator underneath the bar." The more civilized of our kind use animal blood to sustain ourselves, but the human vintage is more fortifying.

I knelt beside Jack's body and tugged on the watch chain attached to his belt. The pocket watch I'd given him one hundred or so years ago fell into my hand. With a flick of my thumb, I removed it from its chain and went to the antique wall unit across from the desk.

"Do you think the shells will work?" Melaphia asked.

"I don't know, but it's worth a try."

Before I could remove the bone box from the drawer, Melaphia gave me a meaningful look and inclined her chin in Werm's direction. I looked him hard in the eye and said, "Forget what you see here." He would never remember seeing me remove the box. Glamour was a trick a vampire could use to enthrall humans and blood drinkers weaker than themselves. It was hard to master and some vampires never managed to. My skills were adequate. Jack's were prodigious. Involuntarily, I glanced again at his motionless body, and my throat constricted. I silently gave myself the same admonishment I had just given Werm. *Keep your wits about you. For his sake.*

"If they work, what can the shells tell you?"

Melaphia asked once she saw that Werm could not follow our conversation.

I forced a smile. "I won't know until I see—and hear. Any small bit of information might prove useful." I didn't say what I really thought: that I merely hoped the shells would tell me if Jack was still undead and could be brought back whole. If he'd already been damaged beyond help, I had a painful decision to make.

I let myself out the double-locked door from the vault to the little courtyard, mindful that I only had a few minutes before the sun rose. As in dreams, while the visions afforded by the shells might seem to span the breadth of a night, they never lasted more than a few moments in real time.

A thicket of bamboo guarded my privacy from the sidewalks beyond the estate grounds. The moon shone its reflection in the Japanese mirror pond, and in the same way that its pull awakened the tides, it stirred the mystical box.

The box had been carved by an African voodoo priest out of the skull of his father. It had been passed down to me by the man's great-great-great-granddaughter, Lalee. The ancient shells within the skull rumbled with the roar of the nearby ocean as they called out to me.

I opened the box and stared at the shells. They were already beginning to rouse themselves. I held Jack's watch over them and they danced. I shook them in their box and they rattled angrily, as if objecting to the disturbance. Then I pitched them onto the stones at my feet.

The roar of the surf in my head became deafening,

and I felt myself transported through space and time. Dark, threatening clouds passed me by on either side, looking like the view out the window of a passenger jet in a thunderstorm. Or perhaps I passed by them. I felt my ears pop as if the atmosphere had changed radically, and I found myself hovering in a clearing in the underworld. The near-total absence of light was the same as it had been the first time I visited, and I would recognize the reek if I lived another five hundred years.

The shells were as accurate as always. The watch had helped them and led me straight to Jack. He was at my feet, almost close enough to touch, and he was wrestling a demon.

Without thinking I reached out to pluck the wretched thing off him, but my hands passed through thin air. I was an observer here, nothing more. Jack threw off his attacker and it writhed upon the ground like a serpent. Its scales glowed an iridescent green— beautiful in their way but ghastly, too.

The power of the shells whirled me about as Jack's nemesis leaped to its feet. I concentrated as hard as I could to manifest myself. Jack needed my help, and I was convinced if I brought the force of my will to bear, I could make myself real in this place—at least enough to help him. The reptile appeared to have another painted upon its body. What manner of horror was this?

A wave of heat hit me as if I had just opened the door of a furnace, and I saw to my shock and revulsion that this creature was Eleanor. She yammered at Jack like a harpy. In my astonishment, the meaning of her tirade eluded me. She rushed at him again, and he flung her up and out into the arms of a pack of demons. Jack, who looked as fit as ever, ran for his life. The shells did not bid me follow him, and despite my efforts I did not feel my corporeal body materialize. However, my concentration did have one effect. Eleanor could see my image.

The shells wanted me to see what I had wrought. This is what I had consigned her to? I knew she would be cast into the underworld, but this? She'd been damned to a fate worse than that of the demons I'd seen when last I came this way.

She was becoming something more vile than anything I'd ever imagined, a fate she would suffer through all eternity. And I was to blame. I tried to help her fight the demons back but found that I still couldn't touch them. I looked down at my hand and it was ghostly and insubstantial. Still, the demons must have decided they were afraid of my image, for they retreated.

When Eleanor was sure they had gone—at least for the time being—she turned to me and began to hiss and writhe. Her hatred of me was palpable. "You— come to rescue your boy, have you? Screw him! Look what you've done to *me*!"

"What are you?" I asked, ignoring her fury.

"Don't you know what happens to vampires who wind up in this place? You've certainly killed your share of them. I am one of the double-damned, the Sluagh. We're not welcome in heaven *or* hell. The management thinks up special punishments just for us. Because of my lovely snake tattoo, now I'm a serpent. I wonder what your special penalty will be."

I wondered why I had never heard of the final death sentence of the vampire, but then I was the only person I knew who'd ever gone to the underworld and come back to tell the tale.

I felt myself fading and was glad of it. I couldn't stand to look at poor Eleanor a moment longer. Her eyes fixed on me; this time she didn't fight back against the others. In fact, she clasped two of the damned to her naked body. Surprised, they began to run their hands along her thighs and torso. "If you can't beat them, why not join them, eh, William? Or fuck them. Once a whore, always a whore."

The last thing I remember seeing of her was a familiar glint in her eye that told me a horrible truth. Somewhere inside that freakish body, the real Eleanor remained.

"William! For the love of the gods, wake up!" Melaphia was tugging at my collar with both hands, raising my head and neck up off the flagstones. I heard Werm's scream and Melaphia's warning for him to go back inside.

A searing pain lit up the side of my cheek. The one facing east. I scrambled to my feet and made it back inside.

Breathless, she joined me in the vault and slammed the door. "I'll pick up the shells later. What happened? What did you see?" she asked, helping me to the easy chair between the bar and the coffins.

"Don't make me speak of it. Please."

"Oh, no! Jack—"

"It wasn't him. I think Jack is all right. For now."

Alarmed by the din, Deylaud and Reyha had come

from elsewhere in the house and were barking in panic. Werm sank to his knees and stroked the two dogs into calmness. Reyha whined pitifully and went to lick Jack's cheek. I could see a vivid red streak across Werm's face from where he'd tried to brave the sun to assist Melaphia with me.

"Let's hurry, then," Melaphia said. "Maybe there's still time."

"Yes. Is everything ready?"

Melaphia nodded. She had arranged the candles in a circle around Jack and Connie. In strategic places, there lay bundles of herbs, incense burners producing fragrant curling smoke, several bottles of my best whiskey, vials of oils and powders, and charms of all kinds.

"Very well. Let us join hands. Melaphia, did you find the information you sought?"

Melaphia shook her head.

"It can't be helped. Let us begin."

The three of us knelt in a circle as Melaphia started to chant. Her head made a rhythmic motion from side to side and I could tell she was falling into a trance. Her chant began in English, changed to an old French dialect and then to an African tongue I had never heard before. She was reaching out and reaching back, entreating any entity who could help us, especially Jack's special *loa*.

After a few moments she began to speak intermittently in a voice that was not her own. If that were not unnerving enough, she then answered herself back in her own voice using one of the strange dialects. I couldn't make out what she was saying, but she clearly became more agitated by the moment.

Suddenly, she jerked her hands away from Werm and me and sprang to her feet. She flung her arms wide, threw her head back, and screamed, "No!"

Jack

I'm not sure how I knew it wasn't a dream. I'd gone knock, knock, knocking on heaven's door and gotten it slammed in my face, so I could understand being a little hazy. But this was real.

It should have been a dream. I knew that I didn't deserve to see something so precious even from a distance. It was like some divine power had said, *Look but don't touch. This is not for you.* But for some reason I was meant to see it.

I understood that what I saw was an abbreviated version, like the trailer of a movie. Connie held her laughing little boy on her lap. They talked and sang. He took her by the hand and showed her his world. It was everything a boy could want. Then he ran off, following a colorful balloon, trying to catch its string. She knew she couldn't follow, and that it was time to leave. Then I saw a glow coming over the horizon like the sunrise. I looked for a place to hide, but there was nowhere. I closed my eyes and waited to burn to a cinder.

But it wasn't the sunrise. It was an honest-to-God band of angels. When they topped the horizon, the glow of their power hurt my eyes. I squinted, but I could still make out that the one in the lead carried a sword. He held it out to Connie, and she looked at it in wonder.

I understood that Connie was about to be told her destiny, given her earthly assignment. But she was also being given a choice. The powers of good knew why she had come to the underworld. They had granted her first wish: that she see her son in heaven. But then there was the matter of the second reason: to wreak vengeance on the man who had taken him from her.

The angels told her she could do battle with whatever remained of her ex-husband's spirit in hell and remain with him there, or she could fulfill her destiny on earth.

Vengeance is mine, sayeth the Lord. Of course she would make the right choice. Who wouldn't, when they put it that way? Yet I understood that the assignment she was about to accept spelled doom for me and my kind, just as Melaphia had said.

She was being sworn in as the Slayer.

A beam of light purer than a ray of sun out of a cloudless Savannah sky struck the hilt of the sword. Just when I was about to turn away from it, I heard Connie ask, "What must I do?"

"You must find the twin of this blade on earth," the angel said. "Look on it well. When you find it, you will be transformed into a killer of blood drinkers. You are to purge the earth of their evil. This is your divine mission. So it has been prophesied. You are the Slayer."

Connie looked the sword up and down from its hilt to its tip, memorizing it. "I will slay them with the twin of this sword," she said, as if in a trance.

"You will also be granted great strength and other

weapons besides," the angel said. "But never forget . . ."

Before the angel could finish, there was a roar louder than forty-three stock cars revving up at the start-finish line. *Gentlemen, start your engines.*

I felt myself tumble backward, spinning like a top. I heard a loud whistle and felt a sting as if gale-force winds whipped all around me. Everything was dark again. It felt like I imagined it would if there was gravity in space and someone pushed me off the moon. I was hurtling toward earth at light speed, out of control.

The last thing I thought before I hit the ground was: *Where's Connie?*

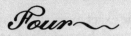

William

An orange-and-blue fireball the size of a wagon wheel sprang from the fingertips of Melaphia's right hand. It caromed around the room for a scant few seconds as if seeking its freedom, bounced once on the hearth, and disappeared up the chimney, spinning like a dervish. The whole display was over so quickly I wondered if my mind had played a trick on me, but Melaphia's earsplitting scream proved it was not my imagination.

Her cry reverberated in the vault loud enough to make the dogs, who had frozen in terror at the sight of the fireball, dive for cover underneath the chaise in front of the bar. Fearing for her still-fragile mind, I stood up and shook her by the shoulders. This trance was too deep, too dangerous. And Satan only knew what the significance of the flaming ball of light had been or what might be next. I couldn't sacrifice Melaphia for Jack. That's the last thing he would have wanted.

I could tell the exact moment Melaphia came back to herself. Her eyes became clear and focused narrowly on mine. "I failed him, William," she wailed. "I couldn't do it." Giving way to sobs, she buried her face against my chest.

Someone tugged on my pants leg and I looked down into Werm's slack-jawed and staring face. He was pointing in Jack's direction with his other hand. I turned and saw that Jack was propped on one elbow, his mouth working like a beached fish, with no sound coming out. A quick glance at Connie proved her condition to be unchanged.

"Jack!" Melaphia shouted. She and I sank to our knees beside him.

"You did it!" Werm shouted, patting Melaphia on the back.

"Welcome back," I said. I gathered Jack into my arms and hugged him briefly before turning him over to a squealing Melaphia.

"Oof," Jack managed, as Melaphia clasped him to her chest. In fact, she had him in a headlock so severe I almost feared for his survival all over again.

I crossed to where Connie lay and saw that she was still motionless. Jack had extricated himself from Melaphia's embrace by that time and joined me at Connie's side. He looked at me hopefully and I simply shook my head. Werm and I stood by Melaphia, giving Jack more space.

"Why didn't she come back with me?" He searched our faces for answers. I, for one, had none, but as I looked at Melaphia, I knew that she did. Jack evidently took the shrug she offered him at face value, but it spoke volumes to me.

He scooped Connie into his arms and urgently patted her cheek. "Connie, wake up!" he pleaded. "It's me, Jack. It's time to come back now." He issued a strangled sob when she didn't respond and stared frantically up at Melaphia again.

"There's nothing more I can do," she said firmly.

"There has to be!"

"No," I said. "There's not. The portal has closed."

"Then I've got to return to the underworld until I can figure out how to bring her back with me."

"No, you will not," I said. "It is too dangerous. It was a miracle Melaphia was able to get you back once."

He looked at Melaphia. "But I wasn't ready. *She* wasn't ready."

"You tried your best," I said gently. "It's over. You have to let her go."

His blue eyes flashed in defiance. "I'll pray to Loa Legba again."

"No, you will not," I repeated. "Melaphia has cast a spell. You will not be able to reach him if your purpose is to open the portal again." I was bluffing, but Jack's wounded look proved he believed me.

Jack swore, his eyes welling with tears. Melaphia and I exchanged glances in wordless solidarity. If she returned, Connie would eventually discover that her purpose on this earth was to destroy all vampires, most likely starting with Jack and me since we were close at hand. The loss of Connie was tragic, especially for Jack, but I hadn't fended off all manner of threats to generations of my family to see it shattered now for the sake of one mortal life.

Besides, with its innate divinity, Connie's soul would

surely find its way to paradise to be with her son for eternity. What fate could be better than that? If anyone had cause to envy that outcome, it was surely I. Both the son of my blood and the son of my heart had already lost their souls and were doomed to eternal damnation should they someday wind up at the wrong end of a stake.

Connie was the fortunate one. Perhaps when he got over his grief, Jack would come to see that. As it was, I'd never seen him as bereft as right now.

"Let us give him some time with her," I said gently. Melaphia murmured to the dogs and they followed her upstairs. Werm hung his head on the way past Jack and joined the others. I replaced the skull box carefully, making sure the latch on the hidden drawer was secure.

I squeezed Jack's shoulder as I passed him and paused on the stairs to look back briefly, still not quite believing he was really here. He clasped Connie's body to his chest and wept as I had wept for Eleanor.

I sighed. Jack and I had come full circle and wound up in the same sad place.

Jack

I pressed Connie to myself and tried to will the warmth back into her cheek as it lay against mine. How could a dead man bring the life back into her body? She was always the one who made *me* feel alive again.

I knew how Romeo must have felt when he entered

the tomb and saw Juliet lying dead. If I'd had some poison on me I would have drunk it. As if that would do any harm to me.

William and Melaphia told me nothing could be done and surely that was so. They would have helped her if they could. I guess the powers of good decided to keep her. She was in a place I could only see through squinted eyes, like someone looking at a total eclipse.

Why, oh why did she have to be taken away from me now, just as we'd truly found each other? I thought about the night we'd spent together, and I yelled out in pain. I held her apart from me and gazed into her face, searching again for some sign of life, but there was none.

I studied her lips, her eyelids, her cheekbones, chin, memorizing her while I could. As painful as it would be, I wanted to remember the lines of her perfect face if I lived to be a thousand.

But I didn't have to live to be a thousand. I didn't have to live at all.

The vault had no windows, but I sensed it was daylight outside. I didn't need poison like Romeo. All it would take to end this pain would be to step out the back door and feel the sun on my face one last time. It would all be over.

With Connie in my arms, I stood. "We're going now," I told her. "I love you. Good-bye." One last kiss, I thought. One last kiss.

I lowered her feet to the floor and held her tightly to my chest. I put my lips on hers, for once as cool as mine, and kissed her long and hard, pressing her body deeper to mine. She still smelled like lilacs, and

I pretended that she was there with me, alive and well again.

I brushed one thumb across the soft skin of her throat and stroked her long ebony hair. I gathered some of the silky mass into my fist and rubbed it against my cheek, savoring the softness. Her every curve and texture was all a woman should be. She was a goddess indeed.

I thought about how we had slow-danced at Werm's club and began to sway with her, playing over and over again in my head the Elvis Presley song we danced to. *Wise men say, only fools rush in.* I'd been a fool to think that falling in love with a mortal would lead to anything but disaster.

I'd had too many relationships with human women to count, but only this one had led me to forget myself and to become reckless. I'd never loved any woman the way I loved Connie, and never would.

I should have left her alone. She'd still be alive if it hadn't been for me. But true to my nature as a demon, I only thought about myself and what I wanted. And, my god, had I wanted her. I saw my red-tinged tears fall onto her gown, staining it, spoiling its pure whiteness, and I cried harder.

I cried for myself and I cried for Connie. My body shook with sobs. The music in my head stopped and I stood still, hugged her, and gave in to my emotions. I thought I'd stopped dancing.

But Connie had other ideas.

I thought I felt an intake of breath against my chest and knew that in my grief I was imagining things, becoming delusional. Then I saw Connie's head move. In another moment she was looking up at me.

"Jack," she whispered.

I covered her cheeks, her eyes with kisses, pausing just long enough to cup her face in my hands and stare into her eyes to reassure myself that I wasn't dreaming. Then I kissed her some more, her nose, her brows. "Thank god," I said. "You're really alive."

"I know I've been on a long journey but I can't remember what it was all about. Wherever I was, you brought me back, though, didn't you?" she asked.

"Yes. Everything's going to be fine now."

"But I can't remember what happened. I think I had a job to do. Something important. Did I do what I . . . set out to do?"

"Yes," I told her. "Everything's all right. You can put all your sorrow behind you." I wrapped my arms around her and gave her a squeeze. "Pinch me so I can believe we're both really back."

Laughing, she reached around me and pinched my butt, and I laughed with her. Then we looked into each other's eyes again and the laughter died on our lips. It was as if I was seeing her for the first time. I saw the same wonder and awe I was feeling mirrored in her face. She flung her arms around my neck and I kissed her again like I'd never kissed anyone before— or been kissed in return.

I carried her to the chaise lounge and sat her down, kneeling in front of her. She cupped my face in her hands and then lowered them to my shoulders and chest, stroking her way to my waist where she grasped my shirt and pulled it out of my jeans and over my head. I reached beneath the white dress and swept it up and off in one smooth motion. She was naked underneath, glorious and perfect. If I hadn't already known for sure that she was a goddess, I would have felt it in my bones. She lay back and I began my worship of her.

Still kneeling at the end of the chaise, I lifted one of her feet and kissed the sensitive arch, making her shiver. I planted kisses up and around her ankle, then along her shapely calf, easing her leg over my shoulder as I did so. I licked the tender little crease at the back of her knee, shuddering with anticipation as my lips moved along to the smooth skin of her inner thigh.

I kissed and nipped, letting my fangs brush her flesh as lightly as the wings of a butterfly. She reached down to weave her fingers into the waves of my hair, massaging my scalp and urging my mouth higher until my lips found the triangle of crisp dark curls that fringed her most feminine place.

I closed my eyes, reveling in the fragrance of her desire for me and let the curls tickle my nose before she spread her legs wider and blossomed for me. Reverently I lowered my head to her rosy flesh, swollen with need. I could feel her pulse beating beneath my mouth as her blood rushed to her blessed womanly parts, making them plump and ready for that splendid dance as old as time. The vampire in me responded to the blood as if I could see it rushing, and my fangs lengthened involuntarily. Mentally, I tamped down my response to the life-giving red nectar and concentrated on my devotion to my goddess.

My tongue teased the dewy petals it found on the way to the little bud at her center. I stroked it again and again with my tongue, lips, and chin until Connie reached down to grasp my shoulders.

She urged me upward until I was braced above her and she went about relieving me of my jeans. "I want you now," she said simply.

My erection sprang to meet her hands and she wasted no time putting me inside her. I felt like I melted into her, onto her, became one with her. As I moved inside her, I braced on one elbow and cupped her breast, massaging upward from her rib cage to the nipple, teasing its tip with my thumb before starting again.

In my unnaturally lengthy life I had made love to more women than I could count, and thought myself *in* love with quite a few of them. I thought I'd known when it was real. And I'd even grieved with the loss of a special relationship when things fell apart, as they always did. Being a creature of the night meant always having to say you're sorry. And always having to say good-bye.

But it wasn't until this woman came into my world that I felt more alive than I had when I was a living, breathing human. She was the only woman who'd ever known what I was. And still she could look past the abominable circumstances that accounted for my existence and love me for the man I still was inside. Or at least the man I tried to be.

And as for the sex—the way we fit together, the way we moved when we found our rhythm felt like something preordained. It was as if this woman who came along so many generations after my death was made especially for me. As I thought this, I remembered the truth. She *was* made for me in a very real way.

She was made to kill me.

That was why I caught fire the first time we touched. She had learned a spell that cured that bit of sexual dysfunction, but the purpose behind it was clear now. I pushed that thought out of my mind, because as surely as Connie and I had passed through hell in the last few hours, we were in heaven now and I wasn't going to let anything spoil that for either of us. We came in a shuddering climax while looking deep into each other's eyes.

"My Consuela, my goddess," I heard myself whisper.

William

I instructed Werm and the dogs to go upstairs and check on Renee. She wasn't expected at her private school—when she'd been kidnapped I'd called the headmistress and told her that we were going to homeschool Renee for the foreseeable future. It's a shame we must go to such ends sometimes to protect our secrets.

"I'll see that Connie is buried in consecrated ground," Melaphia said.

"Yes. Do," I agreed, thinking that Melaphia was now acting entirely too calm for what she'd just gone through. "Are you sure you're all right, my dear?"

She lifted her chin, and I saw a series of differing emotions play across her face. I'd known those various expressions for thirty years now. This child I'd helped to raise had grown into an exceptional woman, a woman who had never used her considerable powers for any cause that wasn't noble and just. She'd never been as conflicted as she was at this moment, and she was hurting.

Finally her reserve crumbled and she hid her face in her hands. "She was my friend." She choked out the words with difficulty. "And I didn't even try to bring her back with Jack. I wanted her to stay."

I was tempted to gather her into my arms again, but I knew that would not help her regain control. Instead I spoke soothingly to her. "Do you remember how we helped Shari to a better place when she was confined to the underworld?"

"Yes. I remember."

"Do you think that Connie is in a lesser place? Consider this. While she was reckless in crossing the portal to the underworld, she lost her life through no real fault of her own, no sin in any case. Would not her divinity ensure that she reached a place of peace with her son?"

"Yes, I suppose it does make sense when you think about it like that." Melaphia wiped her eyes.

"If Renee was . . ." I couldn't bring myself to say the word *dead*. ". . . wouldn't you want to be with her even if it meant leaving this world?"

"Of course I would."

"Then promise me you won't dwell on this. What's done is done. It's out of our hands."

"And you and Jack are out of danger."

I started to say, *From the Slayer at least,* but bit my tongue. Later I would catch her and Jack up on what had happened in Europe. The old lords had been a gathering threat when I'd left for the United Kingdom, but to Jack they were also a vague and shadowy one. I know it was difficult for him to appreciate the menace they posed to us since they seemed to him so far away. What I had learned while in London would *flesh out* the situation, as Jack himself would say.

As glad as I was that Jack was back with us, something still nagged at me about the way he'd returned. "I have to ask you something about what happened down there. Why did you scream just before Jack reoccupied his body?"

Melaphia looked at me blankly. "I did? I don't remember that at all."

"What about the fireball that rolled through just as the portal opened?"

She looked alarmed and shook her head. "I don't know what you're talking about."

"What's the last thing you remember?"

"I remember holding hands with you and Werm and starting my chant. I must have gone into a trance because I remember coming out of it convinced that I had failed and Jack was still in the underworld. What—what fireball?"

"It's probably only some by-product of Jack's crossing. Do you remember anything similar from when I came back from the underworld?"

"No, but it wasn't really the same thing."

"It's probably nothing to worry about."

During the spiritualist movement that began in the 1800s, humans came close to discovering the shadow world of beings other than themselves. A few charlatans gave the legitimate psychics a bad name and the movement eventually all but died out. The mediums who were successful in manifesting spirits during séances found that a residue—ectoplasm, they called it—was generated by the incident. Such is the nature of physics. Perhaps the fireball was something similar.

"Do you think that anything . . . bad . . . came back with Jack?" Melaphia asked.

"Oh, I think we would have known immediately. Demons tend not to play coy."

She visibly relaxed, but her young face showed her weariness. Her emotions had run the gamut in the last few hours. She'd gone from near madness, bereft at having lost her daughter and perhaps me and then Jack as well, to happiness at having us all returned to her. But what should have been elation was tempered by guilt over her part in losing Connie.

"Is it really over, Father?" Melaphia asked, leaning her head against my chest.

In the rare instances when she'd called me that through the years, it was always when she'd wanted reassurance. If my trip to Europe to rescue Renee had taught me anything, it was that our lives were about to become even more insecure, but now was not the time to tell her that. I put my arms around her and hugged her like I did when she was small.

"Yes, little one," I said as I used to. "It's over."

Jack

When I was holding Connie afterward, there were no words for the happiness I felt. I was half afraid I was dreaming. If so, I hoped I never woke up.

Suddenly Connie became aware of her surroundings. "Where are we?" She glanced around the room.

When she saw the coffins, she gave a start and looked back at me in alarm.

"We're in the basement of William's house. Everything's okay. More than okay. It's—" I kissed her again, hard. She broke off the kiss suddenly, her eyes wide. For a blissful little while, we'd both put the underworld behind us. But I saw awareness coming into Connie's face. She wanted answers.

"What happened when we were in the underworld?"

"You still don't remember?" I just stared at her, thinking about all that we'd been through in the last few hours—or was it days? Who knew how underworld time compared to topside time? Where did I begin? What should I tell her? And if she really didn't remember anything, what should I make up or leave out?

She grabbed me by the upper arms and shook me as hard as she could, which wasn't very hard since I was nearly a foot taller and a hundred pounds heavier than she. "I don't remember. Now, *what happened*?" she demanded again.

"What's the last thing you can recall?" I countered. I sat up and helped her on with her white gown. My mind raced as I gathered up my jeans and dressed myself. Hell, how much did I myself recollect about what transpired right at the end? I was pretty sure the angels hadn't gotten around to telling her she was the Slayer.

She gave me a veiled look, on the defensive already, I figured. "I—I came over to talk to Melaphia."

"To talk? Or to get her help changing zip codes and dump me in the process?" The question sounded childish even to my own ears, under the circumstances and considering the mind-blowing sex we'd just had. But gol-dang, I'd just been through hell and back. A man deserved some answers.

"Not everything's about you, Jack," Connie said, putting me in my place.

"I told you over and over it wasn't safe to go to the underworld, and you ignored me."

A look of realization came over Connie's face, and she quit playing coy right quick. "What did you do?" she demanded, her eyes blazing.

"I did what I had to. I brought you back."

She balled her fists and pummeled my chest. I caught her forearms as gently as I could but firmly enough to still them. "You—you—evil bloodsucking bastard! I went there to see my son, and—"

"And you did." She'd never spoken to me of her son before. In fact, I wasn't supposed to know who she had wanted to see. It was a relief to have her finally open up, if only a little.

She stopped struggling and gazed up at me, blinking. "I did?"

I said gently, "It was awesome."

"Tell me," she said.

"There was your . . . son," I began. I didn't want to reveal that I knew how her son died. Seth had warned me that the pity Connie had seen in his eyes after the murder-suicide had spelled the end of their relationship. I wasn't going to make the same mistake. Connie was a proud goddess, and she had told me what she wanted to accomplish in the underworld only in the most general terms. Those were the terms I'd keep things on.

I walked her over to the chaise next to the bar and sat her down. Then I told her everything I'd seen when she'd been with her son. My description of the events didn't do them justice, but I tried my best. Tears ran down Connie's face as she listened, and I did my best to answer her questions. She had lots of them.

When she was out of questions, she took a deep breath and wiped away her last tear with the back of her hand like a little girl. "What about my other reason for going?" After all this time, she couldn't put into words what her ex-husband had done to her.

"You kicked a guy's ass real good," I lied. Thank goodness she didn't ask me for details like she did about her son. I could have made some up, but she might have realized I was lying. A good cop almost always knows when someone is lying even if the liar is as good as me. "The way you cleaned his clock, I hope he had it coming."

"He had it coming, believe me," she said with conviction. "I wonder why I can't remember and you can?"

"Beats me." I wasn't going to admit it, but I knew someone who might know. Talking to him was my next stop after I checked on Renee. I was confident she was back in Savannah, probably asleep upstairs, or William wouldn't have returned to American soil. He'd given Melaphia his solemn vow to return her daughter. That was money in the bank. With Connie and Renee back, all was right with my world. Well, almost all.

As if on cue, Connie asked, "There's something else, isn't there?"

"Why do you say that?"

"I can tell."

For a split second I pictured myself saying *Well, sugar, that's when the heavenly host deputized you to murder me with a sharp stick*. But I decided against it.

The best way to commit a lie of omission is to tell some relevant truth instead. "There *was* some unpleasantness down there. With some demons. I'll tell you about it sometime, but not right now. The important thing is that you accomplished what you set out to do and we're both back here safe."

"You're right. I'm sorry I got testy earlier."

I shrugged. "We've both been through a lot today."

"That's what I mean. I know that whatever happened in the underworld, you risked your whole existence on getting me back here, put yourself literally through hell, and I'm grateful. I'm sorry if you interpreted what I did as . . . running out on you."

She'd been right earlier. Not everything was about me and I shouldn't have taken what she did personally. I just couldn't help it. I shrugged again, not trusting myself to say anything else. I hoped for all I was worth that there would be plenty of time for us to work out all the kinks in our unique relationship.

I'd add my neediness to the list of things I just didn't want to think about right now.

Right after that Slayer thing.

Five

William

Melaphia was about to go upstairs to Renee when Jack entered the kitchen leading a very much alive Connie Jones by the hand. Our shock must have shown on our faces.

"Connie!" Melaphia moved woodenly to Connie's side and gave her a hug. "It's a miracle."

While Melaphia put on a show of welcoming Connie back from the underworld, Jack asked, "How's Renee?"

"Safe and sound."

"Thank God."

By that time, Melaphia had released her hold on Officer Jones.

"Indeed it is a miracle," I said. "We were convinced you were lost to us. Jack, how did you do it?"

"I don't know. It just happened." Jack beamed, unable to take his gaze from his lady love.

Melaphia and I exchanged the most subtle of concerned glances. Our world had just become more complicated by tenfold.

"Are you sure you're quite all right, Officer Jones?"

"Yes, and please, call me Connie."

"This incredible turn of events calls for a celebration." I tried to sound as happy as I could. "Melaphia, we should have some champagne."

"That's very kind of you, William," Connie said, "but I'm really exhausted after . . . everything that's happened. I think I should be getting home."

"If you must," I said. "But there's something I need to say, first. Your reasons for traveling to the underworld are your own and none of my concern. Whatever the reasons may be, the risks are too great. I have forbidden Melaphia to help you or anyone cross that portal again. Is that clear, Melaphia?"

Melaphia looked down at the floor, genuinely chastened, and nodded silently.

"Don't blame her, William. I twisted her arm," Connie admitted. "I promise I won't do it again."

"Good. Because there are not only risks to you, but risks to Melaphia as well, not to mention Jack, who'll always be fool enough to try to go and fetch you back. See that there isn't a next time."

"I understand."

"I must ask for your word." I half-expected Jack to challenge me just on principle for being too bossy, as he would put it, but he nodded instead. He wasn't eager for his girlfriend to repeat the escapade.

"I give you my word."

"Good," I said with a sigh. "And congratulations on your safe journey."

Jack accompanied Connie through the foyer to the

door, all the while offering to travel through the underground tunnels to ensure she made it safely to her apartment. She demurred, but their voices lowered as they continued their good-byes.

Melaphia grasped my arm. "What are we going to do?"

"You're going to go upstairs and go to bed, and Jack and I are going to take our rest as well."

"But—"

"There's nothing we can do at the moment. I'll have a serious talk with Jack first thing tomorrow. We'll both need all of our strength for that."

I heard Jack close the front door behind Connie. Melaphia nodded and hugged Jack as they passed each other in the doorway between the kitchen and the foyer. I heard her footsteps on the stairs up to the bedrooms.

Jack leaned against the doorjamb and regarded me warily. "Mel told you about Connie." It was a statement rather than a question.

"Of course. This is a grave situation, Jack."

"Look, she doesn't even know she's this slayer."

"She will."

"How? Who's going to tell her?"

Jack's defiant attitude was already playing on my nerves. "We're both weary. Let us discuss this when we've had a chance to get our rest."

"We'll discuss it now. Who's to say she'll ever find out? I mean, whose job is it to tell her, anyway?"

"I don't know," I admitted. "Melaphia is going to do additional research."

"She's going to have to look it up? How much *do* you know about slayers?"

"To be perfectly frank, not a great deal. However, I did get some information about them while I was in Europe."

"What information?"

"There seems to be a feeling among the European vampires that a prophesied slayer is or soon could be among us. If she's not already."

Jack ran a hand through his hair in a gesture of nervousness I'd seen a thousand times. "A feeling?"

"The old ones can . . . sense certain events, as you know. Olivia, like Melaphia, is attempting to learn everything she can. Until they know more, you must keep a close eye on Connie."

Olivia was my second in command in Europe. She had recently uncovered a cache of documents she hoped would shed light on the history of the blood drinkers.

"Why? What am I looking for?"

I could tell that Jack was deep in denial, something he would have to snap out of quickly if he was to survive. "You're looking for any sign that your girlfriend wants to kill you."

Jack

"If she comes at me with the pointy end of anything, you'll be the first to know," I assured William.

"Don't be glib. This is serious."

William gave me one of his stern looks, the kind meant to scare me. And I was scared all right. I went the extra mile to block my thoughts so he wouldn't know the secret I was keeping from him right then. If he knew that Connie's learning that she was the Slayer was as simple as her memory coming back, there was no telling what he would do.

"Yeah, I know it's serious," I said, and suddenly remembered another serious subject. "Hey! I saw Eleanor in the underworld. She attacked me and said you killed her. What the hell happened?" At the mention of Eleanor's name William looked so sorrowful I was sorry I'd brought her up.

"I was forced to destroy her. She lied to me about her role in Renee's kidnapping."

Big mistake on her part. You did not ever lie to a master vampire, especially the one who made you. The lie of omission I just told—or rather, didn't tell—was only made possible by the control I'd honed through years and years of blocking out William's ability to read my mind. As a fledgling, Eleanor wouldn't have had the power to do that, at least not for very long. "Eleanor was the one who led Diana and Hugo to Renee?"

"For the purity and mystical qualities of the child's blood, yes. I could not allow Eleanor to live after that."

"William, I'm sorry. Really I am. I know that you made El to be your mate for the long haul."

"Yes, I did. But I could not let anyone threaten my family. Not even the woman I loved and hungered for. I'd loved her like no other in half a century. But my family—Melaphia, Renee, and you—are the most important things to me on earth. And I would do anything it took to protect you all." William gave me a meaningful look. "Do you understand, Jack?"

It wasn't like William to go all touchy-feely. And

goodness knew, if the situation were different, this little speech of his would have made me feel all warm and fuzzy. He and I had butted heads many times over the years because he used to treat me like a hired field hand. It had been only recently that he admitted how important I was to him, like a real son almost. Even though we looked the same age in human years, William was my sire and more of a father to me than my human father had been.

But what he was hinting at was out of bounds. "If you're suggesting what I think you are—"

"You know exactly what I mean."

"I want to hear you say it," I challenged, although in fact I didn't. I really, really didn't. Maybe I thought William wouldn't put it into words, that he'd back off. Perhaps he'd show some humanity. After all, it was William's love of humanity that had led him to make me his offspring, his undead *son*. He'd told me so once. He said he'd seen the kind of humanity in me that would not go away even after he'd made me a fellow demon. It was William who taught me never to take a human life without the most dire provocation. Surely, I thought desperately, he would never, ever ask me to harm the human I loved the most.

"Very well, then," he said. "Maybe you do need to have it spelled out for you. I expect you to do everything you can to preserve this family. I have no doubt that you would lay down your life for me as well as for Melaphia and Renee—"

"I can't make that choice for Connie," I said, interrupting him before he got to the part that would break my heart. "I can't choose to lay down Connie's life for our family."

"The day will come when Connie will try to take your life. That is the point at which you must destroy her. If you can't do it for yourself, do it for Melaphia and Renee. If anything happens to me, who is to protect them from the forces that are coming? They are the last remaining pure sources of the voodoo blood. The old lords will kill them for it, and their deaths won't be quick and painless."

I heard myself make a choking sound. "There has to be something I can do," I murmured, my mouth as dry as ashes. "There has to be a way around this."

William grasped me by the shoulders, getting all up in my grill with those cat-green eyes of his. "This is bigger than you or me. Do you think that you, Jack McShane, can reverse a prophecy of two ancient cultures? Even Lalee herself could not do that."

I swallowed hard and shook off William's grasp. "You can't ask me to kill Connie. You just can't." I staggered a few feet away, desperate to put some physical distance between us before I took a swing at him despite myself.

"That is precisely what I am asking you to do," he said calmly. "For the sake of this family, for Melaphia, Renee, and all the vampires whom you have come to know and love—Werm, Olivia, Tobey, Iban—"

"Stop!" I fought the urge to clap my hands to my ears like a child. "I love her, William. I love her more than anyone I've ever loved."

"The way I loved Eleanor," William said stoically. "And the way I loved Diana."

I'd never seen William's face like it was now—a twisted mask of grief. I'd been so shocked at seeing Eleanor being turned into a sideshow-worthy snake woman and horrified to hear that William had had to kill her that I'd forgotten all about William's former wife, Diana. She and her mate, Hugo, had been the ones who kidnapped Renee. When William had left for Europe, he was so angry that he could have killed her with his bare hands. "What about Diana?" I asked.

"The last I saw of her she was being buried alive." In a movement so fast I could barely see it even with my keen vampire sight, he was on me again, staring at me eye-to-eye. "I would have killed her myself if I could have reached her—drained her like I did Eleanor. Did I tell you I too saw Eleanor in hell?"

"How? The shells?"

"Yes. I used the shells to try to get you back—to see if you could be reached."

"Then you saw . . ." I couldn't even stand to say what Eleanor had become. There's just something awful about snakes. I guess it's human nature to be disgusted by the serpent and what it represents. The story of the fall is part of all of us.

A wave of revulsion showed on William's face and he staggered a step away from me, the reality of what he'd done to Eleanor dealing him a body blow. I reached out to steady him. It was a sign of his condition that he let me.

"I did what I had to do, Jack. I sacrificed the woman I loved, the woman I'd planned to spend eternity with, and even having seen her being tortured in the hereafter, I can swear to you I'd do it again, because she was a danger to my family. I put you and the rest of my family first. And that is what you will do, too. When the time comes, you must kill Connie Jones. It's time for you to be a vampire!"

I tried to look away. I tried to think. "But she doesn't know she's the Slayer," I pleaded again. "Maybe she'll never know. You said earlier that I could keep a close eye on her." I stepped back and this time William didn't close the distance.

He sighed and rubbed his brow, considering. We had all been through the wringer tonight, physically and emotionally, and his exhaustion showed. "All right. Watch her carefully until Melaphia and Olivia can find out more about the prophecy. In the meantime, if she comes for you . . ."

"I know," I said, holding up a hand. I couldn't bear to hear it again.

William stared at me for a long moment, sizing me up, trying to decide if I was made of stuff as stern as he was. But he'd gotten as good at hiding his thoughts from me as I was at hiding mine from him. It was probably for my own good that I couldn't read him now. I probably wouldn't like what I saw.

"Prepare yourself," he said. "What Melaphia and Olivia uncover might be quite unpleasant. If that's the case, I expect you to act and act quickly. As I did."

He turned on his heel and left me standing in the kitchen thinking about the horror of spending eternity knowing that I'd murdered the woman I loved. Just as William had done.

Six

William

I awoke later than usual. Even vampires can suffer from jet lag, not to mention weariness. By the time I rose, both Jack and his black coffin with the number 3 decal were already gone. I knew that now that I had returned from Europe, Jack would go back to his own digs, as he would put it—a unit in a heavily guarded mini-warehouse.

At my request, he had been staying at the house in my absence to look after Melaphia. That was no longer necessary, but I knew his hasty departure had as much to do with the tension between us on the issue of Consuela Jones.

Jack and I hadn't always gotten along. He'd resisted my authority as his sire since I made him some one hundred and forty years ago. Most of that resistance was passive, but we'd come to blows on occasion—certainly not that unusual between a blood drinker and his offspring but troubling nonetheless. Still and all, we needed each other, both to protect our family—the descendants of Lalee—and to defend our territory and the human population of Savannah from any nonhuman threats.

Over the years, as Jack had achieved more maturity and hopefully better judgment, I offered him more autonomy. I don't think Jack fully appreciated this until the day my own sire, Reedrek, arrived in Savannah. With the threat of Reedrek, I'd been forced to share with Jack some of the darker knowledge about our race, information that he had craved but which I'd nonetheless hoped to spare him, because along with this new awareness came responsibility.

I thought about these things as I showered and changed. I had much to accomplish this night and moonlight was burning. The first order of business was to meet with Melaphia and decide how to proceed with our lives now that this vampire slayer was in our midst.

Despite the weighty matters on my mind, I had to smile when I entered the kitchen. The domestic scene that greeted me gladdened what was left of my heart. Melaphia stirred a pot of a stew on the stove while Reyha sorted through the spice cabinet in search of herbs for the mixture. Deylaud sat at the kitchen table with Renee and a very large book, extolling the virtues of the epic poem as a literary form. Anyone who might think this too dry a subject for a nine-year-old doesn't know Renee. Her attention was as rapt as if Deylaud were discussing the finer points of a Harry Potter novel. Actually more—when the head of your household is a vampire, wizards hold less allure.

Their greeting smiles lightened my spirits. Renee

ran to me and threw her skinny arms around my waist. "Deylaud is helping me study my literature lesson," she said, giving me a brief hug before leading me by the hand to the huge volume open on the table.

"*Evangeline,*" I observed. The tragic love story forced the unpleasantness of the last night back to the forefront of my mind. I looked at Melaphia and the look she gave me in return said she followed my train of thought.

"The stew is ready," she said. "Reyha, get the cornbread out of the oven and y'all go ahead and eat."

"But Mama, aren't you going to eat with us?" Renee was at her mother's side in a thrice, clinging in a most uncharacteristic way to Melaphia's slender frame. It would take time for both of them to recover from their recent forced separation and the danger they had both been in.

"William and I have some things to talk about," Melaphia said, stroking her daughter's braids. "I'll be back to get my supper in a little bit. Why don't you butter some cornbread for me while it's hot."

As Renee and the twins settled down to dinner, Melaphia and I retreated to the parlor. "I still can't believe she's really home," Melaphia said, hugging herself. "Thank you, Father."

I felt myself smile. As it was with her mother and her mother's mother before her, nothing pleased me more than to hear Melaphia call me *Father*.

"There's no need to thank me. I'm only sorry that you had to suffer through the ordeal of the kidnapping. How are you feeling, really?"

"I'm fine now." She seated herself on the sofa across from the fireplace. She did indeed look as if the weight of the world had lifted off her shoulders. The stress of the abduction had visibly aged her. Now she looked like a young woman of thirty again, clad in her jeans, sneakers, and blue pullover. Her dreadlocks were pulled back and secured with a kerchief of matching blue silk.

"So, your . . . thinking is . . ." I began, searching for the most tactful way to ask if she believed she had regained her sanity.

She smiled. "My mind is as clear as a bell, honestly. I know we have a lot to talk about, a lot to plan. I promise you I can handle it."

"I'm glad to hear that. Because I need you and your skills as never before, my dear. First, I want you to think back a few months to when I went to the underworld when Eleanor was being made a blood drinker."

"All right." Melaphia's face clouded. It had been a dangerous time. I nearly didn't make it back from the netherworld.

"When I returned to my body, did anything come back with me?"

"You mean like the fireball you said came back with Jack? No, not at all. Why? What do you think it means?"

"Perhaps nothing. Do you think that your texts might shed any light on such phenomena?"

"I'll search for any reference that might be helpful, while I'm researching . . . the other thing."

"Yes," I said as I stoked the fire by prodding a glowing ember with the iron poker. The sparks that shot upward into the chimney reminded me of the ball of fire I'd seen when Jack returned to his body.

" 'The other thing' indeed. Is there any reason to believe that Connie knows any more about her destiny than that she is a Mayan goddess?"

"No, and I don't know how she could. The sources on the Internet only go so far, and I don't believe she would find anything useful in even the best libraries. It might occur to her to travel to New Orleans to talk to some of the best voodoo practitioners, but . . ." Melaphia shrugged but was too modest to continue her thought. She might have pointed out that no other *mambo* on this continent came close to her own skills. And none had access to the sacred books passed down from Maman Lalee herself.

"Good," I said. "Keep on searching the texts for anything you can find on the Slayer."

"And how to kill her." It was a statement rather than a question.

"Perhaps Jack is right and it won't come to that," I said.

"I can only imagine how he reacted when you told him," she said. "You did tell him, didn't you?"

"That he would one day have to kill her for both our sakes? Yes. He's in denial right now, and I've decided not to force the issue until we know more."

"I guess I have my work cut out for me then," she said, and rose to leave.

"One more thing. I spoke to Seth Walker briefly last night."

"I heard he was back in town. Werewolf business?"

"Yes. And he said something strange. He's been having premonitions about serious events coming our way."

"What kind of serious events?" Melaphia frowned.

"He said he didn't know specifics. But, as you know, his werewolf instincts are sharper than any of ours when it comes to phenomena in the natural world, so what he senses is worth listening to, no matter how vague."

"Maybe I should talk to him further about it." Melaphia gave me a sly smile despite the seriousness of the issue. She was as fond of Seth as all women seemed to be and would no doubt welcome an excuse to seek out his counsel.

As Melaphia joined the others for dinner, I returned downstairs and turned on my computer. The phone rang as the PC powered up, the caller ID indicating that Tobey was calling from the West Coast.

When I answered, he said, "William! It's great to hear your voice. I was just calling to see if Melaphia had gotten any word from you and Renee yet."

I thanked Tobey for his concern and gave him a brief recap of what had happened while I was in England, but not about Jack's own adventure to the underworld. He expressed joy at hearing of Renee's good health and genuine sorrow at the loss of Eleanor.

As I listened, I realized I needed to warn him about the Slayer. To keep it to myself would be unfair to the other master vampires.

"Try to go easy on yourself about Eleanor, William. It sounds as if you did what you had to do. We all make mistakes from time to time when matters of the heart are involved. I've made more than my share myself."

"I appreciate the understanding, my friend, but let

us speak no more about that for the present. I need you to come east again with Iban and Travis. I need to share some additional information that I can't get into on the phone."

There was a pause. "Sounds urgent," Tobey said.

"Very."

"I'll talk to my people and reschedule some things. Iban and I will charter a jet and leave as soon as the sun sets. We'll be there tomorrow night. I'll put out feelers to try to find Travis, but you know how nomadic he is."

Travis Rubio, descended from ancient Mayan Indians, roamed throughout the Southwest as well as Central and South America. His value in monitoring nonhuman activity in that part of the world was enormous. "Thank you. Before I let you go, I need a bit of information. I understand you are acquainted with a vampire named Freddy Blackstone."

"Freddy? Yeah. Why?"

"He's here in Savannah. He seems to have made a friend of our Lamar."

"Lamar?"

"Werm," I amended. I explained the nature of Werm's new enterprise. "What does this Mr. Blackstone look like?"

"Medium height, brown hair, brown eyes. No particularly distinctive features."

"Any idea why he came here?"

"I think he has a touch of the wanderlust. He was made here in the West a little after I was and has roamed around from clan to clan ever since. I think he wants to see as much of the world as he safely can, so I wouldn't expect him to stay in Savannah all that long. He's really quite harmless, a bit on the goofy side, to tell you the truth. You won't find him particularly helpful in a crisis, but you shouldn't have any trouble with him either. He knows how to behave himself."

In vampire parlance, knowing how to behave oneself meant not killing human beings unless gravely provoked. "Very well. I'll give him your regards if and when I meet him."

"Please do," Tobey said. "When do I get to hear more about that treasure trove of information that Olivia inherited from Alger?"

"Olivia should be able to give us a report tomorrow night. She hasn't had time to have much of Alger's material translated as yet, but she might have discovered something of value," I said. "By that time Melaphia may be able to supplement the information with some research she's doing on this end."

And, I thought, I'd have had more time to decide what to tell the other master vampires about the Slayer.

Tobey and I said our good-byes, and I scanned my backlog of e-mail for anything that needed my immediate attention. I saw nothing that couldn't wait, so I e-mailed Olivia: *Arrived safely with Renee in Savannah. Please prepare a briefing for tomorrow night on behalf of the Americans on the new information you've uncovered. If anything on the Slayer comes to light, contact me immediately. Yours, WCT.*

I thought a moment and added a postscript: *No more secrets from me. However, you must not tell Jack anything you find out about the Slayer. Leave that to me. I will explain in due time.*

I e-mailed Gerard and Lucius to prepare to attend tomorrow night's meeting as well. I received quick responses indicating that traveling on such short notice would be a hardship due to their schedules and the inherent difficulties of travel.

For the blood drinker, trip-taking was inconvenient at best and outright dangerous at worst. Excursions beyond one's home territory were not undertaken lightly. That is why I prefer sea voyages when I have the luxury of time and discreet private air travel when I do not. For the purposes of tomorrow night's meeting, I decided not to press the matter and agreed to let Gerard and Lucius participate via secured telephone.

I could have allowed Iban and Tobey to attend the meeting remotely as well, but I sensed I might need their moral support in convincing Jack of what he had to do for all our sakes. He would pay more attention to a united front of his friends than to me alone.

I powered down the PC and selected an Italian leather sport coat from the armoire that I kept in the vault. It was time, as the young ones say, to go clubbing.

Jack

An alarm clock in your coffin comes in handy now and then. I was especially glad I had one tonight. The last thing I wanted was another confrontation with William about Connie—at least not until I had more information. But who did you turn to for the 411 on vampire slayers?

Under different circumstances, the obvious choice

would be Melaphia, but Mel's devotion to William meant she wanted to see Connie dead even more than my sire did. Since she'd failed to get rid of Connie by helping her into the underworld, she was going to be on the lookout for other ways to make sure my girlfriend wouldn't kill either of the men who raised her. I couldn't really blame Melaphia. How could I? But I also couldn't let her succeed.

There was only one person in Savannah I could think of who might be able to give me some advice, and it wasn't a person at all. Not a live one, anyway. I had to talk to Sullivan. He had been Connie's friend in life. Maybe he had seen her when she went to the underworld or learned something valuable since he'd been dead.

As the sun was still setting I had hauled my coffin on my back through the garage to the carriage house. I made a quick call to Rennie to make arrangements to pick up the black box and take it to my unit at the mini-storage before hopping into my Corvette for the drive to William's plantation where Sullivan was buried.

I roared to a stop beside the little family cemetery and let myself in through the wrought-iron gate. A cold breeze blew off the marsh waters, swaying the Spanish moss in the branches of the live oaks overhead. I heard the murmurs of the dead rising from graves here and there—greetings, entreaties, warm wishes. I didn't let any of the spirits engage me, not even the ones with sweet, enticing female voices, but made my way directly to Sullivan's little plot of earth.

Visiting people's graves was always a little humbling. Charismatic people like Sullivan cut a wide swath of influence in life. In death, he was reduced to a three by six rectangle of dirt. I sighed. "Sullivan. Are you there?"

"Is a bear buried in the woods?" he asked.

I heaved a sigh of relief as I hadn't been 100 percent sure I'd be able to reach him.

"Say, didn't you bring me any flowers?"

"That sounds kind of gay, dude."

"Just kidding."

"I wasn't sure I'd be able to talk to you," I said absently. I was still thinking about that age-old question of where the soul resides. I remembered how upset the spirits in Colonial Cemetery got when William went on a tirade and disturbed their graves. But that wasn't even the worst of it. My sire went on to kill a couple of innocent people in the tunnels in a fit of rage. I'd never known him to do that in all my existence. It shook me up, to tell you the truth.

"I'm always here. And always in the underworld. It's kind of like having a split personality. A little part of your spirit always stays with your body, just enough to communicate, I guess."

"That makes sense," I said. "One time I was able to raise a bunch of dead people to guard the harbor. It was pretty awesome if I do say so myself."

"I heard about that," Sullivan said. "I don't know if you know what a big deal that was. Getting the dead to walk again isn't easy. If a ghost that is reanimated from the grave gets up and walks topside, then its spirit goes into suspension in the underworld. I'm not sure what happens when someone is raised from the dead directly from the underworld. I don't know if anybody's ever done that before."

His voice had an otherworldly quality. It was a little spooky, to tell you the truth. "Sounds like all hell could bust loose."

"Very funny," he said. "But I've heard that one before."

I really wasn't trying to make a joke. My own power to reanimate the dead had creeped me out. It was a handy skill to have, but I hoped nobody ever asked me to do it again. Things could backfire on you quick; my friend Huey, who was a nice guy but also a smelly zombie, was living—er—lurching proof of that. The law of unintended consequences could be a bitch when you had a power that was hard to control.

"Listen, Sully, I've got to ask you something. It's really important."

"Shoot," he said. "I've got nothing but time."

I explained to him what had happened with Connie, going into as much detail as I could remember about the angels' Slayer ceremony.

"Dude, your main squeeze is supposed to kill you? That's a colossal bummer."

"Tell me about it."

"What are you going to do?"

"I'm not sure yet. I've got to figure some things out. For example, why do you think she forgot what went on there when she got back here and into her body?" I asked.

"Think about it, Jack. Nobody is supposed to be able to go to the underworld and come back to the land of the living to tell about it. It's against the most basic rules of God and the universe. So in the rare instances when it's been done, the people involved are stripped of their memories of what happened in the afterlife."

"But Connie was always supposed to come back—as the Slayer," I said. "It seems like she would need to remember being sworn in. Besides, I can remember what happened."

"Maybe she's supposed to remember at some later time," he suggested. "Or it could be that the shock of the whole experience caused her to have temporary amnesia. The only reason I can figure for why *you* can recall what happened there is that you're not, strictly speaking, a human anymore."

"That makes sense, I guess," I said. "Do you know everything now that you're dead? The meaning of life—all that kind of stuff."

"No, of course not. There's just too much to know. What kind of information do you need?"

"I need to know anything and everything about vampire slayers."

"I guess you do at that. I'm afraid that's one of the things that's not in the handbook."

"There's a handbook?"

"Kidding," Sullivan said. "Although now that I think of it, one would be good to have." His gentle laughter rustled the leaves at my feet, causing them to fly away as if chasing one another on a little updraft of salty breeze.

"You're a writer. You should get right on that," I said. "It would make a helluva movie."

"It would at that. Not a bad idea," he said. "About the other thing, though—I'm sorry I can't help you, Jack."

"Oh well. Maybe she'll never remember that she's

the Slayer and everything will be like it was before Melaphia figured it out."

"I wouldn't count on that."

"Why?"

"Destiny is a powerful thing, my friend. That's one of the things that I *have* been able to learn down here. If Connie's destiny is to be the Slayer, she can't escape it. Somehow, some way, she'll find out."

"Oh, crap."

"You asked."

"I gotta go," I muttered.

"I'll see you around," Sullivan said.

I just love a corpse with a sense of humor.

On the way to check on things at the garage, I wracked my brain for any solution to the Connie dilemma. Olivia might know something, but William would have gotten to her first. Besides, Olivia would be just as anxious to see Connie dead as any other blood drinker. I wondered if any guy in the history of the universe had ever had my problem. What I wouldn't give to have some sort of normal predicament like in-law trouble or money difficulties. If I went to Dr. Phil with *this* crisis, what was left of his hair would stand on end and he'd go screaming out of the studio.

Nope, I was on my own with this one. I had to protect Connie from the danger she was in from my own kind—hell, from my own family. I couldn't even tell her about the threat she faced, or she might try to kill *me*. I just wish I knew more about slayers so I could come up with a plan.

There was one last person I might be able to turn to

for information if I was very, very careful—Travis Rubio, the ancient Mayan vampire I met a while back. He had told me a story about being spared by the slayers who had slaughtered the Mayan blood drinkers he lived with hundreds of years ago. I'd have to see if I could puzzle out how to reach him without William finding out.

When I got to the garage I paused for a minute outside. I'd only been gone from here a few nights, but it seemed like a lifetime. It was good to see the old place again, and I relaxed a little. As I was about to step inside, I heard something around back. I followed the noise, which sounded like a grunt. A zombie grunt, as it turned out.

"Hey, Huey." I greeted the little man wielding a spade. "What you doing here, buddy?"

"Oh, hey, Jack. I'm just digging out the Corsica." Huey stopped long enough to look up at me and grin. At least I think he was looking at me. It was hard to tell with those googly eyes of his. Melaphia had blessed him with some kind of voodoo spell that kept him from rotting any more than he already had in the weeks between the time that he was murdered and the time that I accidentally raised him from the dead. He could still pass for human, though, which ensured that the customers wouldn't run out of the garage screaming at the first sight of him. Usually they didn't, anyway.

"Carry on," I intoned, and stepped inside the back door. We had buried him in his Chevy Corsica with a beer in his hand after Reedrek murdered him. He just loved that car. Like they say, there's no accounting for taste. Especially if you're a zombie.

The irregulars—that is, the motley assortment of misfits who hung out at the garage most nights—were playing cards as usual. Rennie, my business partner and the only human in the place, was there. So was Jerry the werewolf and Rufus, who I was pretty sure was some other variety of shape shifter. I'd never quite figured out which kind.

The only one missing was Otis, who might or might not be human. Us nonhuman types can usually sniff one another out, but sometimes the lines get blurred. Blurred by what, you might ask? Well, maybe genetics, maybe nature, maybe the hand of God or even the fickle finger of fate. It'd always been my hunch that somewhere along the way Otis had gotten fingered.

I poured myself a cup of brackish coffee as the boys greeted me. "So I see Huey's trying to liberate the Corsica," I remarked.

"Yeah," Rennie said as he pitched a quarter into the kitty. "I thought about offering him the backhoe, but I figured that using the shovel would keep him busy and out of trouble for a while. The exercise might be good for him, too, who knows?"

I turned around the chair usually occupied by Otis and straddled it. "Everybody needs a hobby, I guess, but I don't know if enhanced upper body strength is really what you want in your average house zombie. I must admit, though, he does come in handy in a fight."

Recently, Huey had given Seth and Jerry and me a hand in a dominance fight with the local werewolf pack. He was strong but a mite uncoordinated. The fight was at the edge of the swamp and Huey managed to fall in. He had crawled out so covered in muck that when he lurched toward them, the werewolves thought they were facing down the Creature from the Black Lagoon.

"Tell me about it," Jerry said, folding his hand. "He found his way to the fight just in time." Jerry still had some claw marks on his face to show for his own efforts. Werewolves heal almost as quickly as vampires, though. He'd be as good as new in a day or two.

"I'll keep an eye on Huey," Rennie promised. He threw down his cards as Rufus collected his winnings. "Maybe the exercise will help him with his stress."

"Stress? Huey's got stress?" I asked, astounded. "He has a nice place to sleep—or lurk or whatever he does in his off hours—plenty of raw hamburger to eat, gainful employment, everything a zombie could want. What does he have to stress about?"

"I don't know, but he's seeing things," Rufus said.

"What kind of things?"

"Little green men," Rennie said.

"Say what?"

"Little blue men," corrected Jerry.

"Only his hair is blue," Rufus said. "According to Huey, that is." He pointed at his head and made a circular motion with his index finger.

"Who is 'him'?"

"Huey calls him Stevie," Rennie said. "I guess he's like an imaginary playmate or something."

"Well, what can you expect?" I asked. "Huey barely has enough reliable brain power left to tie his shoes. Hallucinations are probably just a by-product of dead gray matter."

"Kind of like carbon emissions are a by-product of internal combustion engines?" Rennie observed. "Maybe Huey needs a catalytic converter for his brain." Rennie could put anything in terms of auto mechanics.

"Well," I said, "if Huey needs an imaginary friend to keep him company, so be it. But speaking of friends—Rufus, where's Otis?" Rufus and Otis were usually joined at the hip. You seldom saw one without the other.

Rufus shrugged and shuffled the cards. "He's back at Werm's nightclub, I reckon. Just like every night since they opened."

Rennie gave me a sidelong grin as he picked up the first card Rufus dealt him. He'd heard the peevishness in Rufus's voice as well as I had.

"Why is Otis hanging out at Werm's nightclub?" Jerry asked. "The only kind of nightlife he's ever been interested in is this here standing card game."

"He hasn't decided to start courting that female impersonator who sings down there, has he?" I asked.

"Otis ain't like that," Rufus assured me with a disgusted look. "There's something else going on with him, though. He's acting . . . funny."

I started to point out that Otis often acted funny. Take those Dickies work shirts with other people's names on the patches. And the fact that he had no visible means of support. I didn't know where he lived or if he had a job. And then there was the little matter of not knowing what he was exactly. I wanted to ask Rufus if he knew, but the garage was strictly a don't-ask-don't-tell zone. People didn't allude to the fact that I was a vampire, and I, in turn, didn't bring up whatever they were unless they mentioned it first.

"How is he acting funny, Rufus?" Shape shifters are very intuitive—sensitive, you might say.

"It's hard to describe," he said. "He's kind of nervous, like."

"I've felt it, too," Jerry offered. "He's stressed out or something."

Rufus started to say something else but stopped himself. "What is it?" I urged him. "What aren't you telling me?"

Rufus and Jerry exchanged glances, and Jerry shrugged. "We—that is, you know, folks like me and Jerry here—we've been sensing that something is going to happen," Rufus began.

"Like what?"

Jerry scratched the back of his head. "It's hard to explain. We just know that something important is coming and . . ."

"It's not good," Rufus finished.

I looked from one of them to the other. "That's it? That's all you've got?"

"Sorry. I know it's not much," Jerry said.

Shape shifters' animal instincts are nothing to sneeze at. I made a mental note to keep my eyes open. With that in mind, I decided to mosey over to the Portal to check on what was happening with Werm and see if he'd heard any gossip that might shed light on whatever was nudging my frequently fuzzy friends. From the look of his opening night clientele, the club was going to bring together just the kind of assorted oddballs that might know a thing or two about otherworldly goings-on. Heaven help Savannah.

I let myself out the back way to check on Huey's progress, which was negligible. In fact, he'd stopped digging altogether and was talking to a crow perched in the live oak beside the garage. As far as I could tell, the crow wasn't answering back, but it looked like it wanted to.

"What's with the crow?" I said to the little guy.

"He flew up just after you went inside."

"Shouldn't he be roosting right now?"

"That's what I asked him," Huey said reasonably.

Seeing little blue men and talking to crows. Poor little feeble-minded Huey. "What'd he say?" I asked gently. The crow cocked its head to one side and stared at me with its beady black eyes.

Huey shrugged, leaning on his shovel. "Nothing yet. I think he likes you, Jack."

The bird hadn't taken its eyes off me since I'd stepped outside. It was downright creepy. "You let me know if he says or does anything interesting," I said. "And good luck with that digging,"

"Thanks," Huey said.

I started to go, but curiosity halted me and I turned to Huey again. "What's this I hear about this Stevie fellow?" I asked.

Huey waved one grimy hand dismissively. "Aw, it's just Otis."

"Huh?"

"Otis and Stevie are the same. Stevie is kind of inside Otis, like that little crow used to be inside a shell."

The guys were right; Huey was one lug nut short of a wheel's worth. I already had to buy his weight in ground beef once a week. Was I going to have to spring for zombie therapy, too?

"You've started seeing somebody inside Otis?"

"Ever since I came back," he said.

"Ooh-kay," I said. "What does Otis have to say about this?"

"I haven't talked to him about it. I just mentioned Stevie to the other guys and they made fun of me, so I shut up. I didn't tell them the part about him and Otis being the same guy, though."

"Uh-huh. If I were you, I wouldn't mention it to anyone else." I hoped Huey's hallucinations would take care of themselves. I had enough to worry about without men in white coats snagging my pet zombie with a butterfly net and hauling him off to the state mental hospital. I would have a lot of explaining to do about his eating habits.

As I pulled away from the building I glanced in the rearview mirror. The crow was still watching me.

Seven

As I entered Werm's nightclub I fought the urge to cover my ears, assaulted as they were by the incomprehensible racket the young people of today called music.

Seth, who was tending bar, motioned me over and I seated myself on a stool. "I called this morning to check on Jack and Connie. Melaphia said they were all right. Congratulations on getting them back." Being familiar with my drinking preferences, he poured me a double shot of single-malt Scotch along with one for himself.

I clinked glasses with him. "Here's to their safe return," I said. The whiskey warmed my throat pleasantly, and the next sensation I felt warmed the rest of my body.

A pair of slender arms reached around my waist and caressed me in a most intimate way. The touch's familiarity sent a shock wave of recognition through my body. *Eleanor* . . . I stood and quickly turned toward the woman, whose arms slid around me even more firmly as I faced her. So sure was I that my Eleanor had escaped damnation and made her way back to me that I was shocked to see Ginger in her place.

As I composed myself, I wondered what had caused her to exhibit such forwardness toward me. Her manner hadn't seemed at all unusual on my first visit to the Portal.

"William, I'm so glad to see you again. I feel like it's been forever."

"Why, thank you," I said. "But I was here only last night, remember?"

"Oh yes. Silly me." She arched her back and pressed herself against my groin, arousing me immediately, as she'd meant to. "I wonder if you could answer a question for me."

"What's that?"

She tossed her head, shifting her mass of red hair to one side, uncovering the creamy flesh of her neck. "I heard a rumor that Eleanor isn't coming back. Is that true?"

I kept my face a neutral mask. "Oh? Who told you that?"

"A little bird," she said. She put one palm flat against my chest and peered up at me with long-lashed blue eyes. "So what's the story? I really have to know." Her perfume was cloying and familiar.

"You heard right. She's not coming back. She decided to stay in Europe indefinitely."

"Ooh, whatever shall we do without her?" Ginger purred. Her hand brushed my swollen cock before coming to rest discreetly on my thigh. "I don't want you to be lonely, William."

Her vermilion lips reminded me so much of blood that I felt my fangs begin to lengthen along with that other part of me. The light blue veins in her delicate pale throat seemed to pulse with the primitive rhythm of the music. I basked in the living human heat her body radiated and felt myself reach out to her.

But then I became aware of two blood drinkers approaching on my left. Werm had appeared with another young vampire.

Ginger must have realized my attention was required elsewhere. "Later?" she asked.

"Perhaps," I said.

She moved away with a pretty pout.

"William," Werm said, "this is Freddy Blackstone, the guy I was telling you about."

The vampire, who looked much the same human age as Werm, smiled and offered his hand. He was of average height and weight, with unkempt dark hair and a scraggly beard. His ragged jeans and worn flannel shirt over a faded tee might have been acquired at any charity thrift store.

I shook his hand. "I understand you're a friend of Tobey's."

"Yeah. Tobey and me are tight," he said.

I looked toward Werm, who offered his interpretation. "They're friends," he said simply.

"How do you find our fair city?" I asked.

"I found it real easy, dude."

"He means how do you like it here," Werm explained to Freddy.

"Oh. It's cool, man."

"That is gratifying," I said. I was struck by the notion that Freddy was not a great intellect, and that inference led me to wonder how he made it across the continent in one, unparboiled piece. "How *did* you get here?"

"I stowed away in the luggage compartment of a jet that was supposed to land on the right coast of Florida in the middle of the night, dude. Turned out it wasn't the baggage compartment at all, and I froze solid when we reached cruising altitude. They opened some kind of hatch or something and I got dumped."

"Dumped? As in, onto the ground?"

"Yeah, man."

"When you were 'dumped,' did some frozen green matter come out with you, by any chance?"

"Yeah, dude. How did you know?"

"Just a lucky guess." I exchanged glances with Werm, whose eyes had gone wide with wonder. He had obviously come to the same conclusion as I. The plane's septic system had jettisoned Freddy along with its chemically treated waste. "What a charming anecdote," I went on. "Where did you, er, land?"

"In some marshland. It cushioned my fall, but I was still unconscious for a while. I'd sunk into just enough mud to protect me from the sun."

"My, but you are a lucky young man," I observed. "Do continue. What happened then?"

"When I came to, I cleaned myself up and followed the smell of food."

Speaking of smell, I imagined that Freddy would have been somewhat fragrant after being flushed with the waste and then marinating in mud for a spell.

"On the subject of food . . ." I began.

Werm interjected, "Don't worry, William, I explained to him about your house rules."

Freddy held up the fingers of his right hand as if he were about to take the Boy Scout oath. "I won't kill any humans. I promise. I don't believe in it, dude. I'm a live-and-let-live guy. You feel me?"

"Indeed," I said, hoping he didn't mean that literally. "I'm sure you're a civilized man if Tobias calls you friend. And if you stay that way, you're welcome to remain here as long as you like."

"Thanks, dude." Freddy smiled, giving the barest glimpse of a mature set of fangs. This blood drinker might seem youthful, but he was no fledgling. I wondered at his background. Since I hadn't brought him to the New World as part of my smuggling operation for peaceful European vampires, I assumed he was a product of the indigenous western vampires like Tobey. Perhaps I'd ask him one day if he stayed in the city long enough.

"C'mon, Freddy, I'll get you a beer," Werm said, and his new friend followed.

When they'd left, I saw Jack's friend Otis sitting on the bar stool directly behind where they'd stood. He was furtively fiddling with an electronic device, and when I greeted him he nearly jumped off his seat.

"Hey there, William," he said, stuffing the gadget in the breast pocket of his workshirt—a shirt bearing for some unknown reason a patch embroidered with the name *Kenny*. If Otis was attempting to secrete the apparatus, he was doing a poor job of it. An earpiece still dangled from his pocket. "Gotta go," he said abruptly, and drained his beer in one gulp. Wiping his mouth with the back of his hand, he disappeared into the pressing crowd.

I turned back to Seth, who refilled my glass. "Strange guy, that Otis," he remarked.

I took a sip of Scotch. "If Jack didn't have strange friends, he wouldn't have any friends at all."

Jack

Hellfire and damnation. My sire was the last guy I wanted to see tonight, and there he was, sitting at the bar. I ramped up the mental shield I used to keep him from sensing my whereabouts and skulked into the shadows behind the wildly gyrating young people on the dance floor. Normally I wasn't the skulking type, but I just didn't want to deal with him again so soon. I'd hang out for a while, and if he didn't run along home pretty quick, I'd skedaddle back to the garage.

The crowd milling about the bar shifted and I saw what looked for all the world like Otis taping a conversation that William was having with Werm and a vampire I'd never seen before. Usually a strange vamp in town was enough to put me on red alert, but I relaxed when William's body language said he wasn't a threat.

Since the new bloodsucker had gotten the Good Housekeeping stamp of approval from my sire, the only remaining question was what Otis thought he was doing with that little voice recorder. I knew what it was because Iban had one just like it that he used to dictate movie-directing ideas.

Werm and his friend cleared out as I made my way

closer. William said something to Otis, who downed his drink and turned to go. He made for the back door and I went after him, reaching him just as he made it there. I got his biceps in a vise grip and dragged him out into the alley.

"What's with the voice recorder, Otis?" I asked without preamble.

"Huh? What voice recorder?"

I plucked the gizmo out of his pocket by the ear-buds. "*This* voice recorder."

"That—well, that's . . ."

Nobody I knew had ever accused Otis of thinking fast on his feet. "Since the cat's got your tongue, let's just skip ahead to the next question. You were using this to spy on William. Now I want to know why."

Then the damndest thing happened. Before my eyes, Otis changed into something very unOtislike. In a little poof of sparkly pastel light, he lost a third of his height and all of his Otisness. In fact, instead of the guy I knew, before me was . . . Stevie Sparkle?

His hair looked like blue-tinted Christmas tree tinsel, only finer, and his skin had an unnatural creamy perfection that glowed like a flawless pearl. *This* was the blue-haired Stevie who Huey had been seeing inside the shell of the homely, oil-streaked Otis! The Otis exterior was only a cover for a fey glitter-rock icon who didn't look a day older than he did when I saw him on seventies TV variety shows.

I looked him up and down, still unable to believe my own eyes. Even Werm wouldn't be caught dead—if you'll pardon the expression—in the skintight outfit Stevie wore. The spangled electric-blue number had been his trademark, as I recalled. A chick I was dating at the time said he wore it to emphasize the color of his eyes, which were as otherworldly a shade of blue as his hair. She had a crush on him.

I can't believe I actually bought that woman drinks.

Otis/Stevie looked down at himself as if he was just as shocked as I was at his appearance, and just like that, he was back to looking like the old Otis again. I'd scared him so badly he'd dropped his glamour by accident.

"Dude," I said accusingly. "You're a *fairy*!"

Otis jumped a little as a skinny goth came out of the men's room down the alley and passed us on the way back inside the club. "Keep it down," Otis said. "Somebody's gonna hear you and think I'm . . . you know."

I nearly laughed. "You're worried that somebody's going to think you're gay? That's the least of your problems, pal. I've heard all about you—you fairies. Real fairies, I mean."

William had told me about the fey a long time ago, but I'd never met one before, and I wasn't sure I believed they existed until now. William had said they were troublesome creatures—a race of charming and supernaturally beautiful thieves and tricksters never to be trusted.

"That's *faerie*," Otis corrected peevishly, pronouncing it *FAY-ree*. "And most of the stories they tell about us are just old wives' tales. For instance, I've never stolen a baby in my life."

Baby stealing? I stared at him. I'd never heard that one before. "God a'mighty!" I had so many questions—and accusations—I didn't know where to start. "*You're* Stevie Sparkle?"

Otis sighed. "That's what I look like naturally. For a little while, back in the seventies, I got a chance to let my freak flag fly, as they used to say."

"So you actually *were* Stevie. You hid in plain sight," I observed.

"Yeah. Kind of like you do."

He was right about that. We vampires have learned to adapt to our environments by taking on what humans consider to be normal lives. Except for not going out in the sun, we hold everyday—that is, every*night*—jobs, like mine. Never being seen in natural light helps us disguise our pallor. Also, I tried to avoid the kind of lighting they have in most retail stores. But hey, a boy has to go to the twenty-four-hour Wal-Mart once in a while just like anybody else.

"So," I mused, "you got to go around in your real skin back then, not having to get by on glamour to hide what you really look like so as not to freak people out."

"Yeah. When glitter rock was popular, my natural look was perfect; I fit right in. In fact, nobody could outshine me. Before that, the only time I got to drop the glamour was on Halloween. And, you know, at parties."

I didn't even want to know what kind of parties he was talking about. "So people thought the shiny hair and eyes and skin were part of the act. They must have thought you had one hellacious makeup artist."

"They thought it was some kind of special effect, like in *Star Wars*." Otis laughed uneasily.

"So what are you doing here?"

Otis shrugged and looked at the floor. "Oh, you know—it's a fun place."

"I'm not talking about the *club,* dammit." For one of the fey, he was a terrible liar. "Try again. What is an undercover faerie fey doing hanging out with a bunch of vampires? And why were you spying on William?"

"Uh . . . ," Otis mumbled.

Now this was just sad. Fairies, that is *faeries,* were supposed to be clever and quick, not as big and dumb as a man can come. I drew back my lips and extended my fangs. "Don't even *think* about lying to me."

Otis froze, mesmerized by my display of badness. People—human or otherwise—never failed to find my full vamp-out mode . . . inspiring. I used it to inspire reluctant people to talk, shut up, stop doing what they were doing, or do exactly what I said to do—whatever my needs happened to be at the time.

"I, uh, guess I just like vampires is all," he said. "Always have."

"*Nobody* likes vampires," I said, leaning close enough for him to see that special quality in my eyes. It's a feature most vampires learn to mask to keep humans from running away screaming. When my eyes dilate completely, my blue irises disappear into blackness, taking on a subtle, doll-like emptiness that says more clearly than words ever could: Do not be deceived, human. Despite the walking and talking and all other evidence to the contrary, this creature is dead. And deadly.

"Um, okay, would you believe . . . I like the coffee at the garage?"

The coffee at the garage looked a lot like the kind of pitch they use for waterproofing down at the docks, and probably tasted worse. I seized Otis by the back of his shirt and hoisted him into the air. "No more games, Tinker Bell. We're going to talk to the big dog."

When I hauled Otis before William and whispered to my sire that we had to have a serious talk, he told Werm to close the bar immediately. Most of the patrons took it in stride, although Ginger seemed a little put out. She tried to cling to William, which seemed kind of strange for her, but he gently shooed her away. Then it was only me, William, Werm, Otis, and Seth. Whatever Otis had to say for himself, Werm probably needed to know, too, and there was no point in keeping things from Seth either as he'd always been an ally.

William looked from me to Otis. "What's this about, gentlemen?"

"I caught Otis taping your conversation with that vampire that was in here earlier," I said.

"I wasn't doing that, honest," Otis argued, drawing himself up.

I snatched the recorder out of his pocket. "Want me to play it for William?"

Otis deflated visibly and hung his head. I was almost sorry for him, especially when I thought about how terrified he'd always been of my sire.

"When I confronted him, he got spooked and dropped his glamour. He's a faerie, and he's been hiding it from us all the time he's been hanging out at the garage."

I heard a little growl from Seth, who came around from behind the bar to stand beside Werm. Werm just looked surprised. "Hey, Jack," Werm said. "I know you're a good ol' boy and everything, but I never figured you for a homophobe." I silenced him with my shut-up-or-I'll-bite-you look. Seth bent to whisper something in his ear. "Oh," Werm said.

William took a menacing step toward Otis. "You are one of the fey?" he asked. He leaned close to Otis and sniffed. His fangs came out. "Yes, you are. Why have I not smelled the Sidhe on you before?"

"Because he never let you close enough," I said. I now knew why Otis avoided William whenever he could. I had always thought it was simple fear. After all, William was the baddest blood drinker on the continent. But part of that fear was of being found out for what he was. The question was, why was he hiding?

"I always knew there was something not quite human about him, but I didn't know what until tonight," I said.

William's eyes narrowed and he jabbed Otis in the chest with one index finger. "You knew Jack was a relative child amongst blood drinkers, and since the fey are almost unheard of on this continent, you were pretty well assured he'd never seen—or smelled—one before. You've been a fixture at his place of business for years now. It looks as if you've been spying on the both of us. And now you'll tell me why."

Otis just stood there, mesmerized by the sight of William's razorlike fangs fully extended.

William leaned closer. "I tasted fey flesh more than once in my youth. I rather liked it. If you don't answer my questions, I'll offer you to my two offspring so they might know that pleasure as well."

I heard Werm whisper to Seth, "What is fey flesh supposed to taste like?"

"Chicken," Seth whispered back. "They say."

Otis started to crumple to the floor, and I got a better grip on the back of his shirt to help him stand upright. "What's it going to be, buddy?" I asked with a wink toward William. It wasn't the first time we'd had to use the bad cop–good cop routine on some recalcitrant bad guy. "You know we don't want to eat you. But you give us no choice if you don't tell us what's going on."

"Okay. Okay. But can I have a drink first? I need a stiff one."

William nodded to Werm, who scurried behind the bar and poured Otis a whiskey. I settled the wayward faerie on a bar stool and we all gathered around him.

He took a gulp of his drink, followed by a deep breath. "I'm part of a secret society among the fey," he began. "We're what you might call . . . watchers."

I glanced at William, who was wearing his poker face. "*What* is this secret society dedicated to watching?" he asked evenly. "Or should I say *who*?"

"Um, you," Otis muttered.

"Say what?" I said.

"That is to say—vampires," Otis clarified.

"What about shape shifters?" Seth asked.

"Not so much," Otis said.

Seth looked a little hurt and walked back behind the bar.

"Although we're supposed to report any unusual activities by anybody that's not human," Otis continued. "But with vampires, we're supposed to document everything. Which ones get made by who.

Which ones die and how. Even who you guys hang out with." He shrugged apologetically.

"That's why you've started hanging out here at the bar as well as at the garage," I accused. "You've been a fixture at my place of business since forever. You know it's my job to help William import peaceful vampires from Europe and ride herd on the ones already here. And when Werm opened the bar, you knew it would attract weird characters, human or otherwise, who might be in Savannah, so you started spending time in here, too."

Otis shrugged, not bothering to deny it. I thought about the fact that it was Otis who always had the latest gossip about the odd happenings in the nonhuman community. It had been Otis, after all, who had alerted me and William to the *Alabaster* being found adrift with its crew and cargo dead.

Just lately I had found out that Jerry liked to pass the time at my place of business because his werewolf cousins—the ones who wanted to eat him for daring to leave the pack—were afraid of me. Now I find out that Otis just hung around to spy on me. And here I thought it was my warmth and personality that kept them coming back. It was all enough to hurt my feelings a little, to tell the truth.

"If something happens, like if a fight breaks out between nonhumans, what are you supposed to do?" I asked. I had wondered why Otis had remained conspicuously out of the conflict when Jerry, Huey, and I had to help Seth out. Rennie had an excuse to stay away; as a human he would have been torn apart. And Rufus got a pass because we still didn't know what he *was* exactly. But as a Sidhe, Otis's powers of trickery alone would have come in handy, like Werm's did.

"I'm supposed to stay neutral," Otis explained. "Like Switzerland."

"Is this cool or what!" Werm said. He seemed really flattered. "William, did you know there was a watcher society for vampires?"

"No, I did not," he admitted, not taking his gaze off Otis. "What is the ultimate purpose of this watching?"

Otis cleared his throat and sat up a little straighter. The whiskey had obviously calmed his nerves. "The nobility don't tell us peons much about that. They just told me to watch you guys' comings and goings, any new vampires that come along, and report back to them."

"You must have some idea," I prompted. I took the whiskey bottle from Werm and refilled Otis's glass.

"All I know is that a few years ago I was having a great time on an oldies tour," Otis began again. "The free booze, the women, hanging with Frampton. It wasn't as good as the seventies, mind you, but it was still pretty sweet."

Werm's eyebrows shot up and he started to interrupt, but I silenced him with a warning glance. "Go on, big O," I said.

"And I got summoned to the old country. A bunch of Sidhe over there witnessed . . . something." A shiver seemed to go down Otis's spine for a moment, but he shook it off.

"What?" I asked. "What did they see?" I was afraid Werm would run plumb out of booze before I could get the whole story out of this guy.

"The return of the Wild Hunt," he said.

William, who rarely betrayed feelings of anxiety or alarm in front of outsiders, actually gasped.

"What is that?" I demanded.

William explained, "The Wild Hunt is a manifestation of phantom warriors and huntsmen that were thought to ride across the sky on thunderstorms, complete with horses and hounds. It hasn't been seen in recorded history. Even the oldest blood drinkers think it's a myth. I admit I certainly always thought it was."

"It's no myth," Otis insisted. "Only one of the five Sidhe who witnessed it returned to tell the tale. The others were struck down."

"Struck down?" Werm asked.

I ignored Werm, even though he looked like he was going to faint any second. What else was new? "So some faeries were dancing around a maypole or something and got struck by lightning. What's the big deal about a pack of ghost riders in the sky?" I asked.

"The wild huntsmen are thought to be harbingers of doom," William said. "Seeing them is supposed to presage something catastrophic—war, plague, famine."

"What did the Sidhe tell you when they summoned you to—where?" I asked.

"Ireland," Otis said, pronouncing it like the Lucky Charms leprechaun. "The leaders of my branch of the Sidhe organized the unattached males and assigned each of us a landmass to cover. We're supposed to watch the activities of any and all immortals in our territory."

"Why?" I asked. "What's the connection between the Wild Hunt and vampires?"

"That's the part I'm not quite sure of," Otis admitted. "It has something to do with how vampires figure into some ancient Celtic prophecies."

Otis was getting quite drunk now, and he was starting to look depressed. For that matter, William wasn't looking any too perky either. His natural pallor had turned downright ghostly. I could tell that he didn't like the way this conversation was going. Not one little bit.

"Ancient Celtic prophecies about what, exactly?" I asked, leaning toward him.

"The end of the freakin' world," Otis said, and did a face plant onto the bar.

Eight

William

Jack accepted a damp bar cloth from Seth and began to swab his drunken faerie friend's face in hopes of reviving him. Otis's glamour had deserted him when he passed out. He now resembled a diminutive circus performer. The transformation caused some hubbub among Jack, Werm, and Seth. Evidently Otis was indeed some sort of recognizable entertainer in his true guise. Werm was especially impressed.

The tumult caused by Otis's revelations and his transformation into fey form afforded me time to gather my thoughts. I now realized there was a preponderance of evidence pointing to a looming disaster of worldwide proportions.

First there were the vague but ominous warnings that Olivia's vampires found in Alger's Celtic scrolls and tablets. Then came the fulfillment of a Mayan slayer prophecy in the person of Connie Jones. Bolstering that was the uneasiness sensed by Seth, which

I'd wager was shared by the rest of the shape shifter community. Finally, and most alarming of all, was this reappearance of the Wild Hunt after thousands of years. The event had obviously frightened the Sidhe, and they didn't frighten easily.

When Jack had succeeded in propping his friend upright once again, he told Werm to brew some strong coffee. I could only hope Werm could make coffee more drinkable than Jack was used to at the garage. Faeries are a hardy lot, and this one had shared some valuable information; I didn't want to see him poisoned.

Jack gently but firmly patted Otis's face until he opened his eyes. As soon as he became oriented to his surroundings, he raised his glamour and became the old Otis once more.

"Whoa!" Werm observed, duly impressed.

Jack thrust a cup of black coffee into his friend's hands and urged him to drink. "What do vampires have to do with the end of the world?"

"Huh?" Otis muttered.

"Focus!" Jack commanded. "You were talking about ancient Celtic prophecies about the end of the world which had something to do with vampires. What's the connection?"

"Crap if I know," Otis said.

"Think hard, Otis or Stevie or whatever your name is," Jack said.

"I've told you everything I know. Honest."

I said, "Jack, why don't you take Otis back to the garage, or wherever he sleeps. I sense that he's telling us the truth. If we think of anything more to ask him, we can question him at another time."

"What—what are we going to do?" Werm asked, naturally frightened.

"Don't concern yourself," I said, trying to sound reassuring. "Melaphia is already researching some related matters. I'm sure we'll know more soon. Until then, try not to worry."

Seth squeezed the little vampire's shoulder in a manly gesture of support. "William will get to the bottom of this, buddy. Why don't you go on downstairs, hop in your box, and get a good day's sleep?"

Werm shivered. "I don't mind if I do." He took a couple of steps toward the door to the cellar but turned back to get the half-empty bottle of whiskey and took it with him.

Jack threw Otis over his shoulder in a fireman's carry and paused at the door. "What are you going to do?"

"I think I'll go and speak with your grandsire to see if he knows anything about any of this."

"Good luck. The last few times I've talked to Reedrek he'd gone as crazy as a shithouse rat from being cooped up in that granite cornerstone. He was talking gibberish."

I said good night to Seth, who showed me the entrance to the tunnels. Werm had cleverly installed the steel doorway to the tunnels from the cellar when he had the building renovated. The web of abandoned tunnels was what remained of Savannah's first street level before the city was raised as protection from high tides wrought by hurricanes. I could have driven closer to the place underneath the hospital where Reedrek was entombed, but I welcomed the walk to help me think after all we had just learned from Otis.

I'd always wondered why Reedrek had chosen last autumn to track me down after these hundreds of years since I escaped him. He'd wanted me to begin killing and turning humans in great numbers to increase his power as my sire. That must have meant that he needed power more than he ever had.

When I reached the slab of granite behind which Reedrek lay, I focused my psychic abilities and found my sire singing to himself in a strange keening voice. I paused to listen to his nonsensical lyrics. Something about a carriage and missing out on leftover lamb. Jack was correct. Sensory deprivation had rendered him quite mad, but that didn't mean he wasn't still dangerous.

The old demon was as contrary as he was treacherous. If I asked him straight out what he knew about the Slayer or the looming catastrophe, he would think it a fine game to try to lead me astray. I had to establish the game myself. To control it.

I allowed him to sense my presence, and he spoke to me as if we stood face-to-face without the layers of granite and concrete between us.

"You've come back, my son. How good to, ah, see you. I hope your journey was a pleasant one."

Had Jack told him I was in Europe? Surely not. We'd agreed not to tell him anything he could use to taunt us. What Jack called head games were Reedrek's specialty. Just because Reedrek was immobile did not mean he was helpless, not as long as he had his psychic powers and anyone in his vast bloodline to use them on. I cursed him silently for casting the first die and rendering me on the defensive from the get-go. I fought the urge to demand how he knew I'd been gone.

"Indeed it was a pleasant visit," I said, falling back into the formal speech of the days when I'd been at my sire's beck and call. "I was able to accomplish much good."

"Is that so?" Reedrek asked benignly. "Do tell. I'm keen to hear of your exploits."

"I won't bore you. I'm sure you have your sources." I hoped he'd tell me who they were, but I didn't count on it.

"I do," he said. I could hear rather than see the mocking grin on his face. "I've learned much from them just lately."

"I learned much as well, about the past as well as the future. Our upcoming travails remind me of the famous Chinese curse—"

"May you live in interesting times," Reedrek supplied, and cackled with insane laughter. "That's a clever way of putting it."

My ploy was not working. I could tell by the brevity of his answers that Reedrek, even in his madness, sensed I was fishing. Just as I was about to turn to leave, he said, "Good news travels as fast as lightning."

Was the mention of lightning a veiled reference to the Wild Hunt? Folklorists explained away the phenomenon by saying it was a myth constructed by primitive Celts to explain electrical storms to themselves.

Human beings, even learned academics, have a clever talent for protecting their fragile minds from truths that would render them mad with fear if they were ever acknowledged. They take great pains to construct reasons to distrust what the primitive parts of their brains instinctively know. But they choose to close their eyes to their reptilian brains. Only the fullness of time will tell if that tendency is a skill to aid their survival or hasten their downfall as a species.

"And what news would that be?" I asked, hoping to provoke some response I could make sense of. He would probably balk at the direct question, but I was losing patience with the game.

"Moving day is almost here!"

"Moving day? Who, pray tell, is moving?"

"Why, me, my boy. First I'll be moving north and south and east and west along with everyone else. Then I shall be moving up in the world. Surely if you've learned about the future as you claim, you've learned about that," he taunted.

"I suppose you could use a change of scene. I guess I should have made your resting place more secure." I hoped to inspire him to tell me what force he thought could break him out of granite, concrete, and steel, but he was too wily to take the bait.

"Nothing you have the power to build can keep me imprisoned when the old lords deem the time is right for my freedom."

So he thought the old lords would free him. "That's funny. I don't seem to recall seeing any of them around."

"They have their agents," Reedrek hissed.

"I haven't seen any of them, either."

Reedrek laughed again, and it had a hysterical quality that put my fangs on edge. "You think to trick me into revealing their identities and plans. But as I said, the time is not yet right. When the time comes, you'll know. And so will everyone else."

I wished I could punch my way through the concrete and stone and throttle my sire, but there was little I could do. I couldn't threaten him, because Jack and I had already subjected him to the worst punishment we could dream up for him—to be immobilized in the dank darkness with the rats and the worms for eternity. We couldn't have killed him, for to destroy one's own sire or grandsire means death to the vampire that does the killing. I had neither carrot nor stick to influence Reedrek to talk, even if he knew anything of value.

"I have better things to do than to listen to the bluffs and ravings of a lunatic."

"Off with you, then. I'll be out of here soon enough. My carriage is coming. I can almost hear the rumbling of its wheels now!"

Disgusted, I turned on my heel to walk away, but then thought of a different tack he might respond to. At this point, what harm would another direct question do? I might get lucky. "What do you know of the Slayer?" I asked.

"Why ask me?" he answered. "Why not ask her?" For the first time in our conversation, he sounded completely sane. That shook me much more than his wild ramblings had.

After I left my sire, I returned to my automobile and drove over to the construction site where Eleanor's brothel was being rebuilt. It was to have been a grand establishment that would have reflected Eleanor's excellent, if exotic, taste. Looking at the half-finished building now, I was tempted to set fire to it myself. It would remind me of Eleanor's treachery and her death and suffering at my hands every time I looked at it.

And that was only part of what weighed on my mind. A worldwide catastrophe, foretold by both Mayan and voodoo prophecies and confirmed by the shape shifters and the Sidhe, was imminent. I had no clue how to avert the disaster, whatever it was, unless Melaphia or Olivia turned up any relevant information in the ancient scrolls and tablets they were studying. Add to that the appearance of the legendary vampire slayer in our midst and my so-called life was complete.

I couldn't recall a moment in my long undeath when I felt as alone and powerless, not even during the time I was under Reedrek's thumb. The calamity would come and there would be nothing I could do about it. Jack would refuse to kill Connie Jones before she killed him, and if I took matters into my own hands, he might just kill me himself.

The framing on the multistory building was almost complete, making it look like a monstrous skeleton lying bleached and motionless in the moonlight. I made my way down the basement steps to the spot where Eleanor had erected her voodoo altars in the old house. As I hung my head and remembered my lover's horrible suffering in the underworld, I felt my old familiar death wish rear its head. I deserved to be in hell right along with Eleanor even if it meant being tortured for all eternity with some foul punishment fashioned just for me. If I had only left her alone, or at least refused her pleas to be made a blood drinker, she would be alive and well and mistress of this house right now.

I spied a pile of scrap lumber and sawdust that some worker had piled up in a corner and seized a three-foot-long piece of two-by-four. It made a satisfactory splintering sound as I broke it over my knee, wood shards flying. One of the fragments had come away with a sharp point, producing the pleasant fragrance of timber. As I tested the weight of it, switching it from hand to hand, I heard footsteps on the new subfloor above me.

"What on earth are you doing down there?" Ginger asked as she made her way down the steps in four-inch spike heels—not an easy task even in the daylight, but she did it with grace by the light only of a nearby streetlamp. I noticed, not for the first time, how shapely her legs were and couldn't help but imagine them wrapped around me.

"Just . . . thinking," I said. "What are *you* doing here?"

"I couldn't sleep after seeing you tonight. I missed you so much while you were away."

Ginger's behavior toward me this evening was totally uncharacteristic, but the change wasn't surprising. She was no fool, and when she heard that Eleanor wasn't coming back, she evidently decided to waste no time making her move on the richest man in Savannah. What was a whore if not opportunistic?

"That's kind of you to say," I stated, tossing the wood back onto the pile. She was near enough to me now that I could smell her perfume as well as the sweet, heady odor of her humanity. "So you decided to take a walk, did you?"

"Yes, and I'm glad that I did, because now I get to see you again. Alone." She stepped closer to me and put her small palms against my chest. I wondered if she noticed I had no heartbeat. Her own heartbeat called out to me like a siren song. "This is very naughty of me, but I'm glad that Eleanor's not coming back," she said.

I captured her hands with my own, squeezed them gently, then brought them to my lips, first one, then the other. "Oh? And why is that?"

"Because I can seduce you," she whispered. I released her hands so she could put her arms around my neck and press herself against me. I was quickly aroused by the feel of her firm, round breasts rubbing my chest. Now, here was something to live for, at least a little while longer.

The chivalrous thing to do would be to take the young woman to a proper place for our very first encounter—the nearby Hyatt perhaps, or at least back to my home. But I wasn't feeling particularly chivalrous this evening. "Let's get on with that, then," I said.

My hands roamed down her body, pausing briefly to squeeze her breasts, then her buttocks, and on to the hem of her black leather miniskirt. I reached underneath it and up to that magical place at the apex of her thighs. My fingertips found a fine barrier of silk and teased their way across it, eliciting a moan of pleasure from the lady. I covered her painted lips with my own, kissed her deeply, and pulled her more tightly against me. I blazed a trail of kisses down her neck while fingering aside the strip of fabric between her legs.

She was dewy with need and shuddered when I penetrated her, stroking the sensitive forward wall of her passage with one finger. What was it the moderns called that magical area? Ah, yes, the G spot. When I touched the swollen bud of her clit with my thumb, her body shuddered with release. I carried her to a makeshift table made up of planks suspended side-by-side between two sawhorses. A circular saw had been set up at one end.

I ripped off her panties and set her bare bottom on the edge of the table. Glancing at the saw, she said, "You're not going to saw me in half like a magician, are you?"

I laughed hoarsely. "I'm not that kind of magician," I said. "Besides, I want you in one piece."

I let go of her long enough to unfasten my pants and free my erection. Meanwhile she threw off her sweater, revealing a lacy bra, and shivered briefly in the winter chill. I saw her squint in the darkness to see me better, but I was blocking her light. She reached out for me and wrapped both hands around my cock.

"Oh. My. God," she said breathlessly and, I thought, a little fearfully. Not an uncommon reaction to my size, even for an experienced whore. She began to stroke me and gasped when I dug my fingers under the brassiere and ripped it off.

"I'll buy you another," I said, pausing to admire the way her nipples rose. I circled them with my thumbs while cupping her breasts. Her skin was the color of ivory, so pale she looked almost like one of my kind.

I slid my hands underneath her bottom and leaned into her body, penetrating her only a little at first. I enjoyed the sound of her feminine sigh and savored the feel of her slick, welcoming heat. Then, in one long, hard stroke I rammed my cock fully into her. The invasion caused her body to stiffen at first, but when I began to work in and out of her, she clung to me like a woman drowning and matched me stroke for stroke. There was something in her movements that reminded me of Eleanor. Perhaps the madam had taught her protégée some of her techniques.

I bent my head to her breasts to suckle there, pulling on her rosy, taut nipples and laving them over and over with my tongue, allowing the serrated inner edge of my fangs to graze them ever so lightly.

The temptation to bite was strong enough to make me quake. Perhaps if I only took a little blood, she would just assume it was one of my individual kinks. She must have regular patrons whose peccadilloes were stranger than that. On the other hand, I didn't want to frighten her away. She might prove to be a satisfying regular plaything. There was time to initiate her into the life of the swan later, if she was amenable. With effort, I sheathed my fangs.

She began to whimper when I changed our rhythm, speeding my strokes until I could feel the crescendo building toward our mutual release. She moaned and arched against me when she came, and my own climax convulsed me to my core. We clung writhing together, wringing every last spasm of satisfaction out of each other.

When I'd separated from her and clothed myself, I gathered the shredded bits of her underwear while she put on her sweater. She let me help her down from the table and onto her feet. I steadied her when she swayed a bit, and then led her by the hand back up the basement steps.

"Well," she said tentatively. "That was—was amazing. If I'd known seducing you would be this much fun, I would have done it a long time ago."

"Indeed," I said. "We must do it again soon. Very soon." I kissed her hand and led her to my automobile to drive her to her apartment.

One night. One reason not to stake myself, for now.

Jack

I stood outside Connie's apartment building and looked up at her window, feeling like Romeo staring up at Juliet's balcony, and just as doomed. Starcrossed lovers, they'd called them, and they both had wound up dead. So much for happy endings.

At least Romeo hadn't had to kill Juliet, but himself. If only that were one of my options.

If I couldn't bring myself to kill Connie, William would do it. I was starting to understand William's death wish. He'd spared me from the worst of what it meant to be a vampire for as long as he could. Coming-of-age was a bitch.

I had to save Connie from both of us—all of us. But how? I'd bought myself some time with William by promising to keep an eye on her while Melaphia figured something out. But what if Mel's research turned up a goose egg? We'd be back to square one. Even if I could talk Connie into running away with me, where would we run?

As a last resort, I supposed I could tell her the truth. What would happen then? I tried to imagine how a conversation like that would go: *Listen, babe, I just found out the damnedest thing. You know how I'm an evil, bloodsucking vampire and all? Okay, well, here's the funny part.* You, *are a vampire* slayer. *And you were put here on earth to kill me and my kind. Now, is that ironic or what?*

My cell phone rang and I unclipped it from my belt and noticed that the charge was almost gone again. I had to get a new battery.

It was William. He had the power to speak to me psychically, but I routinely blocked that intrusion into my mind. He'd long ago stopped bitching about it. A man had to stand up for his rights of privacy. I was blocking him out constantly now so I could mask my thoughts and feelings about Connie.

"Yeah," I said.

"I forgot to tell you earlier, Jack. Be here tomorrow at sundown with Werm. I've called a meeting with the clan heads so we can share the information we've learned."

"Is everyone coming?"

"The westerners will be here. Gerard and Lucius are attending by phone conference. Make sure you and Werm are here promptly."

"Will do, bwana. We'll be there at dark sharp." I heard the line click dead, and as I reclipped the cell to my belt, I felt a little hope. If I could just get Travis alone and ask him more about the slayers I might have some clue about how to save Connie. Travis was the only vampire in existence to have any firsthand experience with vampire slayers. He had been killed by a swarm of them, to hear him tell it. I just hoped he had something—anything—useful to tell me.

I looked up and saw a shape move behind the bedroom curtain. I knew that shape. I loved that shape. Connie parted the curtain and looked out.

But, soft! what light through yonder window breaks?

Hey, just because I'm a southern-fried good ol' boy doesn't mean I'm unacquainted with literature and the fine arts. One of my old girlfriends used to call me the Renaissance redneck. I love me some Shakespeare.

Despite the fact that it was the dead of winter, Connie raised her window and leaned out. Because of the lights on behind her, she still didn't see me.

She looked like a maiden in a painting by one of the Old Masters, framed there by the ornate window in the soft backlighting from the bedroom. Her beauty recalled the next line of the tragedy: *It is the east, and Juliet is the sun.*

The sun. Something that was certain death for me.

Hadn't I always known deep down that Connie would be the destruction of me? The way I'd almost been electrocuted when I first touched her had been a pretty damned good clue.

I sighed, feeling renewed desperation, but I was rooted to the spot. Just when I was thinking I could stand and look at her forever, she noticed me and beckoned like one of those mermaids of legend that drew sailors to their deaths on rocky shores.

I had to go up now, because if I didn't she would know something was wrong. Besides, how could I keep an eye on her like William said if I didn't stay close to her? Yep, that was the ticket.

She greeted me at the door in pajamas with bunnies on them. I hugged her hard, thinking how I'd probably never know which hug would be our last. So it was all hard hugs—and hard everything else—from here on in.

"I was hoping you would come," Connie said. She took me by the hand and led me to the couch. She pulled her legs beneath her and leaned her head on my shoulder. I put my arm around her and pulled her close, feeling her hair as soft as satin on my stubbled cheek.

"I just came by to see how you're doing," I said. "You went through a lot yesterday."

"Yeah," she said. "It's kind of hard to get my head around everything that happened."

"Did your memory come back?" I said, trying to hide my alarm.

"No. But I've been thinking about what you told me, and it's given me a lot of peace and some closure, you know? It makes me feel empowered, like I can face things that I couldn't before."

"Good," I said. "I'm glad to hear that." For a second I thought about asking her to tell me why she needed that closure, but Seth had warned me that his knowing about the murder-suicide had ended their relationship.

"Is William still mad at me?"

"Nah," I said. "It's all good."

"Melaphia didn't get in any trouble for helping me go . . . there, did she?"

I wasn't feeling very warm and fuzzy about Melaphia's actions, but I didn't know what to do about it. I supposed I shouldn't confront her since William had chastised her already. "No," I told Connie. "Nobody's mad at anybody, and nobody's in trouble."

"Good, because I don't want to have to think about anything negative tonight."

"Why's that?"

"I have plans for you. Wait here. I won't be long." She headed toward the bedroom and I watched her perky derriere until she'd turned the corner. When I turned my head back around, my gaze lit on her little shrine on the opposite wall. Religious artifacts give me the creeps under any circumstances, but Connie's cross had set my hair on fire once and I just wasn't digging the scene at all. It all reminded me of what I lacked—a soul. The statue of the Virgin Mary gazed demurely downward as if, in her holiness, she couldn't stand to look at the likes of me.

Connie reappeared in a lacy teddy that made me forget all about religion. She motioned for me to follow her into the bathroom, where she'd set lighted candles all around a deep, narrow tub.

"What is that?" I asked.

"It's a Japanese soaking tub."

The water looked inviting and smelled even better, with the scent of rose oil wafting through the air. A handful of tender pink petals floated on the surface of the water. The light vapor rising from the water fogged the mirror completely.

She undressed me slowly, giving my dangly parts a rub here and a tweak there. The girl knew her way around a man's body. As soon as we were both naked, we stepped into the tub and sat facing each other, up to our necks in the steamy water, slick with scented oil.

I picked up one of the rose petals, curved inward like a delicate shell, and placed it on Connie's nose. "She loves me," I said.

She laughed and puffed out a breath to make it fall again. I replaced the petal with another and said, "She loves me not."

The rose petal fell and Connie floated closer, stroking my thighs. Her hair swirled around her on the surface of the water like a mermaid's and her lashes shimmered with droplets of moisture. "She loves you," she said.

I met her in the middle of the tub and we floated there, exploring each other with eager, oily hands. I cupped her breasts and kissed her, and she arched her back, presenting me with her lovely bare neck. I squeezed my eyes shut, pretending that I didn't both see and feel the pulse at the hollow of her throat. She stroked me with her clever fingers, knowing just where to apply pressure, and I massaged all down her spine from her neck to the place where her bottom gave way to the back of her thighs.

Able to stand it no longer, I lifted her up and sat her on the side of the tub, her back against the tile wall. She raised her knees and wrapped her legs around my waist. Greased with bath oil, I entered her and she clutched my shoulders and urged me deeper, moaning softly. I rocked in and out of her, our movements making gentle lapping waves against the side of the tub. Her body was glossy in the candlelight, and I had to cup her derriere tightly so I wouldn't lose my grip because of the slippery oil.

Her moans increased with our rhythm and I knew I wouldn't be able to hold on much longer. When we came, an explosion of white light filled my vision, and I drew her back down into the water with me until our own internal waves had played out.

We held each other like that until the water cooled, saying nothing. Then we stepped out of the tub and Connie got us each a towel from the cabinet over the sink. We took turns drying each other carefully. She twirled her towel and popped me with it when I became too forward. "I've got to get all your nooks and crannies," I insisted. "I don't want you to have any greasy residue. How would those dress blues look with oil stains?" She tried to pop my thigh and I dodged the blow.

"I'm a detective now, remember? I wear plain clothes."

"Darlin', no clothes are ever going to be plain as long as you're wearing them."

"You fill out a mean pair of jeans yourself," she said, brazenly staring at my package.

"Thank you kindly."

I could tell she had some kind of witty comeback on the tip of her tongue when she glanced to the side and the grin died on her face. The fog had cleared from the mirror above the sink. Connie's face in the looking glass registered a brief flicker of surprise when she realized that she was alone with a dead man who couldn't cast a reflection. In the hairbreadth of time before she regained her composure, I could see the horror in her expression.

You know how sometimes you can't get a song out of your head and it drives you crazy? With me, it was Shakespeare. Lines from *Romeo and Juliet* bumped off the walls of my cranium like steel pellets in the pinball machine of my brain, and I heard the words of Friar Laurence:

> *Lady, come from that nest*
> *Of death, contagion, and unnatural sleep.*

Just step away from the evil dead, ma'am, he seemed to be saying. *He'll be the death of you.* Not bad advice, I had to admit.

Connie took the towels and tossed them into the hamper, forcing laughter over some remark she made about the way her fingers were pruning. I pulled on my clothes as she did likewise with the pajamas she'd hung on the bathroom door.

"It's late. I should go," I said.

"Mmm-hmm," she agreed.

On the way through the bedroom, I noticed that she'd forgotten to close the window. The sheer curtains were swaying in the chilled breeze. "I'll just close this for you," I said, shutting the window. As I did so, I noticed the vampire I'd seen earlier at Werm's place standing under a streetlamp. He didn't look as if he saw or sensed me; he only lounged against the post of the lamp idly smoking a cigarette.

"There's another vampire out there, isn't there?" Connie said.

Puzzled, I turned around. She leaned against the bathroom door frame, her damp hair swirling in corkscrew-shaped tendrils. There was no way she could see out the window from where she stood.

"How do you know?"

She shrugged. "I don't know. Earlier, when I raised the window, I knew you were out there before I could even see you. That's weird, isn't it?"

"Weird." More like terrifying. "Is tonight the first time you've noticed you can . . . sense when there's a vampire around?"

"Yeah. Who knows, maybe I can sense when other people are around, too. Maybe I picked up some kind of extrasensory perception when I was in the underworld."

"Right. Maybe so."

"Do you know who it is?"

"I've seen him before. William knows him. I'll go check him out and make sure he knows how to behave himself. It's nothing to worry about." It wouldn't be when I got through with him. "Then I'll head home."

She looked wistful. "Do you think there'll ever be a time when you'll feel comfortable enough to tell me where you live, Jack?"

I tried to manage a smile. "One of these days." I imagined the wisdom of telling a vampire slayer the whereabouts of my daytime resting place. Not in this lifetime. The thought hurt where my heart used to beat.

I hugged her again, hard, and left. On my way past the shrine, I looked at the Holy Mother. "Please help me," I prayed silently, though I had no right to. She kept on looking down at her white flowing robes.

When I was on street level, I crept around the corner of the building and was able to sneak up on the loitering vampire. I slapped the cigarette out of his hand and threw him up against the lamppost so hard his head made a clanging sound against the wrought iron.

"Ow!" the vampire said. "What the hell?"

"Don't you know it's impolite to spy on a lady?" I asked.

"C'mon, man, I was just hanging out having a smoke."

"Hanging out under my girlfriend's window?"

"I don't know what you're talking about."

"Like hell. Who are you?"

The blood drinker rubbed the back of his head. "The name's Freddy Blackstone. I'm a friend of Tobey's, just passing through town. I met William tonight. He can vouch for me. Hey, you must be Jack."

The vampire offered his hand and after a moment's hesitation, I shook it. The guy looked harmless enough. He favored those beatniks you used to see in the fifties, all sloppy and unkempt in his hair, beard, and clothes. In fact, he reminded me of Maynard G. Krebs on the old Dobie Gillis show. Man, did that date me or what?

"Listen, buddy, you need to give my lady some space," I said. "Understand?"

"Yeah, no problemo. Hey, I date human chicks all the time. You can't be too careful with them, am I right? I'm just going to move on, bro. No harm, no foul, right?"

"Yeah. Sure."

I watched him slouch off down the street and into the darkness. It seemed to be quite a coincidence that an itinerant blood drinker would just happen into town right when the vampire slayer was identified. And then, just by chance, out of all the haunts in Savannah, to get caught loitering around her apartment. I vowed to keep my eye on Freddy. Like he said, you just couldn't be too careful.

Another fear nagged me, though. Something was on the tip of my brain and I hadn't connected the dots yet. If Freddy knew about Connie, then how? From Tobey? Had William told Tobey and the others? Would he?

A wave of nausea hit me. Of course he would tell them, all of them. And he would do it tomorrow night. They needed to know about the threat to their lives and to their clans. And then it would be open season on Connie. Any one of them could and would try to kill her before she started killing us. How had I ever imagined that the only one I had to protect her from was William?

I looked up at Connie's apartment, which was dark now. I couldn't guard her twenty-four/seven, although the thought of sticking around until the sun came up and fried me to a piece of charcoal was not without its appeal.

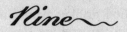

William

Tobey and Iban were at my home as promised shortly after sundown. Jack, looking uncharacteristically grim, arrived a few moments later with Werm in tow.

Iban Cruz, a director of noir movies, had the courtly manners of the Spanish aristocrat he was. He bowed low and kissed Melaphia's hand when we greeted our guests in the foyer. "Thank you again for my life," he said in his lovely accent.

Melaphia curtsied and thanked him for the many gifts of imported delicacies, clothing, flowers, jewelry, and spirits he had sent. "They were not necessary, but very appreciated," she said.

A short time ago, Iban had been stricken with a rotting plague, and only the pure voodoo blood from Melaphia's veins could save him. The process was not pretty, and it had been a heroic effort on her part, one for which Iban would be eternally grateful.

"The gifts are mere trifles," he assured her. "Always

know that if you ever need me, I'll be here as soon as the sun and air travel will allow. I am forever your servant."

"I can't get over his recovery," Tobey remarked.

Indeed, Iban looked remarkable when one recalled how the rotted flesh had been falling from his bones not so long ago. Now he appeared completely normal. That was, if you called his striking dark looks normal. Melaphia told me once that Iban's looks put her in mind of an actor of some note named Antonio Banderas.

"I can't get over the change either," Jack remarked. "I don't mind telling you, buddy, you looked like a guy whose face caught fire and somebody tried to put it out with a hatchet."

Iban laughed. "That was most vivid, Jack. But thank you. I think."

"Tobey, were you able to contact Travis?" I asked.

"I'm sorry, but no. I notified some key people in the western clans to keep an eye out for him and ask him to get in touch with you as soon as he can. Maybe we'll hear from him soon."

I was disappointed that we would be without Travis's counsel, but evidently not as disappointed as Jack, who seemed most disturbed by the news that our Native American friend would not be joining us.

"Are Gerard and Lucius coming?" Iban asked.

"We're going to teleconference them in, as well as Olivia, of course."

Iban and Tobey represented the vampire clans of the West and Pacific Northwest, and Gerard Bouchard the plains and the Midwest. Lucius Dru, an art dealer headquartered in Manhattan, covered the Northeast and mid-Atlantic. Jack and I were the heads of the few blood drinkers in the South and as far west as Texas. Travis covered the southwest and Central and South America.

The vampires of the Americas were an ethnically eclectic mixture of the descendants of ancient indigenous blood drinkers and those whom I had imported by ship from the old world. These last were what Jack referred to as the "Draculas" or the "Count Dracs" because of their often old-fashioned European ways and manners.

One thing all these vampires had in common, however, was a peaceful philosophy. Except for a handful of rogues we'd had to dispose of over the years, the vampires of the New World had adopted a code of nonviolence toward the human population. Feeding on humans was allowed as long as no permanent injury was done and the mortal involved was either a willing swan or someone whose short-term memory could be altered to ensure the act was immediately forgotten. However, our policy of benevolence did not preclude the occasional act of vigilante justice when it was warranted.

Until recently, there was only a loose alliance among the vampires of the New World, dubbed "Bonaventures" by Olivia, who was the leader of the peaceful blood drinkers of Europe. But since we collectively saw Reedrek's recent arrival in Savannah as a sign of the old lords' resurgence, all of us had been communicating more often and formulating plans for mutual defense. The old lords had formed a council with the goal of world domination. Their aim was to use us to eventually turn all humans into blood drinkers, over whom they would rule with an iron fist.

Jack, who had been unusually silent so far, asked Tobey about the racing business and Tobey launched into a discussion of his latest exploits on the West Coast night stock-car racing circuit.

Jack still looked a little pained whenever Tobey's career was mentioned, even though he was the one who usually brought it up. Jack's most treasured dream was to be an automobile racer, and he'd turned several shades of green when he discovered I'd helped Tobey achieve his goals. I think on some level Jack still resented me for that.

I settled us all in the formal parlor, where Deylaud had built a pleasantly crackling blaze in the fireplace. Renee came downstairs briefly to greet our guests. Iban received a particularly warm welcome because of the myriad gifts he'd showered on her recently. "I love you, Uncle Iban," she cooed, kissing his cheek. We all had a gentle laugh at her transparency.

"She'll have you buying her diamonds and pearls before long," I assured Iban.

"That's quite all right with me," he said.

"Me too!" Renee agreed, to another round of laughter.

"Why don't you go with Deylaud and have him help you with your literature assignment. You've got some work to do to catch up on your studies."

With good-bye hugs for all of us, she followed Deylaud and Reyha upstairs to my library, which had somehow evolved into her schoolroom.

"I was so relieved to hear that you got her back safely," Tobey remarked.

"And I as well," Iban said. "William, Tobey told me about the matter with Eleanor. Please accept my condolences. I'm so sorry that . . . eliminating her became necessary."

"Thank you," I said quietly. "You're very kind." Out of the corner of my eye, I saw Jack fidgeting. Werm, for his part, looked both shocked and puzzled but said nothing, evidently sensing the tension in the air. I'd told him that Eleanor was dead, but he had had no idea that I'd killed her myself until now. That reminded me of the reason for the meeting.

Melaphia nodded when she had finished testing the telephone links to Olivia, Gerard, and Lucius.

"I called this meeting," I began, "because information has come to light that we all need to know. We are all aware of bits and pieces, but it's time to make sure that each of us is armed with the complete facts. After all, knowledge is power."

I started by reviewing what had taken place in London. Gerard and Lucius expressed shock and remorse over what happened with Eleanor. They all peppered me with questions, particularly about the gathering of the vampire council of old lords.

"Olivia," I said, addressing the speakerphone, "have Alger's scrolls and tablets turned up additional information on the Council and what they may be about?"

"No. When our coven house burned down, it was a tremendous setback. We had to reorganize all the material and check it against the inventory we had made."

"How much was lost?" I asked.

"We were able to save almost all of it, but the parchments suffered smoke and water damage and they will take some time to restore."

"I know that several of your vampires risked their lives to save the documents, so you must be confident that they will yield valuable information," I said.

"Yes, once we get them translated. So I don't have anything new to report from the texts, but I do have some news from our spies," Olivia said. I thought that her voice sounded uncharacteristically small. Olivia was a strong woman, never afraid to express herself. I chalked up her tentative speech to the long-distance connection.

"Good," I said. "We'll hear your report presently." I went on to describe what we learned from Otis and what Seth sensed with his animalistic instincts.

"Are you sure you're not putting too much store in anecdotal evidence?" Gerard, ever the scientist, asked.

"The shape shifters in New York are nervous as well," Lucius said, and I could hear the controlled alarm in his voice. "And they don't know why."

Jack rubbed the back of his head as if the preponderance of bad news was giving him a headache. "Jerry and Rufus feel it, too," he said.

After a few minutes of discussion, I said, "Before we call on Olivia for her report, I want to return to one of the biggest issues we face. It's something I learned from Ulrich and Diana when I was in the United Kingdom."

My gaze came to rest on Jack. He knew what I was about to reveal and that I had no choice. I had expected defiance, but his eyes held only misery. My bleak narrative was about to get even bleaker.

"The vampire slayer prophesied by the lore and legend of many cultures is in our midst. But rest assured that Jack and I have things under control where the Slayer is concerned."

There was a hubbub of voices, originating both in the room and over the speakerphone, as this dire news sank in.

"Just as you had your son, Will, under control?" Iban asked, only the fire in his dark eyes betraying emotion.

Despite our friendship, I knew he still harbored resentment over the fact that my human son, Will, had murdered Iban's best friend, Sullivan. An evil vampire named Hugo had made Will and my wife, Diana, blood drinkers without my knowledge and kept Will under his thumb for centuries. Will grew up half-feral under Hugo's tutelage, only recently redeeming himself in my eyes by helping me rescue Renee. I'd left him behind in London where Olivia was keeping an eye on him and, I hoped, setting an example of civility. For his part, Iban had sworn to kill Will and I had no doubt that he would one day try.

"We'll discuss Will later," I told Iban.

"What do we know about the Slayer?" Tobey asked. "I thought the vampire slayer was only a legend."

"As did I," Iban said.

Gerard said, "As a boy I remember hearing the Gypsies speak of the *dhampir* as vampire slayers, although I never met a blood drinker who'd ever seen one."

"I remember this legend as well," Lucius said. "The *dhampir* was said to be half-vampire and half-human and the sworn enemy of the blood drinker."

"Wait a minute," Jack said. "How can there be a half-vampire/half-human? Female vampires can't get pregnant and males can't knock up human females."

"Evidently, once in a great while a male blood drinker is made who is . . . gifted in that particular regard," William said.

"What else do these prophecies say about the Slayer?" Lucius asked.

Melaphia said, "It is written that she—"

"She?" Lucius asked skeptically.

Melaphia continued, "*She* will be sworn to destroy every blood drinker on earth, and she'll have special powers to do so, although we don't know what those powers are. I'm still researching the ancient texts." Melaphia went on to describe the birthmark, the Mayan goddess connection, and other signs that led to her being able to identify the Slayer. No one tried to refute the case she made.

"To make matters even more complicated and regrettable," I said with a glance toward Jack, "the Slayer is someone known to most of us." I paused, loath to continue because of the pain it would cause Jack, but surely, I thought, he understood that I had no choice. He sat stone-faced, opening and closing his fists.

"Don't keep us in suspense, *mon ami*," Gerard said. "Who is the Slayer?"

"The Slayer is Connie Jones."

Jack

My first urge was to lash out. I felt my muscles coil, ready to propel me to my feet, but then I felt Iban's cool hand on my arm.

"Jack, I'm so sorry," he said. "I'm in shock. I adore Connie. So did Sullivan."

The others expressed their condolences as if Connie were already dead.

"Death by exsanguination is not the worst way to go, you know," Lucius pointed out helpfully.

"Lucius, please," Iban said. "Perhaps a little sensitivity is in order."

I ignored them. "She doesn't know she's the Slayer. Maybe she won't find out," I said, hearing the desperation in my own voice.

"She will," said a deep voice from the doorway. Distracted by the revelation about Connie, we hadn't noticed that Travis Rubio had opened the door. Or maybe it was because he moved with the silent, graceful tread the Native Americans are known for. I was both grateful and fearful to see him. Grateful because he alone of us all had some experience with slayers past and might offer some alternative that could spare Connie's life. Fearful because that same understanding might prove the old adage that no situation is so bad it can't get worse. Given his opening statement, I didn't feel lucky.

"It's only a matter of time," Travis said. With his angular nose, black eyes, and leathery skin the color of antique bronze, Travis looked like Sitting Bull in that famous photograph of the Lakota chief. "The destiny of the Slayer cannot be denied. She will discover her mission."

That was almost exactly what Sullivan had said. Not good. Not good at all.

The other vampires greeted Travis in subdued tones, given the gravity of our subject. William shook his hand in welcome as I tried to figure out what to say or do next. My plan to talk to Travis in private if he showed up had been blown all to kingdom come. I'd better think of a plan B in a helluva hurry.

Travis nodded toward William. "I got word of the meeting shortly after Tobey left a message with a mutual friend about it. Sorry I'm late."

William invited Travis to tell us what he knew of the Slayer, so the ancient Maya related the story of how blood drinkers came to be established in the land now known as Belize.

"About five hundred years after the birth of Christ, I was a young priest of the Maya's polytheistic religion as my forefathers had been. The Mayan nobility had sunk into dissolution under the influence of peyote, hallucinogenic mushrooms, and coca leaves, all of which it was legal only for them to partake.

"Their rituals rivaled those of the old lords for bloodshed. One of my tasks was to cut the beating hearts from sacrificial victims and anoint the king and queen with their blood. It was thought that the blood of a sacrificed human being could open the portal to the underworld."

I shivered. I knew a little bit about opening the portal to the underworld myself.

"I've read about the Maya," Tobey said. "It was as

if even the humans were vampire wannabes. They even filed their teeth into sharp points."

"It's true that some historians and anthropologists believe that they sharpened their own teeth," Travis replied.

"Wait until you hear the rest of the story," I said.

Travis continued, "Human sacrifices were most often made from prisoners of war. The higher the rank of the prisoner, the more prized was his blood. As one might imagine, the rarest and most valuable vintage was that of a king. As fate would have it, the day eventually came when our warriors were able to capture the king of another city. They kept him alive for months, letting his blood in increments, savoring it, until he grew weak and delirious.

"Finally, our king decided to make the enemy ruler into the ultimate sacrifice, so amidst a great festival I raised the ceremonial obsidian knife and struck him in the heart—but not before he put a curse on our ruler. The doomed king called out to Itzamna, the lord of the heavens, to curse our leader so he could never again see the sun and, since he was such a lover of blood, require that it be the only food that could ever sustain him.

"Our king laughed at the curse and drank the blood of his enemy, but he immediately became ill and fell upon the ground writhing in agony. I sat with him until after sundown on the second day when he awakened and bade me lie on his bed and rest, for I had not slept in many hours.

"No sooner than I had lain down, the king was on me, holding me down with inhuman strength. His mouth opened, showing what looked to me like the awful fangs of an animal. I was helpless as he bit into my throat and drank my blood until I heard my heartbeat dying away. Then he ripped the flesh of his wrist and forced me to drink of his blood in return, thus making me a vampire like himself."

"My God, they *were* vampires," Melaphia said.

"He set about making the rest of the nobility into blood drinkers as well, and they all preyed upon the common people," Travis continued, "who were forced to flee the great city to live in the lush jungles and forests. But when the aristocracy's bloodlust reached its zenith, the slayers came. They slaughtered all the blood drinkers save me. I managed to get away and hide in a cave until they were gone. Thus ended one of the greatest civilizations in history."

"Do you have any idea why you were spared?" Melaphia asked.

"I've been asking myself that question for hundreds of years, but I have yet to come up with an answer," Travis said. "But you were correct when you said they have special powers. They descended on us from the sky like Valkyries and slew the blood drinkers with swords. The ancient Maya were a fierce people, but I never saw blood such as I witnessed the night the slayers came. Blood ran in rivulets down the pyramids and into the streets." The old Maya closed his eyes as if to banish the memories.

"What should we do?" William asked.

"I understand that many of you call her friend, so I don't say this lightly. But my advice is to kill the Slayer as quickly as you can."

I came to my feet, and looked to some of my best friends in the world—William, Melaphia, Tobey, and

Iban—for help, some kind of encouraging word, or a sudden brainstorm that could pry me out from between a rock and a hard place. Instead, I saw my friends looking to *me* for . . . what? Protection? Leadership? It was as if a hand grenade had been tossed into our midst and since I was the closest, I was supposed to fall on it and get blown to smithereens.

And I would have, if it hadn't meant Connie's death. I would destroy myself in a heartbeat for them. As they would do for me. All the excuses that had bubbled up to the tip of my brain died on my lips.

William froze me with one look. "Jack understands what must be done," he said. "And he'll do it."

The vampires listening remotely no doubt believed him. I could tell Tobey, Iban, and especially Travis weren't so sure. I could see by their expressions what they were thinking: that one of *them* might have to fall on that grenade to save us all, because I didn't have the guts.

"Wait," I pleaded. "What if I just go to Connie and tell her all this? She knows us. She knows that we don't hurt humans. When she realizes that we're on the same side, she'll help us fight off the old lords."

"I wish it were that simple, my friend," Travis said, "but you have no idea what you're dealing with. I have seen slayers with my own eyes. Our bloodlust is nothing to theirs. When they are on the hunt, they . . ." He searched for the right words. "They turn into something not human. Something that I hope I never have the misfortune to see again. The essence of the slayers, that which is in them that is not human— once awakened can never be turned off."

"I know you saw them attack and that you got

away," I challenged. "But how do you know about this—this activation, as you call it?"

"The priests brought by the conquistadors destroyed for heresy most of our writings that were left behind when we abandoned our great cities. Priceless texts on mathematics and astronomy were burned and broken in the white men's religious fervor. After I fled the city to escape the slayers, I returned. I stole away with many of those tablets and secreted them in places where not even the most determined of archeologists can find them. I have read the texts that survived the purge.

"I had been unaware of many of these documents before the slaughter of blood drinkers. Some of the ancient ones had prophesied the arrival of the slayers. And they also prophesied a later rise of a single slayer, the greatest of them all. That is what is taking place now."

"What else do these writings say about the Slayer?" William asked.

Travis said, "The Slayer is the product of an unholy union between blood drinker and human."

"That jibes with the European *dhampir* legend," William said. "Is there more?"

"Only that she will not be easy to kill, and that she cannot be turned away from her destiny. The gods alone in their wisdom know how and why this creature is empowered to slay blood drinkers. I don't know why she has not already begun to do so, but she will. There is no doubt," Travis said. "I am not exactly sure what causes the activation and how that activation turns into bloodlust, but I have the impression that it is a distinct process."

"What will it take to kill her?" Melaphia asked in a small voice, avoiding my eyes.

"I don't know. That is where the writing ends," Travis said. "The rest of the tablets on the Slayer were turned to dust."

"Jack, what do you know of Connie's background?" William asked.

I forced myself to think back, which was hard because my head was spinning from so much information I didn't want to hear. "She told me once that she was born in Mexico City and adopted by a couple from Atlanta. She had been abandoned when she was a few days old and left at a shrine to some pagan goddess or other."

Travis's hawklike eyes narrowed. "How old is she?" he asked.

"Late twenties, I think," I said. "Why?"

Travis shook his head and his features took on a stony, inscrutable expression as he stared into space, as still as one of those carved Indians that used to stand outside cigar stores in the old days.

"There's something else," I admitted. "When I talked to her last night, she said that she sensed it when I got close to her apartment. Even before she saw me."

"The process has begun," Travis said. "I am sorry, Jack. There's not much time left. If you wait until activation turns into bloodlust, it might be too late. She will become immortal, and we won't know how to stop her."

I collapsed back onto the sofa beside Werm, beaten. When William first told me I had to get rid of Connie, I hadn't accepted it. I'd refused to believe that there wasn't another way. I'd put my faith in Travis to give me some idea for how to save her, but instead, he had just dashed all my hopes. Because of him, the cold, hard truth was setting in, and I felt like I was barely hanging on to a world spinning faster and faster. I wanted to turn loose and let the centrifugal force sling me into the black void.

"Even after a slayer is activated, it must have some kind of fatal flaw, some Achilles' heel. Is there anything the Mayan writing can tell us about that?" Tobey asked.

"Not specifically, no—at least not in the writings that survived."

"Does anybody know how the Slayer ties into the Sidhe's notion of doomsday?" Gerard asked.

Travis said, "I don't know if there's a connection, but there is always the cataclysm the Mayan calendar foretells. That is no secret, though." He waved a hand. "The end has been extensively written about since archeologists interpreted the calendar."

"What cataclysm?" I asked. Travis took a seat on the sofa on the other side of Werm.

William rubbed his forehead. "Of course. I should have thought about that . . ."

I saw realization dawn on Melaphia's face as well, and Werm spoke up for the first time. "The end of the world," he said. "The Sidhe say the end of the world is coming and that it has something do to with vampires."

In my agitation, I wanted to wring his scrawny throat if he didn't get to the point soon. "What the hell are you talking about?" I demanded.

Werm turned his round eyes to stare at me. "The

Mayan calendar is one of the most accurate in the world. And it ends in 2012!"

There was another hullabaloo where everybody tried to speak at once. Everybody seemed to be formulating his or her own pet theory about whether the end of the world was really at hand and, if so, what it had to do with the Slayer. Finally, William called for order and said, "Let us focus, my friends. We seem to have a number of problems which may or may not be connected. Since we don't know any more about the Slayer and the end times, let us move on to the issue of the old lords."

"Yes," Lucius said from the speakerphone. "Do we know nothing more about how the Council means to attack us? Through the ages they've assembled before to try and force us all to slaughter more humans and create more blood drinkers. Each time their plans—whatever they were—fell through. There was too much infighting among the master vampires, or so the stories go. They were never able to do much more than organize occasional raids against the peace lovers. Are we to believe that the return of the Wild Hunt and the premonitions of the Sidhe and the shape shifters, and perhaps even the Mayan prophecies, signal that they've hit upon some weapon that *can* bend us to their will?"

William opened his mouth to speak but stopped when we heard Olivia clear her throat. It occurred to me that she had been quiet throughout the meeting. Too quiet.

"I think I might be able to shed some light on that issue," she said.

"By all means, enlighten us." The sarcasm in Lucius's

voice set my teeth on edge. He was the kind of man who thought that no woman knew as much as he did.

William glared at the speakerphone. "It's time we heard from Olivia," he said. "She has reestablished the network of spies that Alger used to monitor what is happening with the Council. It sounds as if that effort has borne fruit. Olivia?"

"I suppose you could put it that way," Olivia said. "Poisoned fruit, maybe. One of our spies was able to make a reliable contact who swore he knows the old lords' plan. The Council believes it has discovered how to raise from the dead every vampire who was ever slain at the hands of another blood drinker since the beginning of time. Which is pretty much all of them."

"You mean take them from the underworld back to earth?" William asked. My sire had the best poker face I'd ever seen on anyone, but here among his peers, he didn't bother to hide his alarm. Werm and I looked at each other. If William was anxious, then it was time for us to be terrified.

"Evidently," Olivia said. "The source didn't know how they planned to accomplish this, or when it's supposed to start. But when it does, the Council expects those risen vampires to do their bidding."

"Which means slaughtering humans and any of us standing in their way," William said.

"If it happens all at once," Olivia continued, "the human population can't help but know immediately. It will cause a massive, worldwide panic."

"And spell doom for all of us," Iban said.

"If they all come at once, what can we fight them

with besides our fists and fangs?" Tobey asked, looking around the room.

"There aren't enough of us to fight them hand-to-hand," William said. "We'd be vastly outnumbered. We're going to need supernatural help."

All eyes turned to Melaphia. "I'll try to call upon Maman Lalee to help us," she said. "But as you know, even she cannot go against the elemental powers of fate." She turned to me with a meaningful look that I was sure had even more bad news behind it.

"All you can do is try your best, my dear," William said. "That's all we can ask."

I was sure he hated to put pressure on Mel again, especially since she had just recovered her sanity. I'd had every intention of confronting her about her part in helping Connie get to the underworld. But when I saw her face register the weight of the task William had just assigned her, I gave up on the idea. The trip to the bad place was blood under the bridge now.

"How will we know these dead, er, doubly dead vampires when we see them?" Tobey wanted to know. "Won't they look and smell just like us?"

Double-dead. What had Eleanor called herself and those like her in the underworld? Double-damned, she had said. I remembered what she was like down there, and shuddered. William looked at me, obviously thinking the same thing.

"No," William said. He told everyone briefly about what Eleanor had told him in the underworld—and how she looked. She had called herself a word that sounded like *SLOO-ah.*

"The vampire in the underworld, having died twice, is the most doomed of the damned," William continued. "A special sentence is chosen just for him or her. Eleanor was turned into a half-snake creature. Other blood drinkers could rise as—whatever is their own individual torture made manifest."

"The Sluagh are part of Celtic legend, are they not?" Lucius asked.

"That's correct," Olivia said. "They've been described as the unforgiven dead who were said to have stolen the souls of the living. If the Sluagh are really vampires, it would explain that part of the legend. I had no idea there was a connection between the Sluagh and twice-killed blood drinkers in the underworld."

"Nor I," agreed Gerard. "But it's not surprising when you think about it. William and Jack are most probably the only vampires who've gone to the underworld and come back to tell the tale. This is something that only the handful of us, in all of history, now know about."

There was a hush as each vampire let all this sink in. No doubt they were thinking about what their own personal hells would be if they were ever destroyed. Too bad I had my own individual hell looming in front of me right then. And I didn't have to be staked to get there.

Everyone in this room expected me to go out—as soon as possible—and kill the woman I loved.

Eventually, they all started talking again. As they did, I tried to figure out what to do. If I didn't kill Connie, one of them would, and soon.

"I move we table this discussion until we know more," William said. "Until then, several of us have action items to work on."

William was back in control now, about to conclude a vampire conclave concerning life-and-death issues as if it were a corporate board meeting. In light of what he expected me to do, I think I hated him for that.

"Melaphia, you continue your research and use your spells and chants to try to make contact with Maman Lalee," William went on. "Maybe it's not too late to slam the lid on the underworld. Olivia, keep on working your spy network and step up the transcription and translation of Alger's scrolls and tablets. Travis, search your memory and your holy writings to see if you can shed more light on the issues we've talked about. Tobey, Iban, Gerard, and Lucius, spread the word to your clans to be on the lookout for any manifestations of demons that might have already come up from the underworld. Something like this could signal the rise of the double-damned."

He paused and looked at me, not without compassion. "Jack," he began. I stared at the hardwood floor, feeling as if I was in physical pain. *Don't say it.*

"You know what you have to do," he finished. Then William called the meeting adjourned, and the ones who had attended through the mysterious ether of electronic bits and bytes clicked off.

I've heard people talk about out-of-body experiences. What I wouldn't have given for one of those right then. I wanted to be as far out of my body as I could get. Like in the next time zone.

I sat there, staring into the roaring fire as those assembled, one after the other, patted my shoulders and murmured words of sympathy on their way out of the parlor. I heard Werm say that he'd make his own way back to the Portal. William asked Travis, Tobey, and Iban to have drinks and cigars in the den before they all headed downstairs to the vault to take their rest.

When everyone but William and Mel had gone, I stood and walked to where they stood motionless by the door. "There's something you should know, Jack," Melaphia spoke up. "I meant to tell you earlier, but we haven't have a chance to talk since you . . . came back. I prayed to Papa Legba for another way."

"Another way to get rid of Connie, you mean?" I asked. Sensing bad news, my throat constricted.

"A way to turn Connie from her path," she corrected softly. "I thought that if I prayed to the *loa* Maman Lalee assigned you to, maybe he would help since you are so closely tied to Connie and he was the one who helped you go after her. I'm sorry, Jack. The *loa* Legba can be hard to interpret sometimes, but he didn't indicate a prayer, spell, or chant that we could perform to eliminate the threat Connie poses, short of . . . taking her life. I'm afraid we have to assume that what Travis said is true."

"Thanks for trying," I managed to say. Melaphia started to hug me, but she could tell by my body language that it was not the time. She wiped at a tear with the back of her hand and slipped from the room.

When it was only William and me, he said, "Jack, if you cannot do this, I—"

I held up my hand to silence him. "No, William. It's my responsibility."

"You should do it tonight."

"I'll do it tomorrow," I said. "I have to have some time to think about how . . . it would be best . . . to—"

"Jack, it will best if you get it over with. You heard

Travis. The window of opportunity is short." William lowered his voice and spoke in his most sympathetic tone. "Use your great skill with glamour. Soothe her with your mind. You know how to make it painless and quick. Think of it, Jack. You'll be giving her the gift of eternity in paradise with the son she thought she'd lost forever. If you wait until she becomes immortal, she may never see him again.

"Human beings are transitory, Jack. As much as you and I have loved Melaphia and her foremothers, we knew we would always have to say good-bye and give them up to the loving arms of Maman Lalee.

"You have seen the paradise that Connie will enjoy if she does not become immortal. You can spare her the same kind of fate that we are cursed with. If she continues to exist on this plane, she will have to fight and kill for the remainder of her existence, never able to let down her guard for fear that an enemy may be coming for her. Give her peace. Give her everlasting life."

"Giving people everlasting life isn't in my job description," I said, my eyes burning. "That's up to God, not me."

He put his hand on my shoulder. I thought to wrench away, but I didn't. In fact, I leaned on him, let him be my rock, just as he had been for almost a century and a half, whether I always appreciated it or not.

"If you're honest with yourself, you'll realize that this is not the first time you've been called on to play God, and it won't be the last. In each and every instance you have chosen to do the right thing.

"I've tried to protect you in every way that I could,

but now it's time for you to step forward to protect your family and your kind. In so doing, you will be saving countless other human lives that would be sacrificed if the peaceful vampires are vanquished by the evil ones.

"If Connie could be counted on to fight at our side, things might be different. But by all indications, she would kill us Bonaventures first simply because we are close to hand. Then she would be alone against the evil ones. They would eventually discover how to kill the Slayer. And hear me now, Jack: death at their hands will not be pretty. You know enough of your own grandsire to know that."

I nodded my understanding. All my life as a vampire I'd heard William and many of the older imported blood drinkers tell stories of the savagery and depravity of the old sires. What they were capable of doing to both human beings and to other blood drinkers alike was unfathomable. The moment Connie became the immortal vampire slayer, every blood drinker in the world would be gunning for her. I couldn't, under any circumstances, let the more evil ones get their claws on her.

When I finally spoke, my voice came out as a raspy whisper. "You can stop trying to convince me. I understand what you're saying; I know what needs to be done and I'll do it tonight. I won't let you down."

He hugged me then, actually hugged me. "You never have," he said.

Ten

William

At Tobey's suggestion, he, Iban, Travis, and I visited Werm's nightclub for cocktails. Tobey had hoped that he would run into his old friend, Freddy Blackstone, but the young vampire was not in attendance.

I made discreet introductions of the vampires to Otis of the Sidhe court, and they all retired to a back room to question him further. He seemed to be quite agreeable to answering their inquiries when Tobey produced his black AmEx card and offered to buy rounds of drinks. Apparently Otis's duties for the Sidhe nobility did not afford him an unlimited expense account.

I took the opportunity to depart. The more time I spent with Iban the more I knew he would eventually want to talk about his grudge against Will. But we had more important matters to concentrate on. I still harbored hope that he would one day forgive my son.

For reasons I could not explain at the time, I had the idea to visit one of my antique shops in the city, one whose collection included the sword claimed to be one that Georgia's founder, General James Oglethorpe, used in both the Battle of Bloody Marsh and the Battle of Gully Hole Creek in 1742 during the War of Jenkins' Ear with Spain.

I had always doubted that particular story about the sword, having been convinced that the blade was much older. Still, the story had come with the sword when I'd purchased it from an elderly Spanish plantation owner shortly after I arrived in Savannah in 1778. I thought that presenting Iban with the gift of Oglethorpe's purported sword would make a particularly ironic and lighthearted peace offering for my Spanish friend.

I let myself in the back entrance of the shop and was shocked to see that the sword was gone. It had been in the store for at least a hundred years, since its cost, due to the historical significance, made it out of reach for most collectors. In truth, I had never really meant for it to sell, but I was a businessman and had put a price on it, though one that I knew would be prohibitive. I couldn't help but wonder who had purchased it. I made a mental note to ask the store manager as soon as possible.

The sword's faded outline on the wall filled me with an apprehension I couldn't fathom. I selected a splendid antique dagger from one of the display cases as a gift for Iban instead, and left a note to the store manager to put it on my personal account. I locked the door to the shop, unable to shake my unease. Sentimentality had never been part of my nature, and neither had self-analysis. Still, I couldn't help concluding that the forfeiture of the sword was adding to my overall feelings of loss regarding Eleanor. Or perhaps I just thought it strange that it was gone.

I wrapped my overcoat closer around me and started to walk, not particularly caring where I was headed. Cold, bleak nights such as these would have stirred my blood not so long ago and put me in mind of the hunt. It had been many years since I'd given up the ham-handed barbarism of the old days in favor of a more subtle and civilized stalking. I might have been inspired to stalk a pretty coed walking alone from one of the bars along River Street, entice her to sit awhile with me on a park bench in the shadows. I would ply her with kisses and anesthetize her mind to the bite that would follow. She would awaken shortly, alone, none the worse save for a bit of weakness, a craving for drink, and two tiny puncture wounds on her throat.

But I was in no mood for the hunt this night. My most pressing need, as always, was more for sex than food. I took out my cell phone and dialed a number. "I know it's late," I began. "But as always, I'll make it worth your while. Meet me at your boutique."

An hour later I was standing on the doorstep of Ginger's garden apartment with a gaily wrapped package in my hand. "You don't mind a late visitor, do you?" I inquired when she opened the door. "Especially one bearing gifts?"

"Of course not," she said, offering me a pretty smile. She stepped aside to let me in, and the invisible barrier that would have stopped me had she not issued the invitation melted away. I gave her the gift bag, which had been carefully prepared by the female acquaintance I'd paid handsomely to open her lingerie shop after hours.

Ginger took my coat, folded it over a chair, and invited me to sit. "What on earth can this be?"

"Open it," I said.

Ginger issued a little squeal as she unwrapped the assortment of silk panties and brassieres. "Oh, you shouldn't have."

"They're to replace the ones I destroyed," I said. She was looking quite attractive in the garment she now wore. A teddy, I believed it was called, in a swirly turquoise satin print that put one in mind of the sea.

"Ooh, you bought me a whole wardrobe of them! There's every color of the rainbow here."

"Do you like them?"

"I *love* them," she cooed. "Would you like me to model them for you?"

Slowly I looked her up and down, from the top of her auburn hair down to the swell of her breasts, the hollow of her waist and the curve of her hips. Down to the place where the scalloped edge of the sea-colored satin barely covered her sex, along her fine, long legs to her shapely feet with their pink-painted toenails.

"No," I said. "I want you bare."

"Then bare I'll be."

She smiled and wriggled her shoulders just enough to loosen the spaghetti straps of her garment; she then let it slide down her body to pool at her slender ankles. In the darkness of last night's encounter I hadn't seen her body as clearly as I would have wished, even with my keen, vampiric sight. Now I let my gaze feast on her perfection.

Her breasts were full and heavy. Whether this was a feat of nature or modern engineering I neither knew nor cared, especially when she leaned over me for a kiss. I cupped her breasts in my palms and the nipples responded by becoming erect. I removed my lips from hers and gave them over to her breasts, suckling as if I could wrest from them the life-giving human blood I craved.

Ginger moaned deeply and pressed more firmly against me as she reached to unfasten my trousers. She seized and stroked me with both hands, my own moan involuntarily removing my lips from her nipple. Kneeling before me, she took me in her mouth and let her lips move up and down the length of my shaft in an intoxicating rhythm that put me in mind of ocean waves pounding their way onto the shore.

She released me from her mouth and straddled me, putting me inside her. I cradled her bottom in my hands and drew her closer, fitting my cock inside her as deeply as her body would allow. She gasped and drew her legs up involuntarily and perhaps defensively, but the movement only allowed me to probe more deeply. I pulled back slightly for another stroke and arched my back to go deeper still. She took a deep breath and shifted, trying to relax so she could accommodate more of me.

"That's it," I whispered as I drew out of her, a little more this time. I thrust again, only harder. And so it went until both of us came together in a violent sunburst of sensation.

As I laid my head back against the chair, sated, I let the memories of other times and other lips overtake me, and I could have sworn I smelled the faint fragrance of lavender.

Jack

I wondered if Melaphia knew of some spell or potion that could turn me to stone.

I'd wept until I couldn't anymore. Did you know that vampire tears appear pink against white linens? I guess it's because they're mixed with the blood that animates us. I'd seen my own tears so rarely in my immortal lifetime that their unnatural color always shocked me, made me wonder just for a moment why they looked that way. Then I remembered.

Maybe one day I would stop hating the things that reminded me I was dead. William had been right all the times he told me that I still felt more human than vampire. He told me once that I would wake up one night having put all memories of being human behind me, and only then would I have come of age as a blood drinker.

Only then would I stop being shocked at the color of my own tears.

I stood mutely outside Connie's apartment door with a bouquet of lilacs in my hand. Connie must have sensed me there with her brand-new slayer perceptiveness, because she opened the door I was too much of a coward to knock on.

"There you are," she said. She took the flowers

from my hand and I followed her into the apartment. "My favorite. How in the world did you get them? You don't see them in florist shops very often even when they're in season."

I shrugged in response and sat on the couch while she got a vase from the kitchen. She returned and set the vase on an end table beside us. I put my arm around her and hugged her close when she sat beside me.

"You're awfully quiet tonight," she said.

"I guess so." I held her tighter and took one of her hands in mine, rubbing the pad of my thumb over her smooth, soft skin. Warm human skin. "I don't feel much like talking, but I want to hear you talk."

"What do you mean?" She twisted her head to look up at me quizzically. The movement bared her pale throat, sending a wave of pain and guilt over me. I forced myself to look away.

"I want you to tell me everything about yourself."

"You already know my checkered past," she said. "I told you about being abandoned and adopted, all of that." Her face took on a strained look for a moment, and I knew she was considering the idea of telling me about the tragic event that had brought her to Savannah and to me. And ultimately to her death, although she didn't know it yet.

But I didn't want our last conversation to be sad. I didn't want to see hurt in her eyes. "Your middle name," I blurted. "What is it?"

"Huh?"

I couldn't help myself. I had to smile at the funny expression she gave me, at the way her eyes crinkled at the edges when she came close to laughing. I closed my eyes for a moment, trying to memorize that look so that I could hold it for as long as I might exist, though to conjure it in my memory would only mean suffering.

"Don't you think I should know your middle name? I want to know everything about you. Like—what's your favorite flavor of ice cream? Um, what was your high school like? Why the little toe on your right foot is so ugly."

She punched me playfully on the chest, laughing. "That toe is a badge of honor. I broke it in the state soccer tournament and we *won.*"

"Hey, watch the pecs," I said, rubbing my chest. "I would hate to see what you'd do to me if you'd lost. And the ice cream?"

"White chocolate chunk."

"I've never tasted white chocolate in my life," I said. She opened her mouth to give me one of her witty remarks and then fell silent. There I went again, reminding us both that I was a vampire. "What about that high school?" I said, changing the subject.

"I went to Saint Pius the Tenth high school," she said. "Known affectionately in Atlanta as Pi High."

"That sounds wholesome."

"Oh, it was. The nuns made sure of that."

"And your middle name?"

"I have several. Take your pick. My name is Lareina Senalda Drina Consuela Adalia, but you can call me Connie."

"I'm honored. That's a long name to saddle on a little bitty baby."

"A long, pretentious name."

"What does it mean?"

"I'm sorry to say that I don't speak a word of Spanish. But they tell me it means something like 'the queen with a sign or symbol who helps, defends, and consoles mankind.' "

"The 'sign or symbol' being your birthmark."

"Yeah, the sun birthmark that Melaphia says means I'm a goddess."

That brought me back around to reality. I kissed the top of Connie's head and then she wriggled around to face me. "You can do better than that," she said, "or I'm not Lareina Senalda Drina Consuela Adalia Jones."

I kissed her ardently, deeply, trying to convey everything I felt for her but would not be able to put into words even if I could speak, which I was sure I could not. Her lips held the promise of hot lovemaking, but that would not be happening again. Even if I could have brought myself to make love to Connie tonight, the memory would have skewered me with white-hot shame every time I closed my eyes.

I broke off the kiss and whispered, "I love you."

"I love you, too," she said.

I swallowed hard. It was now or never. Looking deeply into her eyes, I concentrated my glamour on making her know my love for her. *I love you, never anyone as much as you before, and never anyone again.*

"You're getting sleepy." I heard myself say the words like some cheesy nightclub hypnotist, only from somewhere far away, outside my own body.

She nodded, closed her eyes, and slept, her face offering me the most wonderful smile I'd ever seen. No angel's could have been as sweet. It charmed me and froze time for a precious, peaceful moment.

I closed my eyes, too, afraid that if I looked up I would see that across the room the Blessed Virgin's icon had begun to stare at me in revulsion and censure, perhaps even silently crying her own tears. In my remorse I addressed both her and Connie as I whispered, "Forgive me."

My fangs pierced Connie's throat just over her carotid artery, and the blood flowed in the way human blood did, sure but unhurried, like the Savannah River to the sea. The monster in me savored the taste and the aroma, hungering for more while what was still human in my mind screamed in desperation and horror. I felt like a creature coming apart at the seams, sinew by raw sinew, atom by atom. My dual natures warred against each other until I thought my nerves would catch fire.

I felt Connie's heartbeat as the blood flowed into my mouth. I sucked at the artery, wishing it to be over so I could crawl away somewhere and die like I deserved to. But then I felt something else.

Another heartbeat.

I stopped, sealing the wounds on Connie's neck with my saliva, and tried to think of what could account for what I had felt.

William told me once that I was special, that I had powers and gifts I hadn't discovered yet, ones even he didn't understand. I'd always had powers of communication with the dead. I could feel them as I walked close to their resting places. If I was supersensitive to death, could I also be hyperaware of life?

I looked at Connie's sleeping form as I cradled her

in my arms. The bloom of life still blushed her cheeks. I held her close to me and pressed my ear to her chest, hearing the steady if weak *lub-dub* of her heart.

Then I moved my head so that my ear was against her abdomen. I closed my eyes and tried to concentrate the power of my vampiric senses into my hearing. There it was. A tiny heartbeat. Connie was carrying a child.

My child.

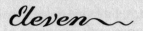

Eleven

William

I arose early the following night and went to my desk to catch up with correspondence and other business matters that had piled up during my recent absence. The evening before, the other vampires and I had returned to the mansion in the wee hours—they from Werm's club and I from my tryst with Ginger. We smoked the Cuban cigars Iban had brought and sipped a fine brandy while listening to Travis's tales of fighting Cortés and the other conquistadors. His deep voice and the gentle cadence of his speech were so soothing, it was almost possible to forget what poor Jack was going through.

His plight still weighed on me this evening, and I wished to occupy my mind to keep from thinking about him and the sad task he'd had to undertake the night before.

I had chosen to stay out of his private affairs over the years, but now I wished I had warned him more strongly against becoming involved with human women. But then, I'd failed to heed that advice myself and paid the price with my peace of mind and my everlasting sorrow.

Despite the fact that Jack could block me from reading his thoughts and emotions directly, he could not always hide his emotions from me when he was in my presence, especially when those emotions were strong. The night he had come back from the underworld, when I first told him he must prepare himself to kill Connie, I knew he hadn't accepted it. I could see it in his face. Jack always thought he could finesse his way out of a bad situation, and many times he could, especially when that situation involved human beings.

But last night Jack had realized that his charm and cleverness were useless against the dire circumstances we found ourselves in. I could tell the instant when he understood that there was no getting around the fact that he had to kill his lady love. The life, for lack of a better term, had gone out of him as clearly and visibly as the mortal verve dies at the point of a fang.

The administrative tasks before me were mere workaday trivialities, but I hoped they would distract me from my morose thoughts. As I sifted through the papers, I could not muster any enthusiasm for my labors.

Melaphia appeared in the vault, bearing a carafe of warm blood and several cups on a tray. "Your guests aren't up yet, I see."

"I suppose they're jet-lagged," I remarked. "They're not used to the sun setting until three hours from now."

"Let me pour you some breakfast while you wait for them."

"Thank you, my dear, but I'm not hungry."

Melaphia set the tray down on the edge of my huge desk and came to stand behind me. Rubbing my shoulders, she said, "It's a sad night."

"Indeed it is."

"I've started my preparations for approaching both Maman Lalee and the gods about keeping the Portal from the underworld closed to the double-deads," she said. "I've sent for the appropriate potions and offerings. I'm still going over the texts and making lists of things I should include in the spells. Deylaud is helping, of course."

"Good. Is he still grieving for Eleanor?"

"Yes, I'm afraid so, but keeping him busy is helping." With a final squeeze of my shoulders, she sat down in the leather wing chair opposite the desk. "How are *you* doing?"

I shrugged. "I may eventually get over her absence, I suppose. But it's difficult to know how much suffering I've caused her."

"But William, there was nothing you could have done differently."

"Not once she was out of control, no. I'm just sorry I let her persuade me to make her a blood drinker in the first place. But let's not speak of it again. I don't want to saddle you with any more of my burdens." By way of changing the subject, I asked, "So how goes the general research into the nature of the Slayer?"

"I confirmed what Travis and the European legends say about the fact that the Slayer is half-human and half-vampire. In the eyes of the Maya, that elevated her to a goddess. I think I've found some passages that may shed more light on what we're dealing with, if I can interpret them correctly. I'm on my way to my little altars in the passageway to say my prayers for guidance now." She paused a moment, and then said, "It's still strange to think of a vampire fathering a half-human child. It goes against every law of nature."

I sighed, feeling each one of my five-hundred-odd years. "True," I agreed. "But when it comes to nature, I believe what Hamlet said to Horatio applies."

Melaphia raised a slender brow. "There are more things in heaven and earth than are dreamt of in your philosophy."

"Heaven, earth, and the underworld," I added. "I hope that in the fullness of time when you reach heaven you will know all and understand all."

"That would be a blessing," she said. She began to speak again, but held her tongue. I sensed that she had been about to wish me the same good fortune.

But we both knew heaven wasn't where I was headed.

Before Melaphia disappeared around the corner to the little altars that lined the passageway to the vault, I said, "Don't forget to get your sleep."

"I'll be burning the midnight oil translating that text about the Slayer. It may tell us something important."

I drummed my fingers on the desk. "Very well, but don't exhaust yourself. You've been through a series of devastating shocks of late. I don't want you to fall ill . . . again."

"Don't worry, Dad. I'll be fine."

I smiled as she left the main room of the vault for the recesses of the stairway and tried to concentrate on the paperwork.

As a first order of business, I called Mr. Murphy, the manager of my antique store. When I inquired about the sword, he became quite flustered.

"Oh, my goodness, Mr. Thorne, I thought that you had taken it. I know you've displayed it in your home from time to time. So when it disappeared—"

"Disappeared? You mean you didn't sell it? When did you notice it missing?" I demanded, not bothering to hide my annoyance.

"It—it disappeared a couple of days ago. I questioned all the help. Nobody sold it and nobody saw anyone take it. One day it was just . . . gone."

"Question them again," I said.

"Should I call the police?"

I thought about that a moment. There was something troubling about the sword's disappearance besides the fact that it was a personal favorite of mine. Some disturbing grain of suspicion irritated my consciousness. "No. After you talk to the staff, go through the receipts for recent purchases and see if anything gives you pause. If not, wait for my further instructions."

As I hung up the phone, I became aware of a mixture of aromas—cinnamon, vanilla bean, and rum— that brought back memories from the night I had first met Lalee. She was standing among a dozen graves, freshly dug for the victims of a yellow fever epidemic. It was midnight, and she was beautiful, glowing with an inner light. Her skin was golden brown and her eyes were like onyx. Her long hair shimmered like strands of jet beads in the moonlight.

She knew me for what I truly was, and yet she was unafraid. In fact, she might have summoned me there. Afterward I was never sure how I got to those graves. Even if I'd wanted to harm her, I couldn't have. I was powerless in the face of her faith in her spirits and charms. She'd come to the grave sites that night to wing penitent sinners to heaven or whisper a dirge to transport the damned quickly to hell. Such was the grandeur of her power, and I was awestruck by it.

We'd made a bargain that night. I would nevermore kill a human being out of hunger, in temper, in pity, or for diversion. If I killed, it would only be for justice. And for that, she would give me the gift of the voodoo blood to strengthen me and my offspring, should I ever choose to make them. The young United States of America was barely past its colonial period; it was long before I met Jack McShane on that Civil War battlefield.

I had broken my promise of late, having flown into a rage upon seeing my wife in thrall to another blood drinker. I took my rage out on a number of defenseless mortals and killed out of anger as I had in the old days.

Later I tried to contact Lalee through prayers and offerings, seeking her forgiveness for breaking our bargain. My pleas went unanswered. I was left with only the unwavering suspicion that my broken bond could spell my doom. I told none of this to Jack, and especially not to Melaphia, but the feeling was growing stronger and stronger that my own downfall might be at hand.

I shivered. Clearly, while I had not been successful in manifesting Maman Lalee, Melaphia's efforts were bearing fruit. I could not only smell the fragrance of the great woman, I could sense her nearness as well. I rose to join Melaphia, hoping to bask in Lalee's aura.

Time seemed to expand as I felt myself coming closer to the lady. When I rounded the corner, I saw a ghostly form, swathed in a flowing gossamer robe, the unmistakable likeness of a very agitated Lalee.

"I heard you have spoke to de trickster," she said. "I should have tole you not to pray to him, no. He is not your spirit guide. Did I not say it to you long ago? He is de guide of de blue-eyed blood drinker, not you. That handsome boy can see through de trickster's lies without he even try, but 'tis not in your nature to do so, gentle one. You are gullible. You are de light."

It was exceedingly rare for the Maman to appear in her true form. When she blessed us with her presence, her voice issued from a chosen one. Once and only once it was Jack. I knew that she favored him with her love, sensing the goodness in him.

"Dat *loa* has led you astray wid de lies and half-truths. Why you want believe him? You he would fool with his tricks just to make himself laugh. What did you ask him exactly?"

"I—I don't remember . . ."

"You must take care when consulting de *loas*. You must choose your words careful or he will twist dem to suit his mischievous ways. Dis you know already, but you got careless in your fear. He made you tink it was righteous to send dis vampire to slay de Slayer. It was a trick, yes. No one must kill de slayer of blood drinkers. She is sired of greatness and carries greatness within her."

Melaphia's eyes went wide. "Should the blood drinkers not fear her then?"

Lalee shimmered, becoming more transparent and insubstantial. "By de gods, dey should fear her power indeed!" she said.

Even though I could barely make out her features, I could swear she looked directly at me. Ordinarily I would be thrilled to make eye contact with the demigoddess once more, but this time, something indecipherable in her gaze shook me and made me want to turn away, but I did not.

I started to speak—to thank her for helping Melaphia save Renee in the bowels of London so that I could bring her home safely. I wanted to apologize and beg her forgiveness for breaking the oath I had made to her. I tried to form the words to ask her to guide us in our current dilemmas. But I was frozen in place as she began to disappear.

"Wait!" shouted Melaphia. "We need your advice! What can we do to stop the old lords? They are ready to open the portal to the underworld so the worst of their demons can prey on us. What should we do to stop them?"

"I do not have power over de kind of elemental forces dat it will take to free de basest demons, no," Lalee said, her voice becoming fainter. "And I do not have dominion over de ones most damned. You must beseech de most powerful beings in de heavens, and even dey may not be able to help you. May de gods have mercy o'er de souls of you all who I love."

In an instant the apparition was gone, and Melaphia and I looked at each other too shocked to move for a moment. We both knew that Lalee would not be back. "Quickly!" Melaphia shouted. "We've got to stop Jack before it's too late!"

"If it's not too late already," I said. I ran to my desk to call Jack on his cell phone. The other vampires, who had been in the process of rousing anyway, were startled fully awake by our shouting. They emerged from their coffins demanding to know what was happening. I dialed the phone while they peppered me with questions.

"Jack!" Melaphia shouted. I turned around to see him descending the stairs, and we all ran to him.

Jack

"Jack, please tell us you didn't do it!" Melaphia cried while grabbing the lapels of my jacket.

"No, I didn't do it," I said. "I couldn't kill her. I—"

"Thank God," William said.

"Why wasn't Jack supposed to kill the Slayer?" Tobey asked.

Iban and Travis exchanged worried glances.

Melaphia slumped against my chest. Her breath was coming fast and in hitches. She seemed to be on the verge of breaking into laughter. Not the good kind, but the hysterical kind you go into when you almost step off a cliff into thin air and something stops you. I knew how she felt.

"Lalee just appeared to William and me. She said the *loa* Legba tricked me when he made me think you were supposed to kill Connie."

The relief I felt was indescribable. Not only did I not have to kill Connie, but I didn't have to worry about any of my friends killing her either. I hugged Melaphia and kissed her on top of the head like I did when she was small. *Thank you, sweet Maman.*

"How then are we to deal with the Slayer when she is activated?" Iban asked.

"She didn't say," Melaphia said, righting herself. "She just said that the Slayer was sired of greatness and carried greatness within her."

"What is that supposed to mean?" Travis asked.

"I think I can answer the last part about carrying greatness within her," I said. They all looked at me expectantly. "Connie's pregnant."

It sounded strange to hear that out loud. It was all I'd been thinking about for the last twenty-four hours, but as I said the words I still couldn't reconcile myself to their meaning. Could it be possible? Had I fathered a child?

Melaphia's dark eyes went wide. "You? I mean, yours?"

"I'm sure she hasn't been with anybody else."

Everyone but William was stunned into silence. "What happened last night, Jack?" he asked.

"I put her under glamour like you said. Then I . . . did what I had to do," I said, not able to put the awful truth into words. "Then, while I was listening to see if she still had a heartbeat, I heard another one. A small one, and I knew. I sealed the wound, woke her up, and told her she got sick with the flu and passed out. Then

I told her she was dehydrated and started forcing her to drink fluids. I stayed with her until just now to make sure she was going to be all right."

"How could she possibly survive blood loss like that?" Tobey asked.

Travis, looking stonier than one of the carvings on Mount Rushmore, said, "The Slayer's powers of healing will be as great as ours. This is another sign that she is close to being activated."

"How far along is she?" Melaphia asked.

"A few days is all."

"How can you detect a life that small?" Iban wanted to know.

William said, "Jack is a very sensitive creature. I've known it all his life. We all know about his power to feel out the dead, even reanimate. It seems he is also as sensitive to the presence of life. I doubt if any medical device could detect a heartbeat at this stage, but with his gift, Jack can."

My sire and I just looked at each other. It was as hard to read William as ever, but I could swear I saw something like awe in his face. "It looks as if Jack is much more special than even I understood. He has just fathered a child." One corner of his mouth turned up in the barest suggestion of a smile.

"If all this is true," Travis said, "he has sired another vampire slayer." Travis looked like he wanted to spit on the ground. "How do we know this voodoo spirit has the interest of the blood drinkers at heart? Has she seen the slayers at work as I have?"

"She has your interests at heart because William made a pact with her a couple hundred years ago," Melaphia said, lifting her chin. "And sealed it with the gift of the blood." Melaphia took any offense to the Maman personally.

"She's never let us down before. Remember who saved us from Reedrek not long ago," I said. "The voodoo blood has saved my bacon more times than I want to remember."

I turned to William to see why he hadn't jumped to Lalee's defense, but he was looking worried, too, in a way I found unsettling for some reason. Finally, he said, "I trust Lalee. Jack did the right thing by refraining from killing the Slayer, even though he may not have known why at the time."

Travis was finished speaking, but he didn't look any happier. Everyone else looked uneasy, too, and they were staring at me. None of them was familiar with the old religion that Melaphia practiced, although they'd seen a pretty good demo the night when we captured Reedrek.

"Maybe there's another explanation for this," I said. "Could there have been some kind of immaculate conception thing going on in the underworld?"

"That hasn't happened in more than two thousand years, and I don't think we should expect to ever see it again," William said.

"I'm sorry, Jack, but somebody has to say it. Could Connie have had another lover?" Tobey asked.

For some reason that didn't make me mad. I guess because I understood that Tobey didn't know Connie like I did. "No," I said. "No way."

Travis said, "I still don't like it. Nothing in my own culture's lore and writings indicates that a slayer should be allowed to live."

"I don't know what to think at this point," Tobey said, scratching his head.

Suddenly my relief was gone. I was no longer sure that Connie was out of danger at the hands of these blood drinkers. She still needed my protection. I had to think of still another plan, dammit.

Melaphia, William, Travis, and the others started debating the relative trustworthiness of voodoo and Mayan and Celtic spirituality and prophecies. Melaphia said something about the word *sire* in some prophecy possibly having more than one meaning. Then they speculated on who Connie's vampire father might have been.

It was all too much for me. I hadn't slept any in the last day because of having to nurse Connie, and my head was starting to hurt. I went to the wet bar at the far side of the room to pour myself some blood, and while they were all talking at once, I backed out of the room and took the stairs up to the main floor two at a time.

I drove to the garage and saw through the window that the irregulars' card game was in full swing. It was kind of comforting in a goofy way. My whole life had been turned on its head the last couple of months. It was good to see that part of my world was still normal. As normal as a human, two shape shifters, and a faerie playing cards could be, that is.

Speaking of things kind of normal but really not, I heard the scrape of Huey's shovel as he continued to despoil his own grave. I went around back to see him laboring under the watchful eye of the same crow that had been there the other night. It seemed Huey had made little progress, but this activity at least gave him a purpose in life—that is to say, death—when he wasn't otherwise busy detailing cars.

I wondered if I'd done Huey any favors by accidentally raising him from the dead. He appeared to me as a ghost once shortly after Reedrek had murdered him, and he had reported that in heaven, he had all the beer he could drink. And it was good imported stuff, too.

Then I got drunk during a voodoo ritual and misapplied a prayer to the god of the underworld—and Huey was reborn, after a fashion. He'd dug his way out of his own grave with his bare hands, to my and Werm's drunken horror. Sending him back seemed too grisly to contemplate, so here he was, a sort of mascot of the business you might say. Besides, he was proving to be useful. The next time he said he saw little blue men, I was going to sit up and take notice. He could speak shape shifter and see through fey glamour. Who knew what else the little guy could do?

"How's it going, Hugh-man?" I greeted him.

"All right, I reckon," Huey reported.

"Haven't hit pay dirt yet?"

"No sir. I ain't seen no sign of that car."

The crow made a screeching noise, startling us both. I looked at Huey sheepishly. A vampire and a zombie shouldn't be afraid of anything, much less a crow.

"It's tryin' to tell us somethin'," Huey said.

"How do you know?"

"It's been trying its best to talk to me all night. Just listen."

The crow flapped its wings and made some other noises, and they weren't any sounds I'd ever heard come out of a crow before. "Maybe it got ahold of some bad roadkill," I speculated. My remark seemed to agitate the crow even more. It beat its wings furiously and fixed its beady eyes on me in a creepy fashion.

"My uncle Elroy had a crow that could talk like one of them talking birds," Huey said.

"Like a parrot?"

"Yep. But only after Uncle Elroy had split its tongue with a knife."

"Don't get any ideas," I said. "I don't want you picked up by the ASPCA." I was glad Huey didn't have a penchant for getting in trouble with the law. If the authorities were inspired to examine him too closely, especially that loose eyeball, there'd be a lot of explaining to do.

"Naw. I wouldn't do that to a dumb animal."

The crow probably had more IQ points than Huey, but I refrained from pointing that out.

"Ain't you going to join the poker game?" Huey asked.

"No. I had to find someplace to think."

"You got problems?"

"Yeah. You could say that."

"Why don't you run them by me? Sometimes it helps to talk to somebody." Huey leaned on his shovel thoughtfully.

I wondered how many vampires had a zombie as a therapist. What the hell? Huey would probably be as good a sounding board as anybody. I told him the predicament and he listened as if he understood.

"That there's a hard one, Jack. Let me think." He scratched his chin sagely. "Do you think you could talk Connie into leaving Savannah?"

"That might work for a while, but some rogue vampire somewhere will eventually track her down. Besides, I don't know if I could convince her to go."

"What if she had a reason to go? And what if she changed her name and went to a place that was way back in the country or somewhere she was hard to find?"

I started to reply that I couldn't think of a reason she'd go to a hick town and change her name. But then it hit me that Huey was right. There was a way I could accomplish those things with one scheme.

But it would mean losing Connie and my child forever.

Speed helped me think, so I didn't go straight to my storage unit near Bonaventure Cemetery. Instead I raced along the back roads, close to the intracoastal waterways that snaked their way between Georgia's barrier islands and the tidal marshes fringing the shoreline. Known as the inland passage since the first European set foot on what would become Savannah soil, these water highways protected small craft from Atlantic nor'easters and tropical storms bubbling up from the Caribbean.

The waterways where Spanish traders and Franciscan friars used to travel now sported marinas boasting high-tech wireless Internet connections and digital TV at every slip.

As much as I loved fast cars, I now longed for the old days when I rode a black horse with silver-studded tack through the marshes. I used to scare the piss out of night fishermen and anybody else who crossed my path, creating legends all my own. I was the stuff of children's nightmares and the star of young girls' dreams, or so I've been told.

Those were the good old days before I met Connie Jones.

When she was still a patrolwoman, she'd come upon me lying half in a ditch where I'd wrecked my car. Vampires never bother with seat belts. My injuries would have been lethal to a mortal human being, and yet to her astonishment I did survive. She'd had her eye on me ever since, a nagging suspicion in the back of her mind telling her that there was something strange about me.

In those months when she'd dogged me, her curiosity aroused, I hadn't wanted to discourage her attentions because I was drawn to her by another kind of arousal. If I could turn back the hands of time, I would have done things differently. Maybe if during one of the many times she'd stopped and ticketed me for speeding, I had scared her with my fangs or put some negative glamour on her, I might have frightened her away or discouraged her enough to leave me alone. But no, I encouraged her attentions, egging her on for my own selfish reasons.

Because of me, she had been led to the edge of an abyss, and one more step would give her the deadly knowledge that would put her on a bloody course of destruction—either mine or hers or both.

It was time for me to put my selfishness aside and do what needed to be done for her sake and for the sake of my child. But I couldn't do it alone. I needed the help of the only other man who I knew for sure loved her and would, I was convinced, lay down his life to protect her if need be.

My friend Seth. To whom I'd have to lie like a dog for this whole scheme to work. I couldn't let him know that Connie was pregnant, and I couldn't let him know that I'd almost killed her last night. All the explanations in the world about how it would have been best for her would not make a difference to Seth. If he knew I'd tried to kill Connie, he would try to kill me. There was no doubt in my mind.

When I got to the guarded storage unit where I spent my daylight hours, I found Seth asleep on the couch in sweatpants and a T-shirt. He had been bunking at my place since he came to town to shape up a wayward pack of werewolves before they got out of control and into trouble with the law.

I shook him, and he came awake as quickly as every good predator should. He blinked his yellow-green wolf's eyes at me expectantly and sat up. "What?" he said.

"We've got to talk," I said, sitting down next to him.

"Oh, man, I just hate it when a conversation starts that way. What did I do wrong, huh? Just tell me. It's my hair, isn't it?" He pawed his sleep-tousled brown mane. "I went running in the woods earlier tonight, so maybe I picked up some burrs. No, it's my butt. It's too big."

"Shut up, doofus. This is serious."

Something in my tone convinced him. "Am I going to need coffee for this?"

"You're going to need whiskey for this, but it's too early for you and too late for me."

Seth cleared his throat. "This does sound serious." He eyed the kitchen area.

"Want me to make the coffee? I could use some myself," I said.

"No!" he said emphatically. "I've tasted your coffee. I'd sooner drink formaldehyde. I'm not immortal like you are, you know. *I* can be poisoned."

Seth ambled off to the kitchen, which was separated from the den by a Formica-covered bar. I followed him and sat down on one of the bar stools. "This is a long story," I began. "And you're just going to have to trust me that I know what I'm talking about."

"Okay," Seth said warily. He'd put the coffee and filter in place and was pouring the water into the coffeemaker's reservoir.

"Connie's in danger, and you have to help me get her away from Savannah."

Seth froze. "In danger from who?"

"From me. And the other vampires."

He narrowed his eyes. "What are you talking about, Jack? You love Connie. What the hell's going on?"

As best I could, I explained about the prophecies, the birthmark, what happened in the underworld, all of it. I also laid out the reasons Travis said that trying to get her to hook up with the vampires to fight the bad guys wouldn't do any good. Of course I left out the part about Connie's pregnancy, the fact that I already tried to kill her, and what Melaphia and William had found out from Lalee.

"And so now William expects you to kill her, just like that." A murderous look came across Seth's face. He stalked the length of the small kitchen and back again, flexing his fists as if he would welcome the chance to destroy something with his bare hands.

"And if I don't do it—*when* I don't do it—one of the other vampires will." That last part was true, anyway.

"So you want me to take her away?"

"It's the only thing I can think of. I mean, do you have any other ideas?"

"Yeah. I could kill me half a dozen vampires," he said.

He was big, powerful, and lethal, but he couldn't take on all of us. "Even if you could—"

"Oh, I could."

"Even if you could," I insisted, "it's already too late for that. By this time all the European vampires know from Olivia that the Slayer is a Savannah cop named Consuela Jones. I even caught a vampire hanging around outside her apartment the other night. Who knows how that guy found out? I'm telling you, she might as well have a bull's-eye on her back."

"Jesus," Seth muttered. "So when are you going to tell her?"

"Tomorrow night I'll tell her she's the Slayer."

"And how are you going to make her leave town with me?"

"Have you gone soft in the head or have you never tried to explain Connie why she *has* to do a thing?"

Seth looked at me dumbly and sighed. "Oh. Yeah," he said. "I forgot how stubborn she can be. And how incapable she is of backing down from a fight. We had a helluva time keeping her out of the dominance fight with the werewolves that night."

"Yeah. She was ready to wade right in. Connie's got to have a good reason for leaving Savannah or there's no way in hell she's going to go," I said, giving Seth a meaningful look that he could not mistake.

"Dude," he said. "She has her own feelings. You can't just *give* her to me, no matter how much you want to. No matter how much *I* wish you could."

There it was. The confirmation that he still loved her. As if I'd had any doubt. For an instant I hated him a little. "I'm going to break up with her," I heard myself say. "And then I want you to convince her that the reasons she came to Savannah in the first place are gone now."

"What do you mean exactly?" he asked, pouring a cup of coffee.

"It was you who told me she left Atlanta because of the murder-suicide, because everyone she knew, including you—*especially* you—pitied her. And she couldn't deal with people's pity. In the first place, you can take her back to Podunk County or wherever the hell it is you're from, where nobody knows her. In the second place, she told me that what happened in the underworld—seeing her son in heaven and all—has helped her come to a kind of closure about what happened. So her head's in a better place about all that now. She's not running from it anymore. That's why I think you can get her to take you back when I'm out of the picture. She won't care that you know about what happened."

Seth handed me the coffee and poured a cup for himself. "That makes sense, I guess. So how are you going to break up with her?"

"Just leave that to me."

"Don't hurt her."

I gave him a murderous look. If only he knew what I'd been through in the last couple of days. "I'm going to do this the best way I know how."

"And what way is that?"

"Never you mind." We glared at each other over the coffee cups, resentment on my part and mistrust on his, simmering like redeye gravy that's about to boil over.

"When are you going to do this?"

"Tomorrow night. Be ready to . . . do your thing." The coffee tasted like battery acid in my mouth.

Seth regarded me soberly. "Seduce Connie, you mean?"

"Well, just, *damn*. Did you have to say it out loud?" My nerves were stretched to the breaking point. I had to calm down. Maybe I should switch to decaf.

Seth stopped glaring and started looking all sorry for me. I don't know which was worse. "This must be killing you, Jack. I'm really sorry," he said.

"No, you're not," I said miserably. "You always wanted her back."

"Yeah, but not this way."

I looked at the ceiling. "Yeah, well, this is the way it is. You take her, make her fall for you again, change her name to Connie Walker, and hide her up there in the wilds of the north Georgia mountains so the vampires can't find her. Have a whole litter of fuzzy half-werewolf puppies or whatever you call them and live happily ever after."

"I should probably be insulted by part of that spiel, but I'll let it slide since you're in such bad shape."

"I'll live." I sighed.

He gave me a skeptical look.

"In a manner of speaking."

"I know you don't want to talk about it, but how *are* you going to convince her that you're not the man for her?" he asked.

I rubbed my chin, thinking about what I'd said just a minute ago. Then I snapped my fingers. "That's it. Why haven't I thought of that before?"

"Thought of what?"

"The puppies."

"Seriously, man. That's a slur. Don't make me come over there and—"

I ignored him. "Has Connie ever mentioned wanting to have more children?"

"Not to me. Remember, she cut me out of her life right after the tragedy."

"But you just know she does, right? I mean, women are like that. They always want to have kids."

"I'm not following you."

"I can't have kids." I didn't make eye contact with him when I said this. I hoped like hell he would never find out I was lying.

"Oh, yeah. I forgot that about vampires. You guys are shooting blanks."

"Talk about a slur." I sniffed.

"Sorry. So you think that if you tell Connie you can't give her a child, that will put her off the idea of a future with you?"

"That's what I'm saying."

"I don't think that will work."

"Why not?"

"For starters, she could just get artificially inseminated or something. There's all kinds of ways around that sort of thing nowadays."

"Okay. What do you suggest I tell her so that she'll fall out of love with me? I mean, I'm a hard man for a woman to get out of her system."

"Uh-huh. Gee, I don't know. You could start with being an evil, bloodsucking demon, that you'll never grow old while she will, that you'll never be able to go out in the daylight, that you'll never—"

"Oh-*kay*. I get it."

"But the best of those is the blood thing. It's just gross."

"She's already seen me go all fang-face on somebody."

"Yeah, but that was to defend *her* when Will killed Sullivan. How about in the Beauty and the Beast story? Not the Disney version, the real one. Where Beauty sees the Beast eating some animal that he's run down and killed and gets really grossed out."

I looked at him for a second. "Beauty and the Beast? How gay are you?"

"I'm just saying. And Beauty and the Beast is not gay. By God, we're about to have to settle all this outside."

"The sun's up by now."

"I know. Why do you think I want to go outside?" After a moment, Seth broke into one of his broad grins, and even though our talk had been about life-and-death matters, I found myself laughing as if I'd never laugh again.

And considering what I had to do tomorrow night, I probably wouldn't ever *want* to laugh again.

I stopped laughing and rested my head on the cool countertop, suddenly so weary I couldn't sit up straight.

I believed in Connie's love for me. Deep down, I knew there was only one way to make her hate me enough to let me go.

She had been the victim of domestic violence in the most cruel way and had spent most of her adult life helping other woman battle it. There was something I could tell her that would set off a firestorm of raw and deep-seated emotions in her gut and make her curse my name forever.

I had to tell Connie I tried to kill her.

Twelve

William

I watched Tobey and Iban circulate through the crowd. They mixed easily with the patrons, not having to resort to glamour. Travis, on the other hand, stood apart from the throng. Evidently, the young ladies thought his striking looks went a long way toward canceling out any perceived aloofness. All the vampires were accomplishing their stated goal for this evening: meeting attractive women.

My own chances for procuring sex tonight were better than even, what with Ginger taking care to brush against me with her ample bosom or squeeze my thigh each time she passed me with her tray of drinks balanced with one hand on her shoulder. Not to say that I was in the mood for games, sexual or otherwise.

The events of the previous night were disturbing on levels the others, even Melaphia, couldn't even guess at. Lalee had forbidden us to kill our sworn enemy, the Slayer, and I knew that at least part of the reason was because I had broken my vow. Did that mean she had abandoned my bloodline altogether? No, I thought not. By her words I could tell that she still had some affection for Jack. Thank heaven for that measure of goodwill at least.

Her negativity toward me shouldn't have come as a surprise, even though not a fortnight earlier she had aided me in saving Renee from a terrible fate. But after reflecting upon the incident I realized that she had done her work through Melaphia, not through me. And her goal was to save Renee, not to do any particular good turn for me.

I felt myself sinking into a mire of melancholia and foreboding. Just a few hours ago, I thought the threat the Slayer posed to us was over. Now Jack was forbidden to kill her, and I knew he would not allow anyone else to do so either.

I had been worried about Jack. I supposed he was overwhelmed, and I only hoped that whatever scheme he was plotting to save Connie was one he felt he could share with me. In his younger days particularly, Jack had a penchant for not thinking things through.

As if on cue, Jack walked into the nightclub, looking almost as grim as he had when he'd left us the night before. When he saw me at the bar, he sat down next to me.

Werm approached him with something very like awe, as I had filled him in on the revelations of the previous night. The fledgling was learning discretion, however. He refrained from mentioning anything to Jack about his current situation, but only asked him for his drink order.

"I'm sorry I ran out last night," Jack said, accepting a draft beer from Werm.

"Things were getting rather intense, and you had already been through hell in the last twenty-four hours," I said. "I don't blame you in the slightest."

"Really?" He seemed to relax a little and took a healthy drink of the beer before looking over his shoulder at Travis, who was conversing with two pretty coeds. "What got decided after I left?"

"About how to proceed where the Slayer's concerned?"

"Yeah. It was looking like everybody was going to be cool with letting Connie live except Travis."

"I had a talk with him," I said. "I told him that we were going to do as Lalee instructed. I further told him that you would inform Connie that she was the Slayer and fill her in on everything we know about what that entails. Perhaps he's wrong when he says she'll lose her reason when she activates. If not, at least we will have tried to appeal to her to fight at our side. Travis seemed to accept my decision."

"Do you think he's wrong?"

"I'm not sure. For now I've decided to give Connie the benefit of the doubt."

"Man, that's a load off my mind. But I have to warn you, Connie might not be anxious to throw in with us after I tell her the rest of it."

"What do you mean?"

"Hang on—I'll explain in a second. Hey, Werm, where is Seth tonight? Is he going to be tending bar with you?"

"Yeah, I sent him for a couple of cases of liquor from the supplier. He'll be here later." Werm then walked away to serve some customers at the other end of the bar.

"Why are you inquiring about Seth?"

"Because he can't hear what I'm planning with Connie. I'm going to tell her I tried to kill her last night."

"Why in the name of heaven would you do that? There is no need."

"Yes, there is."

Jack went on to make his case. He outlined his plan for at least temporarily removing the threat that Connie faced for us. That's the interpretation he put on it, at any rate. I knew that his plan was primarily to protect Connie and his unborn child, but it happened to serve our interests as well. However, it hinged on Connie's being willing to let Jack go and return to the arms of Seth.

"What do you think?" he asked when he'd finished.

"I think the plan is good for everyone." And although I didn't say it, I was glad that he'd chosen to trust me and seek out my counsel.

"Really?" he asked me again.

"Yes. Really. I'm not going to fight you on this, Jack." He opened his mouth and a stern glance from me stopped him from saying *Really* again. "I presume that Seth was amenable to your proposal."

"You presume right. I didn't tell him that I tried to kill Connie, though."

"I don't blame you. I do have one question, though. What do you presume is going to happen when Connie realizes she's with child?"

Jack drained his beer and refrained from meeting

my eyes. "It's so early in the pregnancy, I figure if she and Seth get together quick enough, they can both just assume it's his." He looked down at the polished wood of the bar as if, after all these years as a blood drinker, he were looking for his reflection and put out by its absence.

"I see." I could only imagine what the forfeiture of his child, not to mention the woman he loved, was costing Jack. I had never been more proud of his self-lessness. So I chose not to point out the obvious flaw in his scheme, and in any case it would be years before anyone would have cause to wonder how a *dhampir* and a werewolf produced another *dhampir*. Perhaps by that time, it wouldn't matter for any number of reasons. "I'm sorry you have to bear this, Jack. But I do believe you're doing the right thing."

"I guess," Jack muttered, and rubbed the back of his neck. He looked like he hadn't slept in an age.

"When are you going to break up with her?"

"Tonight."

"Good luck," I said, and squeezed his shoulder. "I'll pick up your tab."

"Thanks." Looking like a man on his way to the gallows, Jack left.

The visiting vampires observed Jack's departure and approached me to see what state he was in. Werm stepped out from behind the bar to join us. Without going into detail, I told them Jack was on a sad mission to prepare Connie, to try to influence her to support us, and to remove her from our midst if possible. They didn't need the details of Jack's scheme; it wasn't a decision to be made by committee.

Iban and Tobey stated their support while Travis said nothing.

Just then the other vampires turned toward the front door, sensing the presence of an unfamiliar blood drinker. "Ah, here's your friend Mr. Blackstone," I said to Tobey.

"That's not Freddy Blackstone," Tobey hissed, and we all moved as one toward the club entrance.

As soon as he saw us, the blood drinker fled. The dance floor was between us and the entrance, so we were impeded by having to dodge the other patrons. By the time we reached the outside, whoever was posing as Tobey's friend had gotten cleanly away.

"Damn!" Tobey unholstered his cell phone and began to dial, presumably one of his clan members, while the rest of us fanned out across the parking lot. There was no sign of the other blood drinker or which way he had gone.

"How long has he been missing? Did he say where he was going?" Tobey asked the person on the other end of the line. After some additional questioning, he clicked off the phone and addressed us as we gathered around him. "They haven't seen Freddy for weeks," he said. "They assumed he was off on one of his wanderings, but now there's the possibility of foul play. They're going to put on a search for him at some of his hangouts."

"Werm, in your conversations with this impostor, did he tell you anything about himself that aroused your suspicions?" I asked.

"Uh—about what?" He looked as if he also wished to flee the scene.

"Anything."

"No. He just talked about stupid stuff—places he'd been, things he'd seen. Nothing you'd ever think twice about," Werm insisted.

"Did he seem overly curious about us—here in Savannah, or any of the other clans in the Americas?"

"Not really, no. I mean, not that I can remember. If he started asking too many questions, I would have told you, honest. I didn't tell him anything about you guys."

"Very well," I said. Werm would not have been able to lie to me if he tried.

"It looks as if your clan has been under surveillance, at the very least," Iban said to Tobey. "It would take some research and knowledge of your people and their habits to determine which blood drinker would not be missed if he left suddenly."

"So that another blood drinker could assume his identity," Travis completed Iban's thought.

Tobey, clearly flustered, ran a hand through his hair. "What did you mean by 'at the very least,' Iban?" he asked.

"I believe what Iban was getting at is the likelihood that your clan has been infiltrated by someone working for the Council," I said.

"Like Will infiltrated my own clan, leading to their deaths," Iban added bitterly.

"Let's not jump to the worst-case scenario," I said. "Tobey, have you ever seen that blood drinker before?"

"I don't think so, but I couldn't swear to it. I concentrate on my racing most of the time. I have underlings who do the administrative work for the clan—keeping track of them, keeping a roster up to date, that kind of thing. We don't have all-hands meetings or anything. It's possible that the guy himself has been circulating among us using another name altogether."

"And another persona," I suggested.

"I've got to go to them," Tobey said, looking stricken. "Iban, will you come with me?"

"Of course," said the Spaniard. Iban had joined Tobey's clan since his own West Coast family had been wiped out. "Do you have any objections, William?"

I said that I did not, although the moment I spoke I felt another wave of what could only be described as impending doom. Perhaps it was due to all the recent talk of catastrophic scenarios.

If the Council did figure out how to strike out at us, who was to say their first target would be Savannah? There were only three of us here, not counting Reedrek. The clans elsewhere on this continent were much bigger targets. Was it a conceit on my part to presume that I was so prominent on their agenda that they would strike at me first? In any case, I could not ask the other vampires to stay with us in the east when their own people might be in danger.

"Perhaps I should go as well," Travis said. "I should warn the blood drinkers in my territory to be on the lookout for strangers, as well as any signs and portents of trouble."

"Of course," I said with a conviction I did not feel. "You must see to your own people."

They left at once, and I as their host made to follow them, but Werm stopped me. "I've got an idea," he said.

I told the others I would be there to see them off, and they went to make their arrangements. Then I followed Werm back into the club. He led me up to a perky-looking female drinking a fruity concoction at the bar.

Werm introduced me to the young woman, who was named Giselle and looked very much like the drawing of Heidi in one of Renee's books. That is, if Heidi had been all grown up and sporting a full rack of double Ds, as Jack would say. She wore a blouse whose puffy sleeves gave it an innocent and feminine look, but whose neckline was cut low enough to show a generous amount of cleavage. All she needed was lederhosen to complete the look. Platinum-blond braids framed a cherubic and carefully made-up face. Her eyes were as pale a blue as any Alpine maiden's.

"Giselle draws caricatures in the parks around Savannah," Werm explained. "She's a regular here. Giselle, you've met Freddy Blackstone, right?"

"Sure. I've talked to him lots of times," Giselle said in a high little-girl voice. With this I got the gist of Werm's plan, and had to admire his cleverness.

"Do you think you could draw him from memory if I got you some paper?" Werm asked. "Only not a caricature this time, but as realistic a drawing as you can do of him in a small amount of time."

Giselle put her pert nose in the air. "I can do realism," she assured Werm. "I *am* a graduate of SCAD, you know. And I've got my sketchbook right here."

She reached beside her and produced a voluminous bag from which she took the promised sketchbook. I thanked her in advance and instructed Werm to put all her drinks for the night on my account. I then called Deylaud and told him to come to the Portal immediately.

In twenty minutes Giselle had produced an excellent likeness of the blood drinker who had passed himself off as one Freddy Blackstone. By that time, Deylaud had arrived. He was panting slightly, and I knew that he had run the whole way. He loved to run whether in dog or human form, and the excuse to do so had made him smile for the first time that I had seen since I'd broken the news to him about Eleanor. I was also delighted to see that he had recovered enough to feel like running once again.

"I want you to take this sketch and fax it to Olivia immediately," I told Deylaud. "And follow up with a phone call. They will be in their coffins, but perhaps one of them will answer if you let it ring long enough. If not, leave a message. Ask Olivia if she or any of her vampires have ever seen the man in the photo. If so, have her tell you everything they know about him so that you can report it back to me. I should be home shortly."

"Got it," Deylaud said, and took the drawing.

Just as Deylaud turned to leave, Ginger stepped around a throng of customers with a tray so heavily laden with full beer mugs she had to use both hands to carry it. She was being careful, watching her step lest she trip over some obstacle, like Giselle's gargantuan bag.

Then she looked up and made eye contact with Deylaud. My faithful half-canine companion went rigid, and the drawing floated to the floor. I stooped quickly to pick it up before someone trod on it, and when I stood once more I noticed that Ginger had frozen as well.

She looked as though she wished to run, but the tray and the throng gathered around the bar prevented her flight. She turned to the right, then left, spilling some of the beer from the mugs onto the tray, but there was no way out.

As soon as she knew she wouldn't be going anywhere, she looked Deylaud directly in the eye. If I hadn't known better, I could have sworn that she was trying to work glamour on him as a vampire would have. If that was her aim, it wasn't working.

Deylaud's nostrils flared and he stepped closer as if to get more of her scent. He stepped back again, confusion written across his narrow, guileless face.

By that time, Ginger had seen an opening between two burly customers and wedged herself through it as if she'd been greased.

"Deylaud, what is it?" I asked, handing him back the drawing.

He took it, still looking confused. The music, which had been mercifully absent for the last few minutes, started up again. "Nothing," he said hastily. "The music just hurt my ears is all. You know how sensitive my ears are."

Indeed. I also knew that the music hadn't been playing when Deylaud's eyes had met Ginger's. "Very well," I said. "Along with you then."

Deylaud ran out of the building, startling the clubgoers he brushed past. Ginger, for her part, was out of sight. I had remained at the Portal rather than taking the sketch home myself in case the opportunity for a quick tryst with the redhead presented itself. I thought perhaps it was time to seek Ginger out and see what developed.

I stood and made my way around the little crowd of people that Ginger had squeezed through and found her standing at the computer set up against the back wall. I slipped my arm around her waist, lifted her barely off her feet, and spirited her away and into the establishment's back meeting room.

"Hey, I have to run tabs for some customers," she protested.

"Not until you tell me what went on with Deylaud just now." I set her on her feet.

"Who?" She blinked her wide eyes, but I could tell she knew very well whom I was talking about.

"I refer to the slender young man who was just here. The one I handed the drawing to. You two made eye contact, and he ran out."

"Oh, William," she purred. "You don't have anything to be jealous about. I don't even know him."

"I'm not—" I began, but then decided not to play along. I knew she would not admit to anything unless I tortured her, which I could surely do. It was unnecessary in any case; when I got home, Deylaud would tell me what I wished to know. Still, I could not let the young woman off the hook. Human or vampire, no one lied to William Cuyler Thorne and got away with it. "I don't like being played," I said.

She had the good sense to look properly chastened, but in an instant her expression turned coquettish. "Don't you?" She put both palms against her thighs and slowly slid her skirt upward, revealing one of the pairs of panties that I had given her the other night.

"Does this count as being played? Or being played with?"

I reached her with such preternatural swiftness that she would not have been able to see me move. I invaded the wispy undergarment with one hand while I freed my erection with the other. She gasped as I raised her off her feet and entered her, pinning her against the wall with the force of my shaft. I bore down with punishing strokes, causing her to issue little rhythmic cries with each one. "Tell me," I said. "What dealings have you had with Deylaud?"

"I told you," she said, her hands against my shoulders. "I don't know him."

"You lie." I grasped her by the waist, trapping her between my rock-solid frame and the wall. She pressed down against my shoulders, whether to urge me closer or to try to work her way up and away from me I neither knew nor cared. She arched back from me, which only served to afford me access to her breasts. I pulled at the elastic neckline of her peasant blouse, hooking my fingers into her brassiere at the same time, dragging them both downward. Her right breast sprang free as if it had a mind of its own.

I pulled hard on her taut nipple with my lips and tongue, grazing it with my fangs, causing her to cry out louder. My cock felt as hard as a jackhammer, working in and out of her tender flesh. "I can keep this up all night," I whispered cruelly. Perhaps it would be fun to torture her a bit after all. I wondered if she had a taste for it. As a seasoned prostitute, she would have been asked to participate in all manner of deviant scenarios. But I had no doubt she would never have experienced a night as brutal as I could give her. The only instrument of torture I needed was between my legs.

The betrayals I had suffered at the hands of Eleanor and Diana came back to my mind in vivid relief and stoked my anger. I didn't yet know what Ginger was playing at, but I soon would, by the gods.

"Oh!" Ginger cried out once more and collapsed against me, sagging like a wilted flower against my chest, her legs limp and dangling. I came in bucking spasms, struggling to remain on my feet to support us both. What a shattering orgasm it was to have robbed me of my strength if only briefly, I thought, shaken. With my vampiric might, Ginger's weight was as that of a fly, but I staggered a moment before I could remove myself from her and set her down. I couldn't determine why I felt so strange. I certainly hadn't had that much to drink.

Ginger came back to herself quickly and I suspected that, unlike me, she'd been faking her sudden weakness. Setting her clothing to rights, she managed a sly grin. "You were like a beast," she observed. "Where did that come from?"

"Let's just say it's the real me," I remarked, fastening my trousers.

"Eleanor said you were kinky."

"Oh? What else did she tell you about me?"

"She said you like to play blood games."

Eleanor had procured swans for me on a regular and discreet basis, but they weren't selected from the ranks of her regular girls. I wondered how many of the other women in Eleanor's stable knew about my proclivities. "And what games would those be?" I asked.

"Don't play coy. You know the ones—where you bite a girl's neck and drink her blood."

"Oh yes," I said. "Those."

"I had hoped you'd want to play that game with me." Ginger moved forward, sliding her pretty, manicured fingers down her neck from her ear to her shoulder. "Why do you think I wore this blouse?" She ran her fingers under the elastic, pushing it down to expose her flesh from neck to shoulder.

I reached out and stroked her perfect white throat with my fingertips. I could see the bluish vein that pulsed beneath her flawless skin. The blood flowing through it called out a siren song as old as time. "As you wish." I pulled her to me and bit down. My sense of taste and smell sharpened as it always did with that first hit of the intoxicating life fluid.

Her blood had a familiar tang, as did her scent. She reminded me of . . . but no, it couldn't be. My mind, my memory, my guilt were all playing tricks on me.

In the same way you see the face of a lost loved one in the crowd, imagine you hear the whisper of their voice on the breeze—so I imagined I tasted my Eleanor and smelled her signature scent. I harkened back to the night I made her for myself, the dark sanctity of the act almost like a black wedding, to have and to hold until death do us part.

If I'd only known that her final death would come so soon. And at my hands.

Ginger's sigh brought me back to reality, and I reluctantly broke contact with her flesh.

"My turn," she said, and stood on her tiptoes.

"What are you doing?" I asked, feeling strangely intoxicated.

"Now I want to drink your blood."

"That's not the way it works," I said. "This is a one-way transaction." I was a natural top, in sado-masochistic parlance, and did not submit to blood donation—not that it had ever been an issue. Of all the young women I had thrilled with my blood sucking, none had ever asked for blood in return. If I were mortal, I would not have objected. Fair was fair, after all. But even though no victim would be drained to the point of death, there was always the possibility of a two-way blood exchange activating the forces that birthed vampires to some bad end.

She pouted for a moment and then shrugged. "Oh, well, have it your way, selfish." Then she turned on her heel and walked out of the room.

I was left alone wondering exactly what had just happened, and if I was in as much control as I thought I was.

Jack

I knocked on Connie's door empty-handed. No flowers this time. *She loves me; she loves me not.*

Connie opened the door. "Hey, you," she said. Except for the dark shadows under her eyes she didn't look any the worse for wear after her ordeal at my hands.

"Hey." I walked past her into the living room. "Are you all right?"

"I'm still a little weak, so I took today off," she said. "I didn't hear from you last night."

"Yeah. Sorry."

"What's wrong, Jack? You don't seem yourself." She closed the door and came to stand in front of me. She reached out to me, but I backed away.

"There are some things I've got to tell you," I said.

"Sounds serious."

I had paced to the window. I turned around to her and said, "You should sit down."

For once she didn't argue with me, but sat down on the couch.

"Things are getting kind of intense between us," I started out. I'd rehearsed what I was going to say, but my mind was a blank. I was going to have to wing it.

"I guess you could say that," she said cautiously.

"Do you remember when we first started to think about . . . seeing each other, and you knew there was something I was keeping from you?"

"And you didn't decide to tell me until I saw you go after Will the night he killed Sullivan," she recalled. "And I saw your . . . fangs." I could see her work hard to suppress a shudder.

"You told me that I couldn't ever lie to you again."

Connie's eyes narrowed slightly. "Yes. I remember what I said."

"There's some things I've got to come clean about—some stuff you've got to know."

"About what?"

"About you. And me." Even as I spoke to her about coming clean, I knew I'd be lying. I was thankful that, as close as we'd gotten recently, she hadn't learned to read me like William could.

"Go ahead. Out with it. What do I need to know?" No-nonsense Connie was back. She reached for a sofa pillow and hugged it to her chest, bracing herself, I figured, for something bad. She'd correctly surmised from my manner that what I had to say didn't involve sunshine and daisies.

I jammed my hands in my pockets to keep from wringing them. "First, Melaphia has figured out what you are, and William's people in Europe have confirmed it by looking at prophecies in some old Celtic records that they have."

"What do the Celts know about Mayan goddesses?"

"It's a little more complicated than you being a goddess." I had decided to shield Melaphia from blame. I didn't want Connie to figure out that Mel had helped her get to the underworld in hopes that she would never return.

"What are you talking about?"

"You are a goddess, as far as that goes," I said. "But what makes you a deity are your specific powers."

"Which are?"

"You're a vampire slayer. *The* Slayer."

Connie chuckled, but her eyes didn't smile. "You're kidding me, right?"

"I wish."

"You're talking nonsense. Vampire slayers are only in the movies and on television."

I raised my arms and let them fall to my sides. "That's what you said about vampires, remember? And yet, here I am, fangs and all. Remember how you nearly burned me to death with a touch before you found that spell that let us get physical without frying me? That was no mistake, no accident. It's who you *are*."

Connie took a deep breath and considered this. "I see what you're saying," she finally said. "I mean, I guess it would explain what happened between us. But what does being the Slayer mean *exactly*?"

"It means that one of these days real soon you're going to have some kind of superpowers that are going to make you really, really good at killing blood drinkers. And it's going to be your solemn duty to kill as many of us as possible. And you're going to *want* to."

Connie looked at the carpet for a moment, her eyes wide. "Are you sure about all this? Maybe there's been some kind of mistake."

I reminded her about the birthmark and told her about the prophecies Melaphia and Olivia had found. "But what removed all doubt was something that happened in the underworld—something I didn't tell you about."

"What did you hold back? What happened?" she demanded, angry now, and I didn't blame her.

"It was right after you were with your son—I didn't lie about that part, I swear. When he went running off and you knew you couldn't follow him, some angels came down to you and showed you a sword."

"My god. Angels? With a sword?"

"They said that you . . ." I stopped, realizing I was about to literally put a weapon in her hands she could use against us. I decided to keep to myself the angel's instruction to find the twin of the shiny sword. "They said you'd be given special powers and weapons to fight the vampires." I stopped, to give both of us time to take a breather. Connie looked as ill as she had been when I revived her the other night, and I expected I looked just as sick as she did. Sometimes it was good not to be able to see your own reflection.

Connie rubbed her temples like she'd just developed a headache. "I think I'd remember if a band of angels showed me a sword and told me to kill my boyfriend."

"Just because you don't remember any of it now doesn't mean that you won't someday."

"Answer me this," she said. "How did I get to be this—this slayer? I mean, why me?"

"Evidently, your natural father was a vampire and your mother was a human woman."

She looked at me as if I'd just slapped her. "*Natural?* What the hell is natural about having a vampire for a father?"

Damned if she didn't have a point there. "I know how you must—"

"No, you don't! You chose to be a bloodsucker! I don't want this. I don't want any part of this!"

"Believe me. I don't want it for you." I changed my mind about telling Connie the rest of what happened in heaven—that she didn't get to beat up her ex-husband. She'd have enough to absorb tonight. I felt a fresh wave of guilt wash over me for having started out my talk by saying I was going to tell the whole truth, all the while knowing I would pick and choose what to reveal.

"What if I just said 'no thanks'?"

"I don't think you can say 'no thanks' to a band of angels, considering who they work for."

"But I don't feel like a vampire slayer."

"You may not feel like one now," I said. "But according to the lore, there's going to come a day when your powers will activate, and then it'll be open season on the likes of me. And I don't think you can turn this assignment down like it was a normal job offer."

She stood up from the couch, came to me, and put her arms around my waist, laying her head against my chest. "I'd never hurt you. You believe me, don't you?" she said, looking up at me with her trusting dark eyes.

I wished with everything in me that her powers could be activated at this very moment and that I wouldn't have to tell her the rest of it, even if it meant she got to kill me now. *Especially* if it meant she got to kill me now.

I wanted to hug her back, to lay my cheek against the silkiness of her hair and tell her everything was going to be all right as long as we had each other. Instead, I kept my arms at my sides and steeled myself.

"You will," I said. "You'll try to kill me and William, and Iban, and all the other vampires you know. And then you'll go after the rest of them. Only by then us good vampires will be dead and you'll have to take on the really vicious ones by yourself."

"How can you say that?" she shouted, and held herself apart from me. "I couldn't kill any of you. How can you think that I could?"

"You're not going to be able to help yourself after you're activated. But even before that, you're going to want to slay us all after I tell you what I came here to do the other night. What the rest of them sent me to do."

She backed away from me slowly. "What are you talking about?"

I could tell she was figuring it out. The horror on

her face left no doubt. I could turn and run now and she'd know without my suffering the pain of telling her. But I couldn't take the coward's way out. I had to finish what I'd started. "You didn't pass out because of the flu. You passed out because I drained most of your blood." I heard myself say these words as if I was somewhere far away, like my brain didn't want to take the meaning in. Connie's eyes went wide with shock and hurt.

"Connie," I said. "Two nights ago I tried to kill you."

Thirteen

William

When I arrived home from the Portal, Tobey and Iban were on their way out. Their charter pilot had been on standby, ready to go at a moment's notice. We wished one another well and they departed. Travis had already left by whatever mysterious means he traveled.

Deylaud was waiting by the telephone in my office. "Any word from Olivia or her people?" I asked him. He shook his head and said nothing. I could tell he was troubled. "What is the matter, old friend?"

"I don't know." He stared straight ahead of him.

"Are you ill?"

He looked at me then. "There's nothing wrong with me. It's that woman I saw at the Portal."

"I saw your reaction to her. What the devil is there between you?" I asked.

"The devil!" he repeated, standing up from my desk chair. "Devil possession! That is the only thing that can reconcile what I took in with my senses this evening to what you told me is true."

"Explain," I said.

"The woman I saw tonight at the nightclub—I don't know who you believe her to be. But mark me, that is Eleanor!"

"What? That woman's name is Ginger. I've known her for—" Before I could finish, the accuracy of Deylaud's assertion hit home. Her scent, the taste of her blood, her style of sexuality, the change in her personality. It all suggested that Deylaud was right.

"How could it be?" he asked.

I began to pace the room. "When Jack came back from the underworld, he was accompanied by a ball of fire that flew up the chimney. It could have been Eleanor's life force escaping from the underworld."

"How did Eleanor's spirit get into this Ginger woman?"

"Ginger worked for Eleanor. Perhaps Eleanor's spirit went to the site of her old home and found Ginger there. It was her home, too."

"If that is what happened, then what became of this poor Ginger's spirit?"

"Poor Ginger is right," I said. "I am loath to think of it. I must go confront Eleanor."

"Confront her?" Deylaud asked, puzzled. "I feel sorry for the other woman as well, but William, surely this is joyous news. Even though she doesn't look the same, we have Eleanor back with us!"

I hated to burden this sensitive creature, but the time had come for me to tell him the truth. "Deylaud, you don't know everything about Eleanor and her death."

"What do you mean?"

"Before she . . . died, Eleanor betrayed me. She betrayed all of us. It was she who put Hugo and Diana up to kidnapping Renee. It was she who told them the value Renee could be to them through her magic blood. When I found Renee, she was within a hairbreadth of being sacrificed to the Council of old lords. And it was all Eleanor's doing."

Deylaud issued a choking sound and tears spilled from his eyes. "It can't be. She wouldn't have—"

"But she did."

A look of horror crossed Deylaud's face. "You—you killed her, didn't you? You killed her yourself!"

I nodded, unable to bring myself to say the words. I decided to spare Deylaud the most painful part of my tale—the way in which Eleanor had been disfigured and tortured in the underworld.

Deylaud bared his teeth and issued a deep, rumbling growl as if he wished to rip me to shreds. It was a disconcerting thing to see, as he was in human form.

"Deylaud, no!" I showed him my fangs and he whimpered, giving me my due as his de facto pack leader. "Remember your love for Renee, and ask yourself how you would have felt if I'd brought Eleanor back here alive after what she had done. Could any of us ever have trusted her again? Or, even worse, ask yourself how you would have felt if Renee had been murdered in the most cruel way imaginable.

"But most of all, remember how Eleanor led you astray, taking you with her to her brothel when you were sworn to stay by my side or face the punishment of a cruel curse. And think of how she left you behind to die. If Jack had not saved you, you would have. Your sister, Reyha, surely would then have died of a broken heart."

Deylaud burst into tears and came into my arms. I stroked his sandy hair and held him, murmuring words of comfort. After a few moments he stood apart from me and, his head downcast, asked to be excused.

"Of course," I said, and Deylaud ran upstairs, no doubt to seek solace in the arms of his littermate.

I slumped into my desk chair, still plagued by a weariness I couldn't remember ever having experienced before. By the gods, I thought, she had sapped my strength. Female blood drinkers draw power from their male counterparts during sex. It is the reason there are comparatively few female vampires. Before they become more powerful than their paramours, they are usually murdered. I had reconciled myself to becoming less powerful than Eleanor one day. I had trusted her that much. But now it seemed that the demon she had become could somehow weaken me much more quickly than was natural.

I remembered then how Eleanor had tried to trick me into a blood exchange in the back room of the Portal. She was making a bid to turn Ginger's body into that of a vampire. She had failed in her attempt to use glamour on Deylaud, so she lacked the full power of a vampire. Yet she still had the ability to weaken me. I could only conclude that the power to benefit from a male blood drinker's essence must reside in the spirit, since her spirit now occupied the body of a human being.

I had to find Eleanor and kill her before she could

do any damage—even if it meant that Ginger's body must be sacrificed. What in the world had happened to the poor girl's spirit when Eleanor took over?

I was preparing to go to Ginger's apartment when the phone rang. It was Olivia. "William, I just got Deylaud's message and looked at the fax." She spoke rapidly, and her voice was unnaturally high.

"Do you know who this vampire is?"

"Unfortunately, yes. He goes by the name of Damien, and we have it on good authority that he works directly with the Council."

"Do you know him personally?"

"Again, and even more unfortunately, yes. He tried to join our clan about six months ago. He was on his best behavior at first, and everyone liked him. Then Alger caught him stealing some of his more sensitive documents, and they had a row. Damien left, but not before we saw his true colors. He's a very nasty and dangerous character. Surely Alger must have told you about the vicious fight they had."

"No, I'm sure he didn't. I would have remembered."

"Male pride," Olivia muttered.

"What do you mean?"

"Alger probably didn't want you to know how close Damien came to killing him. My sire thought he was invincible, you know. He was convinced no one short of one of the old lords could have bested him in a fight."

"Until one of them did," I said, thinking of how Reedrek lay in his granite sarcophagus, slowly going more and more insane.

"Do you know what was in the documents he stole?"

"I wish I could tell you I remember. At that time, I wasn't too concerned with Alger's research. He was secretive about it anyway, and I just didn't make it my business to keep up with it. Of course, I thought my Algernon would live forever, and so did he. Now it seems so long ago that he was here with me . . ."

I could hear the sorrow in her voice. It occurred to me that she must have suffered terribly the other night hearing me recount what I'd discovered concerning a twice-killed vampire's experience in the underworld. I hoped that Alger had somehow managed to escape so cruel a fate, but I didn't see how it was possible.

"I'm frightened for you, William," Olivia said. "If this man is still working directly for the Council, he may have come there on a mission for them."

"I'm afraid you're right. He has impersonated someone in Tobey's clan, someone who's gone missing. The plot took some time to set up. He'd already become friendly with Werm. My guess is that his ultimate plan was to work his way into my inner circle as a spy."

"That must be the way he operates," Olivia said. "He certainly seemed harmless enough when he tried to join our ranks. I wish I knew of some advice to give you besides—be careful."

"Thank you, we shall. Before I let you go, my dear, may I speak to my son?"

"Uh, Will left here shortly after you did."

"But he told both of us that he planned to stay there with you." I had been glad when he and Olivia had started getting on well, and had hoped she would be a stabilizing influence on him. "Why did he leave?"

"He and Donovan have some blood feud that goes back centuries. I believe that Will might have murdered one or more of Donovan's loved ones. At any rate, Donovan wouldn't let it go, so Will decided it would be best for him to leave before one of them got hurt."

This was troubling news indeed. Donovan was as civilized and intelligent as any blood drinker I'd ever met, but I remembered his reaction on seeing Will the night that I left London. "Did Will say where he was going?"

"No, not specifically. He indicated that he intended to roam around for a while. He's been under Hugo's thumb and under the influence of his mother for so long, I think he wanted to see something of the world and be on his own."

I had wanted for my son the protection afforded by a strong clan of right-thinking blood drinkers. Now that security was lost to him. "It can't be helped, then. If you hear from him, tell him that he is welcome in Savannah." By me, at least. Jack was another story.

"Have your informants reported seeing any sign of Diana and Ulrich?" My wife and her new lover had been buried in a landslide the last I'd seen of them. I liked to think the lance I'd heaved into Ulrich's throat had killed the evil blood drinker, but he'd survived the last time I'd nearly severed his head, so I couldn't count on it.

"No sign whatsoever," Olivia said. "Let's hope

they're being tortured in the underworld as we speak."

"Indeed." I bade Olivia good-bye and hung up the phone. Perhaps it had been a mistake to beckon Will to Savannah through Olivia. My city was looking more and more like one of the most dangerous ports of call in the world for vampires.

I made my way upstairs and Melaphia met me in the kitchen. "You're up late," I said. "You haven't been staying up all night researching again, have you?"

"Deylaud woke me with his weeping. I'm sorry you had to tell him about what happened to Eleanor. But what is this about her being back in Savannah? Surely Deylaud became confused in his grief."

As I put on my coat to go out, I caught Melaphia up on the matters with Ginger's possession and Damien the impostor.

"My lord," Melaphia said, and sat down at the kitchen table as if she would faint were she to remain standing. "What are we going to do?"

"Try not to be overwhelmed," I told her, patting her shoulder. "This too shall pass."

"I don't hear a lot of conviction in your voice," she said wearily.

I shrugged. "I must admit we've had a lot to absorb lately."

"Want to hear some good news?"

"More than you can imagine."

"It's actually one of those good news/bad news situations to tell you the truth," she admitted.

"Start with the good news. Please."

"I hoped you'd say that. I think I've found a way to

send the double-deads—to coin a phrase—back to the underworld where they belong."

"That is wonderful news. Well done."

"You haven't heard the bad news yet."

"Tell me."

"The catch is, once they're there, there's no coming back here. Ever."

"I thought you said you had *bad* news," I said, puzzled.

"Think about it. If you or Jack ever decided to travel there again, the gods forbid, you couldn't unless you're prepared to stay there for eternity. If one of you gets in trouble and winds up there . . ." Melaphia shuddered and rubbed her arms. "The other will not be able to save him."

I sighed. "Inasmuch as I have forbidden Jack to visit the underworld again for any reason, and I am certainly not anxious to go back there, I think we can live with those terms. How soon do you think you can accomplish this?"

"I'll have to work around the clock. I haven't nailed down the exact formulas, but with luck and with Deylaud's help I hope I can get the spells prepared by the time we need them."

"Good. I can't thank you enough. But I don't want you working twenty-four hours a day. It's time you got some rest." I kissed her good night on the cheek and left by the front door.

When I entered the hallway leading to Ginger's apartment, I could see that the door was ajar as if she had left in quite a hurry. As I drew closer, I saw that a note had been pinned to the door with a stiletto. I pulled the paper free and read its terse message.

> *William, by this time and with Deylaud's help, you will have figured it out. Don't try to find me. I'll find you when the time is right. And then I'll kill you. Eleanor.*

Jack

"You—you tried to kill me? That's impossible! Don't you think I would remember a vampire trying to rip my throat out?"

"I used glamour on you. To . . . anesthetize you."

Connie backed away from me, and the terror and pain in her eyes ripped me apart. I wanted to gather her back into my arms and tell her I was sorry, tell her all the reasons William had given me for why she would have been better off. But I couldn't because of the chance, however so slight, that she might harm herself in order to get back to her son. And because I had to leave her hating me.

She looked wildly around for a weapon. I decided anything was better than the panic I saw on her face. I turned to the table with the little shrine and picked up the wooden cross. I tossed it to her as quickly as I could, but it had seared itself into my flesh by the time I could release it. She caught it and held it up in front of her.

"Good girl," I said softly, gripping my burned and smoking hand with my good one. "I'm not going to hurt you anymore, but that will make you feel safe."

"What stopped you?" she demanded, tears of pain and anger beginning a path down her cheeks. "Why didn't you kill me like you were supposed to?"

I had anticipated this question, but with the pain of the cross seared in my hand, I couldn't think straight. "I don't know," I said lamely. "I just couldn't."

"I thought you loved me," she said, choking back a sob. "You said you did."

I do. I do. I do. I nearly doubled over, not so much from the pain as from wanting to tell her how I really felt. *Stick to the plan, Jack.* "It could never have worked out for us anyway, not in the long term," I ground out through gritted teeth. "I mean, I couldn't have even given you children 'cause vampires are, like, sterile. All chicks want kids, right?"

She blinked a few times as if she couldn't believe her ears and the cavalier attitude I was putting on. "You never loved me at all, did you?"

That question, and my inability to answer it honestly, completed my demolition, molecule by molecule. I couldn't have spoken at that moment if I'd had to. I only shrugged and looked away, hoping Connie would assume the moisture in my eyes was from the pain in my hand.

"So what am I supposed to do?" she said. "Just wait here for another vampire to come along and kill me? One who's got the guts?"

I felt as if the hatred in her voice had flayed the flesh from my bones. I forced myself to say "My advice is to leave here as soon as you can. And watch your back. Good luck."

Blindly I staggered to the door, crashing into the little table that held the shrine as I went. As I twisted the knob with my good hand and slipped out, I heard the little statue of the Virgin Mary crash to the floor and shatter into what sounded like a million pieces.

"I'm sorry, Blessed Mother," I murmured as I ran down the hallway. "Me and my heart are right there with you."

Fourteen

William

I arose from my coffin at sundown feeling out of sorts from lack of sleep. I'd lain awake most of the day puzzling out what to do about Eleanor and the vampire Damien.

Trying to shake off the gloom, I took a walk through the tunnels to where Reedrek was entombed in the cornerstone of the new hospital. Perhaps I could goad some information from the old bastard yet. Not that I'd had any luck before, but I honestly couldn't think of what else I might do. It was better than just sitting around.

Eleanor and Damien could be anywhere. I tried to reach Eleanor through our psychic sire-offspring connection, but she was either out of range geographically or was successfully blocking my thoughts. As for Damien, I felt there was little I could do other than wait for him to resurface. In a best-case scenario, he might have left the area since we had found him out, but best cases were few and far between these days.

As I reached the tunnel wall behind which Reedrek lay, I projected my thoughts. "Rise and shine."

"Eh?" my sire said telepathically. "What do you want, offspring?"

"I've awoken in a good mood," I lied. "I thought perhaps you might enjoy an outing."

I perceived nothing from Reedrek for several moments, then: "An outing? What do you propose?"

I couldn't help but note that he sounded much more lucid than in our last conversation. "You give me information; I give you a measure of temporary freedom."

"I suppose you mean to tether me like a cur for a nice walk."

"Something like that, if you cooperate."

"What makes you think I know anything that might be of interest to you? It's not as if I have anyone with whom I can share news and gossip."

"Don't you? I thought you might have had visitors lately."

He laughed. "Is that so?"

"You can begin by telling me everything you know about those two." This baiting was a shot in the dark, but I reasoned I had nothing to lose.

Initially I had assumed that Werm had unwittingly given Damien information about us over drinks at the Portal and that Damien had told Reedrek of our activities. But now I suspected that he had connected with Eleanor through Reedrek. Since Reedrek was her grandsire, Eleanor could easily have sought him out and given both him and Damien any information they wanted about us. If I'd had any doubts about Werm, they were officially dismissed.

"And *you* can begin by kissing my ass. I will be out of here soon enough, and when I'm free I shall kill you."

It wasn't often that I received death threats, and two within a few hours seemed excessive. Not that I was overly worried. A vampire trapped in a granite slab and a deceased fledgling were not of much concern.

"I'll leave you for the worms then," I said. "And the rats. Think about my offer, but don't think too long. My good mood can't last forever."

"And neither can you, boy," Reedrek said, and cackled wildly.

Disgusted, I turned on my heel and left, the sound of his braying laughter ringing in my mind.

My restlessness had not left me by the time I reached the mansion, so I decided to visit Jack at his garage. The front bays were closed against the winter wind, and I headed for the back door. The first sight that greeted me as I rounded the building was that of Huey the zombie standing in a large hole in the earth, earnestly digging deeper with a spade.

Caw! I looked up to see a large crow on a pine branch above Huey's head. It hopped furiously back and forth across the branch, as if its feathers were infested with mites.

"Have you a new pet, Huey?"

"I reckon," he said. "She's been here a couple of days now."

I wondered what had convinced him it was a female, but didn't ask. I wasn't in the mood to immerse myself in a discussion on avian sexing techniques with a zombie. Huey had been a few neurons short of a synapse even before he passed. Now, according to Jack, he had even fewer functioning brain cells.

"What is it you're digging for, if you don't mind me asking?"

"I'm trying to dig out my Chevy Corsica," he said.

"Of course you are," I said. "I wish you godspeed with that endeavor."

"Thankee, sir."

When I walked into the establishment, the motley group of men Jack called the irregulars looked up from their poker hands and murmured greetings. I could smell their fear of me, even though of late, as my world spun more and more out of control, I hadn't felt like a particularly fearsome creature.

Jack was working under the hood of an SUV, making him look as if he were being eaten alive by some prehistoric forerunner of the crocodile.

"Throwing yourself into your work," I observed.

"Yeah. I might as well," he said, his top half still buried within the maw of the machine. "You don't come here much. What's happening?"

I brought him up to date on what had happened last night with the Freddy Blackstone impostor and Ginger-Eleanor. This last piece of news made him bang his skull on the underside of the SUV's hood as he shimmied out to look at me.

"Ow! Dammit!" He rubbed his head. "You're bull-shitting me, right? Eleanor is back, only in Ginger's body?"

"I bullshit you not," I assured him.

"So do you know for sure if Eleanor has managed

to vampirize Ginger's body or do you think that she could sap your strength just through her spirit without going whole hog?"

"I don't know. Ordinarily I would propose seeing if one of our human friends could lure her out into the sun or trick her in some way to find out if she truly is a vampire. But now that she knows we're onto her, she's not going to show herself unless and until she thinks she has an advantage."

"What are you going to do?"

"I don't know what to do other than wait for Eleanor and/or Damien to surface, but I'm entertaining any and all suggestions," I stated.

"I'm fresh out of ideas." He shrugged and sighed. "When it rains, it pours."

I knew he was referring to his own situation with Connie. "How did it go last night?"

"I told her she's the Slayer," he said, wiping grease off his hands with a shop rag. "I broke up with her, and now she hates me. Then I went back home and told Seth it was time to do his thing. He should be at her apartment right now."

"Jack, I'm—"

"Sorry. I know."

I sighed, wishing there was something I could say to ease his pain. "Let me know if you get any ideas about how to deal with Eleanor and Damien. And keep me apprised of what's happening with Connie. Hopefully, in a few days we'll be out of danger from her, at least temporarily."

Jack nodded. "Is it going to be this way forever?"

"What do you mean?"

"One crisis right after another. We had so many

years of peace and quiet, except for the occasional rogue vamp or human criminal we had to get rid of. Now it seems like the whole world is caving in."

"I honestly don't know. I think for now the best thing to do is to take things one night at a time."

"Isn't that the slogan they use in Alcoholics Anonymous?" Jack asked.

"Something like that." I had a feeling Jack was beginning to wish there was such a thing as Vampires Anonymous.

Jack must have read my thought as he picked up a wrench and dove back under the hood. As I turned to go, I heard him mutter, "Hello. My name is Jack, and I'm a vampire."

Jack

I scrubbed at the grease on my hands with the abrasive cleanser Rennie kept by the sink until the burned one started to bleed. I had to work out some of this nervous frustration I was carrying around. Throwing myself into my work wasn't helping. Maybe I should take another fast drive up and down the back roads, get some wind in my fangs. But for some reason that didn't appeal to me tonight.

William said I should keep him apprised of the Connie situation. How could I do that unless I was watching it closely for myself? I reasoned. With that, I climbed down to the entrance to the tunnels from the oil pit and took off at a jog for Connie's apartment.

I surfaced through a grate near the corner where I'd

seen Freddy Blackstone—or should I say Damien—skulking around the other night. Parked against the sidewalk was Seth's vintage Chevy pickup. He hadn't wasted any time, like I'd known he wouldn't.

I used glamour to cloak myself so that Connie couldn't sense my presence. It was the same trick I used to keep other vampires from sensing I was around, but I'd never used it much, and I didn't know if it would work on the Slayer in the same way.

I looked up at her apartment window. There was a light on in the living room, but other than that I didn't see anything. Rubbing my arms from the chill, I realized how silly I felt and how much sillier I *would* feel if Connie came to the window and saw me. I'd made sure Seth was on the job, but anything further was just punishing myself. Was I really prepared to see two shapes behind the curtains come together in an embrace or a kiss? How would I feel if the living room light went out and the bedside lamp went on? Pretty damned bad, I decided.

As I turned to go, I felt the approach of another blood drinker, but not anyone in my bloodline. Had that Damien guy decided to show his face again? I crouched in front of Seth's truck; the vampire was coming from the other direction and wouldn't be able to see me. As he grew nearer, I noticed how little sound his footsteps made. Travis.

He rang the bell of one of the apartments and a voice, not Connie's, answered. He whispered something, and I could hear the glamour in it. Whomever he'd selected at random fell for the trick and buzzed him inside. I sneaked out from behind the truck and ran to the door, catching it with my fingers just before it locked itself behind Travis. I peered in and saw that he had entered the stairway to the second floor.

I followed him, keeping out of sight, still covering myself in glamour. It was a blessing I was good at it because Travis was old, powerful, and not easily fooled. He looked neither right nor left, obviously set on a single goal—to kill the Slayer. He'd been bluffing when he told William he was leaving town. He'd had no such intention.

When he'd reached the hallway to Connie's apartment, I made my move, running at him as hard as I could. He wheeled to face me and delivered a roundhouse kick to my midsection. The force of the blow flung me against the wall hard enough to crack the plaster.

Connie opened her door and peered out. "What's going on out here?"

"No!" I yelled. "Go back!"

But it was too late. With the same preternatural speed with which he'd knocked me into the wall, Travis was on her. I scrambled to my feet, but I knew I was too late. I saw Seth entering the doorway and realized that though he was closer he wouldn't be fast enough, either.

As I hurtled down the hallway, I saw Connie's horrified face as she made eye contact with the vampire who would take her life.

William

I was at the mansion going over accounts when the phone rang. I could see by the readout that the call was from the home of my old friend Tilly Granger. It was Tilly's faithful butler, Dawson.

"Mr. Thorne, could you come quickly, please?" Though his voice was calm and professional, I could hear the strain of anguish in it.

This was the call I had dreaded for the past twenty years. "I'll be there in ten minutes."

I ran to my vehicle and jumped behind the wheel. As I headed for Tilly's house on Orleans Square, I cursed myself for not checking on her as soon as I returned from Europe. I'd met her more than seventy years ago when she was a debutante, and had in fact spirited her away from her own coming-out party. I'd taken her to the Cloister on Sea Island, and then I'd taken her virginity in a thrilling night of the most joyous lovemaking I'd known since my wife, Diana, and I were alive.

She was the first woman I'd offered to make a blood drinker. In truth, I'd begged her. She would have made the perfect companion for me, and I doubt if I would ever have looked at another woman for all eternity had she taken me up on my offer of immortality.

She'd turned me down and our affair had ended, but not before we'd become the talk of Savannah society. Our friendship never wavered, however, and I was always there for her. Decades ago I had tried to talk her out of what I knew would be a disastrous marriage, but she went through with it anyway.

One sweltering summer's evening I sipped mint juleps with her and her husband on their veranda and wondered why Tilly wore a shawl even though the heat was oppressive. She'd reached for the pitcher and the fabric had slipped, revealing purplish bruises. I discreetly bade them good night, and with a meaningful nod to Tilly, I made as if to take my leave. Instead, I waited in the shadows of the square until the lights of the mansion went out and Tilly met me on the veranda in the dark.

She told me everything, and we made a pact. The next morning, her husband's body was found in an alley in the industrial district. The poor drunken sod had been robbed, beaten, and garroted so violently that the ligature had nearly severed his head. The wound was so messy that any fang marks could not be distinguished. Funny how that happened.

The merry widow and I remained friends, and some twenty years ago she had extracted a promise from me that I hoped I would never have to fulfill.

She wanted to be able to choose the time and place of her own death, and she wanted me to be its agent.

I drove like a man possessed and reached her mansion sooner than I would have wished. When Dawson opened the door for me, I asked, "What has happened? I saw her only recently and she was well."

"She became ill shortly after your friend Mr. Cruz left us."

"She couldn't have caught what ailed him," I insisted. Tilly had cared for Iban when he suffered from the rotting plague. When Gerard had developed a vaccine, I made him inject Tilly and her staff with the serum as a precaution. When we told Tilly's servants that Iban had suffered from an aggressive flesh-eating bacterial infection, they were more than happy to submit to the vaccination.

"It's not that," Dawson said, and I could see the worry on his brow. "It's pneumonia. She's so frail. The doctors tried all the antibiotics, but they didn't catch it in time, and she insisted on coming home to die. She has even refused supplemental oxygen. She says it's her time."

I mounted the stairs to her bedroom as if I were going to my own doom. I had to pause at the doorway when I saw her, my undead heart at the breaking point. She rested against the embroidered pillows, so thin and frail I would hardly have recognized her. She was as pallid as a creature of the night, and still beautiful in her way, dressed in a silk nightgown of her favorite color, peach. Her breath came in shallow wheezing gasps that pained me to hear.

I knelt beside her and gently lifted her hand to my lips. "My darling," I said.

She opened her eyes. "My handsome swain," she whispered, the glimmer still in her eyes. "You know why I sent for you, don't you?"

"You want me to fetch you some pralines from the candy store on River Street," I said. *Please tell me you want no more than that.*

"Not this time, although it's tempting." She suffered a fit of coughing that left her even more breathless. Her cheeks took on a momentary blush of effort as she labored for oxygen.

It is not often a master vampire of my power feels helpless, but I did then. There was nothing I could do for her save what she had called me for.

"Do you remember your promise?" she managed to whisper when she'd regained a measure of breath.

"Yes."

"It's time," she said.

I pursed my lips as if forbidding my fangs from showing themselves. "Are you sure, my dear?"

"I am." She smiled a peaceful, beatific smile and managed to squeeze my hand. "Thank you for everything you've ever done for me, including this. Especially this."

I nodded, unable to speak. I looked her in the eyes for several long moments before I managed to say, "It doesn't have to be this way, you know. I could still—"

She held up a hand to silence me. "I could hardly enjoy everlasting life in this old body, now could I?"

"But there might be an answer." I had wracked my brain for a solution on the drive to Tilly's mansion and had come up with an idea, though it was a long shot. "I know of a case of demon possession. If I can banish the demonic spirit from a young woman's body, perhaps Melaphia could help you inhabit it. The spirit of the woman whose body it is can't be found, and—"

Tilly tried to laugh and almost succumbed to another coughing episode. "No," she said firmly. "If I wanted immortality by unnatural means, I would have let you make me into a blood drinker while I was young and strong. I am happy with the choice I've made, both then and now, to lead a mortal, human life. But thank you for the offer."

I sighed. "So this is it, then?"

"Yes, please," she said. "If you would be so kind, may I have one last dance before it's time to go?"

"I wouldn't have it any other way," I assured her.

I lifted her, feather-light, from the bed and held her tenderly against me. I pressed my lips to hers and projected the full power of my glamour onto both of us.

We were back on the beach the night we met, music wafting its way to us from the bandstand. She wore a gauzy, peach-colored dress that clung to her girlish figure like a second skin. Her hair was cut in a bob, the style of the time, and she held a half-full champagne bottle in one hand as she beckoned me into the surf with the other. "Dance with me in the sea," she said.

I caught up to her and grasped her around her slender waist, pressing her close and swaying to the music as the waves crashed against our thighs. I kissed her and she put both arms around my neck, letting go of the bottle as she did.

The bottle shimmered shamrock green in the ocean and floated away, perhaps to be found by some beachcomber on a distant shore after time had reduced it to a bright gem of polished glass.

Jack

I reached Travis and grasped him by the shoulders, hauling him backward, amazed that I'd gotten to him in time. His fangs, terrible to see because of his ancient power, were at full length. But he had frozen. Had the power of the Slayer caused him to go into some kind of suspended animation?

By that time, Seth had reached Connie and put himself between her and Travis—but not before I could see a look in her eye that was as strange as his.

I turned the other vampire to face me, and my own fangs came out. He blinked and sheathed his daggerlike teeth. Then he brought his hands up to cover his face briefly before glancing back at Connie as if he'd seen a ghost.

A middle-aged woman peered out from her apartment door down the hall. "What's all this commotion?" she asked.

I fixed her with a look full of my magic mojo and said, "You're really sleepy. You have to go to bed now." Just like that, she yawned and closed her door.

I faced Travis again, still gripping him by the shirtfront. "I'm going to kill you." He didn't resist as I started to haul him away toward the stairs.

"Jack, wait!" Connie said. Before Seth could stop her, she slipped out of his grasp and came to stand in front of Travis. "Who are you?" she demanded.

"He's the *second* vampire who's come to kill you," Seth said. I could only guess that Seth had spent the first part of this evening trying unsuccessfully to convince Connie to leave Savannah with him.

"He's somebody whose throat I'm going to rip out," I added.

"No. Wait. I want to know *who he is*," Connie insisted.

To my astonishment, she came closer to Travis, looked deeply into his eyes, and reached up to touch his face. "I've never met you, but somehow I know you," she told him. "Tell me who you are."

Travis, who looked just as shocked as she did, shrank back from her before she could touch him. He blinked as if to clear his vision and said, "I'm your father."

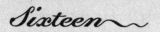

Sixteen

William

I roamed the streets on foot, my mind still immersed in the past. This night would haunt me the rest of my existence. Amid my sorrow and reminiscences about my friend, I couldn't help but remember what she had said, not so long ago, when she'd met Eleanor for the first time.

She's trouble. Tilly was never one to mince words and, of course, she'd been right.

I found myself walking toward the structure that would have been Eleanor's new brothel. The establishment that had burned down on the same location had been the site of many an evening's lively entertainment for me. I seemed to be waxing nostalgic on a number of levels tonight.

More work had been accomplished in the few days since I had been here. I entered the building to examine more closely the work for which I was paying. As soon as I'd crossed the threshold, I heard the sounds of sex.

I followed the animalistic cries and grunts downstairs, masking my presence with my glamour. The evil Eleanor had presented poor Ginger's naked body to the vampire called Damien, who was using it cruelly to Eleanor's evident delight.

The congress halted as I stepped into sight. Damien hitched up his trousers, but Eleanor stood defiantly bare, clad only in thigh-high, stiletto-heeled boots of black patent leather so shiny, the reflection of her nakedness would show in them if Ginger's body was still human.

"I see you're back in uniform," I observed, wishing I could get close enough to look for that reflection. "Aren't you going to introduce me to your friend?"

"We've already met," Damien said with a sneer.

The blood drinker had changed his style since I'd seen him. His hair and beard were now well groomed and his clothing was fashionable and new.

"Oh, that's right. You were using a false name at that time. What kind of coward doesn't even give his real name, Damien?"

The sneer left his face and his fangs came out. "I'll show you who's a coward."

As he flew at me, I dodged him. He was agile and landed on his feet for another assault. In the meantime, Eleanor was edging toward me, angling for a way into the fight.

"I told you I'd kill you the next time I saw you, and I meant it," she said, and hissed like a cat.

She displayed her hands, revealing fingernails newly sharpened to points like claws. They were painted bloodred. "Like 'em?" she asked. "They're all the rage in the underworld where you sent me to suffer."

She swung at me and I dodged, but I was uncharacteristically slow and she managed to rake my cheek with her claws, drawing blood. "You should never have betrayed me," I said.

"I was supposed to be your mate through all eternity. You were to protect me and see to my needs. You should never have betrayed *me* with that bitch Diana!"

She kicked me so swiftly I didn't see the blow, stabbing me in the abdomen with the heel of her boot. I cried out, and she pulled the weapon back from my flesh, leaving me with a gaping wound.

She was fast and powerful. I hadn't remembered her weakening me this much after I made her. There was only one thing that would account for such a dramatic surge in her might and in my weakness: she had been having frequent sex with this Damien, and he must be an ancient and powerful blood drinker indeed. But that didn't address the question of whether Ginger's body had transformed to that of a vampire.

"We've been over that ground ad nauseam," I said. "I suppose we'll just have to agree to disagree who was more at fault—me for letting Diana distract me from your needs, or you for turning over my Renee to be sacrificed to the old lords. In any case, I must congratulate you for your ingenuity on engineering a resurrection for yourself."

"Why, thank you," she said sarcastically. "I'm glad you're finally giving me credit for having some cleverness. The last time I saw you in my original body, you accused me of being an idiot for choosing to trust Hugo instead of you."

"That is another point on which we will always remain at odds. Be that as it may, I am curious about one matter."

"And what is that?"

"Ginger's—that is, your present body—is it the body of a vampire or are you human?"

"Wouldn't you like to know? I am as strong and fast as a vampire, aren't I? Maybe you'd like another kick, a little lower this time."

"No thanks," I said. "But you still didn't answer my question."

"Enough of this foolishness," Damien said. As if to confirm my theory about his age and power, he opened his mouth to reveal a set of fangs scarcely shorter than those of a saber-toothed tiger. Fortunately for me, though, Eleanor would have weakened him as well. I decided to create a diversion to help me escape the double attack.

"So this is the great William Cuyler Thorne," Damien spat. "You're being bested by a woman, and you haven't even landed a blow. You don't look so invincible to me."

"Thanks to yours truly," Eleanor said.

I ignored their taunts, but Damien was right. I was alarmed at my new limitations. I suspect my problem was as much spiritual as physical. Losing Tilly only an hour before had renewed my old death wish. A part of me wanted to go with her spirit, but I knew that was never to be.

They were approaching from my right and left. The stairs were behind me, and I stepped onto the bottom riser, which at least gave me the psychological advantage of towering over them even more than I had before.

"Eleanor tells me you've got quite the inside track with the Council," I said to Damien, holding my wound together as best I could.

His head whipped toward her. "You were to tell him nothing about me!"

"I didn't! Don't listen to him," Eleanor insisted.

I took a step higher, still not ready to turn my back on them and run. "You know how women gossip. She even told me about your plan," I bluffed.

"Why, you bitch!"

"He's lying, you fool! He must have been in touch with Olivia."

Damien narrowed his eyes at me. "Of course," he said. "Nice try, but I should have realized you were lying. You know about nothing of our plan."

Eleanor exchanged a knowing glance with the other vampire and smirked. "If you did know our plan, you sure as hell wouldn't be here right now."

"Oh? And where would I be?"

"As far away from here as you could get," she said.

Damien looked at the moon and then at Eleanor. "We've toyed with him enough. It's time to get the party started."

"I think you're right." Eleanor moved away from me and reached for her clothing.

I gathered my strength to launch myself up the stairs and out the front door, but instead of coming for me as soon as Eleanor was dressed, the two of them went to the cellar's entrance to the tunnels.

"We'll let you live so that you can enjoy the fun later," Damien said.

"Yes," Eleanor said. "Besides, our partner in crime would never forgive us if we denied him the pleasure of participating in your downfall."

"Time to rock 'n' roll," Damien said, and they both laughed maniacally.

"I'm still going to keep my promise," Eleanor told me.

With that, they disappeared into the tunnels, leaving me to wonder what manner of evil was about to befall us. I couldn't read Eleanor's thoughts, as hard as I tried to, but I sensed enough to know she had not been bluffing.

I gave them a few seconds' head start and then, using my hand to stanch my bleeding wound as best I could, followed them into the tunnels.

Jack

"What are you talking about?" I demanded as Connie gaped at him.

"I can see it in your face," Travis said.

"See what?" Connie asked.

"You are the very image of your mother."

I didn't want to have to deal with any more curious neighbors, so I inclined my head toward Connie's door and Seth nodded. We each took one of Travis's arms, steered him into Connie's apartment, and sat him down at the kitchen table.

"Start with the beginning," I said. I didn't have to prompt him again.

"Jack, the other night at William's, when you were asked what you knew of the Slayer's background—"

"*Connie*. Her name is Connie," Seth said, muscling up beside Travis in case he tried to make a move.

Connie held up her hand to silence Seth. "Go on," she said to Travis.

"When and where you born?"

Connie rattled off her birth date and everything she knew about her first few days of life. The name of the orphanage, the slip of paper with her crazy-long name, what little the nuns had told her adoptive parents.

"Were you there then?" I asked Travis. "I mean, nine months before then?"

"Yes, I was there," the ancient blood drinker said. He had been avoiding Connie's eyes. I mean, who wouldn't be ashamed to look at somebody you just tried to murder, especially your own child? But now he looked at her very closely, and then squeezed his eyes shut again.

"I was in love with a human woman," he said mournfully.

"Wait," Connie said. I could see skepticism and curiosity at war on her face. "How do I know you're telling the truth?"

"Because you'd be dead right now if he weren't," I said grimly. "He stopped himself from killing you. He's too powerful and too fast. I don't think Seth and I could have stopped him."

Seth started to interrupt, but he paused and I could tell that what I had said rang true with him, as much as he might want to deny it.

Seeing that Seth and I were convinced, Connie

looked back at Travis. "Tell me about my mother. What was her name? What was she like? Why did you leave her before I was born?"

"I thought she was pregnant by another man," Travis said, answering her last question first. "After all, no blood drinker I had ever known in my long life had fathered a child. I left my beloved, reasoning that, as a blood drinker, I could not give her the life she deserved, and that with me out of the way, she would be free to go to her mortal lover, whoever he was. She was a rare beauty and any man would have been, should have been, grateful to marry her and raise the child—you—as his own."

"Why didn't you tell her you loved her and let her make up her own mind?" Connie asked.

"I was afraid that she was in thrall to me, although I was not intentionally using glamour on her. No human woman had ever loved me before, and I was mesmerized by her. I thought that the only way to free her was for me to leave."

Connie paused a moment for this to sink in. "What was her name?" she asked again in a small voice.

"Maria. She was as intelligent as she was beautiful. She was a university student, and I ultimately didn't want to stand in the way of what I was convinced would be a brilliant future for her."

"What became of her?" Connie asked, her eyes glistening. "Why did she give me up? Is she still alive?"

"I don't know the answer to any of those questions," Travis said. "That is what saddens me. I am afraid for her now, because I know that she would never have given up a child unless some tragedy befell her. And if she had no other lover, then I left her alone and with child."

"Did you know Connie was your daughter when you came here to kill her?" Seth wanted to know.

"No. I thought what I learned at William's was only a coincidence. It truly did not seem a possibility. But then I saw your face, and I couldn't go through with it. I am sorry, my child."

"You say . . . you loved her?"

"More than my life," Travis said.

Connie swallowed hard and stared at Travis for a moment before she turned away. "My father," she murmured. "I have a natural father."

"There's nothing natural about me, my girl," Travis said.

"Then I suppose there's nothing natural about me either," Connie murmured.

"So what now?" Seth asked. "Are you going to try to kill her as soon as my back is turned?"

"No. I cannot," Travis said, directing his words at Connie. "Although, for you to return to the underworld now, Connie, would be—"

I had stayed pretty much out of the conversation, unneeded but now I managed to catch Travis's eye and shook my head sharply. He took the hint and hushed up.

Connie didn't seem to notice. She was lost in her own thoughts. "I'm the daughter of a vampire," she said, sounding out the words as if she was trying to learn something out of an unintelligible foreign-language phrase book.

"I must leave," Travis announced.

"Wait! There's more I want to ask you," Connie said.

"Perhaps we will have the chance to talk at another time," Travis said, "if the gods will it, and if you don't kill me first. I must leave here."

"Where are you going?" Connie asked.

"I am going back to old Mexico to learn what became of your mother."

"Let me go with you!"

"You cannot." Travis inclined his head toward Seth. "I feel that this young man loves you. Let him take you to safety. Besides, even though you don't think you will now, in time you will wish to kill me. And Jack, and every other blood drinker you can find."

"Why do the two of you keep saying that? Am I going to lose my judgment? My ability to think and reason?"

"At first, you very well may," Travis said. "If you survive long enough to mature in your destiny, you will develop a measure of restraint. But initially, you will wish to strike out at all vampires. For the sake of Jack, William, and Werm, see that you go far away from here as quickly as you can. Perhaps your young man here can keep in touch with Jack, and through him I will send to you any word that I can find of your mother's fate."

That stopped Connie cold. I could see that her mind was reeling with the implications of her staying in Savannah. What stopped *me* cold was the assumption that Connie and Seth were already a couple. It was what I had wanted, what I'd engineered. But it didn't hurt any less.

Travis stood. Awkwardly, he raised his hands and touched Connie's face. A flash of fire like an electrical arc jumped from her to his hands and he drew his palms away from Connie's cheeks. "It's happening," he said. "The Slayer in you is ripening. You must leave quickly for everyone's sake, mostly yours. I hope I see you again, my daughter. In the fullness of time, perhaps we can coexist."

His weathered face had become unreadable again, but I could tell he didn't really think that was going to happen. He headed for the door, and the three of us just stared after him. He turned back as he was leaving and said, "A word with you, Jack?" Dumbly, I followed him. We were out on the street before he spoke again.

"Give her up, Jack," he said.

"I have. Didn't you see? She's with Seth now," I said bitterly.

He put his palm flat against my chest. "You have not given her up in here."

"I don't think I'll ever be able to do that."

Travis sighed and stared into the cold darkness. "Then you have not begun to know sorrow."

Seventeen

William

Damien and Eleanor did not know the tunnels as I did. I was familiar with each and every nook and cranny that could be used as a hiding place, and I employed that knowledge along with my best cloaking glamour to follow them without their noticing me. It soon became clear that they were on their way to where Reedrek was entombed, and a deep sense of dread filled me.

When they had reached him, I hung back, peering around an abandoned piece of milling machinery. What in the world could the three of them be about?

"It's time! It's time!" sang Reedrek. "Time for me to rise and shine!"

"Whatever, dude," Damien said.

"We have to hold hands," Eleanor said.

"Yes, dearest," Damien said.

"I want to feel the earth move," Reedrek said.

"We already did." Eleanor giggled.

Damien reached into his shirt pocket and withdrew

a timepiece such as I had never seen before. He examined it and asked the others, "Are you ready?"

"Yes," Eleanor and Reedrek said in unison.

"Then let's begin."

The three of them began to chant in a foreign tongue. Its sounds were a mishmash of ancient and some extinct Celtic languages—Cumbric, Gaulish, Cornish, Breton. I understood only a phrase or two here and there, but it made no sense.

Though I didn't know exactly what they were trying to accomplish, I sensed it involved more than simply freeing Reedrek, though that would have been bad enough. Was this ritual the trigger for the cataclysmic event that the shape shifters and the Sidhe had warned about?

Then I remembered something Olivia had said while I was in London: *According to one of Alger's more recent contacts, the Council was learning to use their combined power to harness elemental forces. Do you remember when the last rogue country claimed to have tested those nuclear bombs underground? Those were earthquakes, not nukes. The Council caused them.*

Of course. Their scheme to cause an earthquake had been right in front of me all along. It explained some of the gibberish that Reedrek, Damien, and Eleanor had been talking. And it was clear that the information Reedrek spouted the last time I'd talked to him—the news he by rights had no way of having—had come from Damien and Eleanor. All three of them had been working together. Only their combined power could release such a cataclysm.

I looked around me for some sort of weapon. All I

saw was my life's blood seeping out of the wound in my abdomen and pooling on the floor of the tunnel.

Still, I had to try to break up that wicked ritual. I knew in what blood of mine remained that my family's survival depended on it.

I stepped out from my hiding place and dove toward the linked arms of the two vampires standing in front of the slab of granite, behind which lay my evil sire.

Jack

I hadn't even had a chance to say good-bye.

After Travis had left, I'd followed Connie and Seth without their knowing it. They'd driven to a little airstrip right outside of town, and I'd sneaked into the hangar nearest the little prop-driven four-seater that was idling on the tarmac. A man who looked old enough to have flown with Eddie Rickenbacker had taxied the plane into place.

Seth loaded Connie's bags from his pickup into the plane, leaving her standing on the runway, rubbing her arms in the cold. I cloaked myself from her recognition, and had to hold myself back from running to her and telling her everything I wanted her to know. That I never would have tried to end her life if it hadn't been for the fear that she would lose her chance at eternity with her son. That I would have plunged a wooden stake into my own heart in exchange for a way out.

But I couldn't tell her that. I couldn't create more conflict for her after everything she'd been through the past few days and with everything she had to face in the future.

A future without me.

Watching her and Seth on the runway, I thought about the last scene in *Casablanca*. I felt like Rick after Ilsa had told Rick he should do the thinking for both of them. There was no way in hell Connie would ever have told *me* to do the thinking for *her*. But I felt that I'd been doing it anyway, and my head hurt from the strain. I just hoped I was doing all the right things.

The old man had hobbled back into the office while Seth was loading up and now came back out with some papers on a clipboard. Seth shut the baggage compartment and came closer to the hangar to sign the papers, probably a flight plan or something.

When the old man turned to go, I said, "Pssst!"

"Eh?" The old man said, turning back to Seth.

You didn't hear anything, I projected. The old man continued his trek to the office.

Seth came over to where I was standing, still out of Connie's line of sight.

He handed me the truck keys. "I knew you'd be around here somewhere. Take care of my truck, will you? Throw my stuff in the bed and I'll send for it when we're settled."

"I'll treat it like it was my own."

"Damn. Give me the keys back, then."

"Wiseass. Hey, are you sure you know how to fly that thing?"

"Hell, yes. Don't worry about a thing." Seth's expression grew serious. "I'll take good care of her, Jack. You're doing the right thing. If you ever doubted it, I think Travis put the nail in that coffin, if you'll pardon the expression."

I couldn't decide if I wanted to give my old friend a man hug or hit him on the jaw. I decided to do nothing. "See that you do take good care of her. If you don't I'll hunt you down and bite you, you old fleabag."

"You could try, you dead bastard." Seth tried to grin and couldn't quite pull it off. Our usual repartee didn't quite feel the same.

"You should get going," I said.

He nodded, then said, "Listen, take care of yourself and all William's people. You know that feeling the shape shifters have been sensing?"

"Yeah?" I asked apprehensively.

"Well, tonight I've got it in spades. It's like an itch I can't scratch. I feel like I'm about to jump out of my skin."

I sighed. "Just as long as you don't jump out of that airplane," I said. "We'll take care of one another down here. Don't worry. Keep in touch, like Travis said. I'll let you know if he finds out anything about Connie's mother."

"Will do. Take it easy, man."

"You too."

I watched Connie waiting by the plane as Seth walked back to her, and I tried to remember Rick's last words to Ilsa on the tarmac in the movie. Something about the problems of two little people not amounting to a hill of beans in this old world. So for everyone's good she gets on the plane with Victor Laszlo.

Connie's profile was lovely as the wind blew her

long silken hair around her shoulders. I tried to imagine her as she would look in a few months, her womanly figure swelling with my child.

Here's looking at you, kid.

I had to stop thinking of Connie's child as mine. It was Seth's now, and always would be. I felt my eyes sting as Connie stood there, waiting for her new man.

We'll always have Savannah.

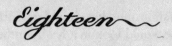

Eighteen

William

Damien flew in one direction and Eleanor in the other, their physical connection broken, their chanting interrupted.

But it was too late.

The earthquake had begun.

They scrambled up and came toward me at the same time, but none of us could keep on our feet because of the violent shaking.

"Let's get out of here," Eleanor shouted to her friend. She knew the tunnels better than Damien, so she led the way around the bend and out of sight, presumably to the nearest opening to street level.

Soil began to rain down from above, causing my mind to flash back to a scene not long ago in which I thought Renee and I were buried in a cave-in underneath London. That had been the work of the Council, too. My every instinct told me to run, get to the surface as quickly as possible, as the other two had done, but I forced myself to stay to see if I could keep Reedrek from escaping.

The rumbling of the earth made an ungodly noise, as if the underworld were attempting to belch up the contents of hell. Each time I tried to stand I wound up on my knees again amidst the growing pile of rubble that was showering down.

After what seemed like an eternity but was probably only a few seconds, came a higher-pitched noise of breaking stone. To my horror, I saw fissures spread out from the middle of the granite slab to each of its corners and through the center, the cracks becoming wider as the seconds ticked by.

With grim fascination, I watched the spiderweb of crevices grow, all the while knowing that there was nothing I could do to prevent the rupture that was about to happen. If I could only stay on my feet, perhaps I might manage to keep Reedrek in his coffin. But just then, a chunk of earth weighted down with asphalt from the street above came crashing down on me, pinning my legs beneath me.

I struggled, trying to wriggle out from under the ton of earth and pavement that had trapped me. I was right in front of Reedrek's granite cornerstone, but I could not move an inch. Mercifully, the ground had stopped shaking for now. I could hear shouting and sirens above me, as well as other sounds I couldn't identify. Geysers of water from burst pipes? Automobiles running into crevasses in the pavement? Chunks of mortar falling from buildings?

I thought of the patients in the hospital above. But most of all I worried about Melaphia and Renee. I reminded myself how smart and resourceful they both were, and that eased my mind, if only slightly.

I flashed back to the great Charleston earthquake of 1886 and remembered how the strong tremors could be felt in Savannah. How could one who "lived" through it ever forget? Not even one hundred years later, I had noted with disbelief the selection of the Savannah River for a site where the government would process tritium and plutonium for nuclear weapons during the cold war. The site stood near several faults, including Pen Branch, the one that had caused the great Charleston quake. Was there no end to humans' folly?

My reverie was interrupted by a more ominous noise. Just when I thought I'd been saved by some miracle of fate, the granite slab gave way, splitting into a million shards. I covered my head with my arms and managed not to be pierced by the razor-sharp splinters of rocks; they flew at me as if from Travis's stories of the merciless Maya and their obsidian knives.

When the landslide was over, I uncovered my face and realized that the shift in the earth had barely missed burying me. I would have felt fortunate had I not been fairly certain that my blood loss was getting worse. With my diminished strength, I just couldn't heal fast enough.

I twisted my body as best I could to look upward at the mound of rock, dirt, and debris in front of me. Reedrek's coffin, complete with the chains Jack and I had bound it in, lay teetering on top of the pile.

I watched the coffin rock this way and that. From within, I sensed Reedrek's song.

Rock-a-bye Reedrek on the treetop
When the bough breaks the coffin will rock . . .

And then the aftershock began.

Jack

At first I thought some huge plane had gotten the little airstrip confused with the international airport. But the trouble wasn't from above but from below.

An earthquake? Well, just—damn! What else could go wrong?

I'll bet this never happened to Humphrey Bogart.

I fell on my behind, and as I was scrambling to my feet, I saw to my horror that Connie and Seth hadn't taken off yet. In fact, Connie had gotten out of the plane and had whipped out her cell phone.

The hell with secrecy. I stalked toward the plane, ready to physically put her back on board if necessary. She flipped the phone closed. "I've got to go back to town," she announced to Seth, who had gotten out of the pilot's seat and reached her side.

"Get back in the plane," he told her.

"No way. This is an earthquake. I've got to go to work! People are hurt, trapped all over the city. They need me!"

"You're leaving now!" I said, charging out of the shadows toward her.

"What are you doing here?" she demanded.

"I'm here to make sure you fly out of here like you're supposed to."

"I'll handle it, Jack," Seth said menacingly.

Connie ignored both of us. "One of you drive me back to town, now!"

"The only place you're going is back on the plane," Seth said.

"I'm a *cop*! I'm sworn to protect and serve, Seth, just like you are, remember?" she said, looking hard at him. "*You*, of all people, should know what that means."

Seth put his fists on his hips and strode away a few steps, letting fly a stream of curses I hadn't heard since I worked the docks.

"Didn't you hear anything that Travis said?" I asked her.

"You're not listening. It's my responsibility to go back and help in any way that I can."

I made a move to grab her, and she shook her finger at me. "Don't you *dare*!"

Another trembler sent all three of us to the ground, and knocked the keys to Seth's pickup right out of my hand. Connie got to her feet first, lunged for the keys, and sprinted for the truck.

"Hey!" I yelled.

"Where's that vampire speed, you toothy sonofabitch?" Seth taunted me as we raced after her.

"It went the same way as those werewolf afterburners, you fur-bearing bastard."

She'd gotten in and locked the doors by the time we reached the truck.

"Let me in," Seth yelled.

"You can ride in the truck bed or ride with Jack. It doesn't matter to me. But you're not going to stop me from going back to Savannah, you hear?" She cranked the truck and put it in gear.

Seth jumped in the truck bed before she could take off, still cussing a blue streak. He was in for one rough and chilly ride, especially if the quake had damaged the roads. I ran back to my Corvette, hoping that no new potholes between here and town would damage the undercarriage of my prized vintage Stingray. I knew it was awful for me to think of my car at a time like this, but I couldn't help it. I'm not just a vampire. I'm also a *guy.*

As I was at a complete loss as to what I should do, I opened my mind to William. Before I could project my news to him, I heard him trying to reach me.

Jack! I'm in the tunnels next to Reedrek's crypt. He's about to get away. Come as quickly as you can!

I changed my mind about hoping the roads were open. Suddenly I wished a big old crack in the ground would open up and swallow me whole.

Nineteen

William

I'm coming, William, Jack told me.

Hurry, I replied.

As the tremor continued, I watched the coffin bounce on top of the pile of earth once. Twice. The third time it became airborne, it slid from its perch and hit the floor of the tunnel hard.

Hard enough to pop the chains on one end. Inside, Reedrek must have thrown himself against the side of his box with everything in him, because the last lurch of the steel coffin caused the chains to slide completely off.

I heard one more thump from the box and its lid flipped open. Like a particularly grisly jack-in-the-box, out popped my sire.

"I'm baaaaack!" he roared.

He looked like something out of a bad horror film. The months of starvation had rendered him nothing more than bone and sagging, sallow skin. He was covered in dirt, dust, and mold, his clothing in tatters.

He smelled like a corpse that had been baking in the sun for a week. I had been sure I would never lay eyes on my sire again, but, to my shame, I'd underestimated him.

"I'm sorry I'm late, but I've been . . . tied up." He dissolved into insane laughter. "Has your sense of humor deserted you along with all your vampire friends?" He drew back his sagging lips to unsheathe his awful yellow fangs, and flexed his fingers to display his talonlike nails.

"Where's the rest of you?" he taunted as he crept toward me. "I can only see your top half. You remind me of a stuffed hunting trophy like those that hung in the great halls back in the day." He laughed heartily at his own joke. "Perhaps I'll hang you up on my wall when I kill you. What's the matter, boy? Cat got your tongue—along with the rest of you?"

"What did your cohorts do?" I opened my mind fully so that Jack, if he was still listening, could hear whatever explanation I might wring out of my sire. If I was to die at Reedrek's hand beneath this pile of rubble, I wanted Jack to know what had happened.

"Why, the Council's bidding, of course," he said. "Damien came to Savannah on their instructions. They had sent a cohort to develop a cover story, complete with an identity for Damien to assume. He was to perform the ritual that would free me. Little did he know that he would acquire such a lovely helpmate."

"That sounds like a lot of trouble to go through just to free the likes of you," I said.

His eyes flashed his rage but only for a moment. He was too wily to rise to the bait. "You cut me to the quick, boy. I'll have you know the Council chose

Savannah for this event precisely because they knew it would free me. And to make an example of you, of course. But I must admit, there was another objective as well."

"Which was?"

He clapped his hands together in glee, and a shower of dust and dirt rose from them. "It was supposed to be a surprise, but since you're trapped you might miss the show. So I'll go ahead and tell you just to see your face when you hear what the Council has wrought."

"Do enlighten me," I said, trying to mask my dread.

"Since you and your friends have been so naughty as to shirk your responsibilities to your sires, the Council decided to enlist the aid of some more reliable blood drinkers."

"What do you mean?"

"A deal was struck with the ones who have gone on before you."

I felt suddenly sickened; I didn't know whether from the blood loss or from the comprehension of the disaster that was beginning to dawn on me. "You mean—those in the underworld."

"Just so, my boy. Just so. You're not so stupid as I had begun to think."

At the meeting of vampires the other night at my home, Olivia had said the Council was rumored to have discovered how to raise from the dead every vampire who had ever been slain at the hands of another blood drinker since the beginning of time. I recalled her exact words: *massive, worldwide panic.*

The nightmare of every civilized blood drinker in the world was upon us.

"How does the Council know that they can resurrect dead vampires to do their killing for them?"

"That is the truly marvelous part," Reedrek said, his putrid face splitting with a fiendish grin. "An agreement was reached with the Dark Prince—"

"Satan?"

"Bingo! He agreed to let our people go if the Council could engineer their means of upward mobility, if you get my drift. My continental drift."

I grimaced. What passed for Reedrek's sense of humor was getting on my nerves. "How did they know the vampires would be viable once they returned to earth?"

"That brings me to the marvelous part I just alluded to, my dear boy. They didn't know it would work until *you* proved it to them."

"What the hell are you talking about?"

"Eleanor, of course. Your bringing her back by accident played right into their hands. It provided a test case. She is a prototype, if you will. The scenario that you set in motion could not have been more perfect for the Council's ends if I had planned it myself. Of course, you used different means than the Council, but the result was the same."

I knew that Jack was hearing Reedrek's rant through our psychic connection, because I could hear him cursing. At this moment he would be racing his automobile toward where I lay trapped.

I'm sorry. All my fault, he said.

Can't be helped now, I told him.

"So the ritual Damien and Eleanor performed was

to cause the earthquake and to call the twice-killed vampires to the surface."

"Double bingo! Give that vampire a prize! They called for the others of their kind to rise up from the underworld and inherit the earth!"

I thought of all the evil rogue blood drinkers that Jack and I had personally dispatched to hell. Ones who had had decades or more to suffer the punishments of Lucifer himself, all the while wishing for a way to revenge themselves on me and my offspring.

Jack—

I know. I heard. Shit.

Go to Melaphia. Tell her what's happening.

What about you?

Forget me. Just go. Melaphia is working on a way to close the portal to hell. If she's close enough—

I'm on it.

I could feel that Jack was changing direction. Thank the gods he hadn't chosen to argue with me.

"You seem unusually pensive, my son," Reedrek observed. "A penny for your thoughts."

"You said the Council wanted to make an example of me. What does that mean?"

"They're aware that you've led the efforts to thwart their goals for hundreds of years. So naturally, they wished to unleash the twice-killed vampires on you and yours first."

"So the earthquake isn't happening everywhere? Just Savannah?"

Reedrek turned peevish at this. "I'm sure in time they will develop the ability to produce worldwide events. But for now, they are satisfied with striking specific targets with precision. You should be honored that they selected your home first. Why, I suspect your guests from the underworld are making their way to the surface even as we speak."

If the damage was confined to Savannah, and if Melaphia had made progress developing her spells, there might still be a chance of limiting the destruction. I remembered the implications of Melaphia's research and her admonition about what it meant. If Jack or I were to be killed by one of the risen vampires, that would be our end. There would be no way back from the underworld for any of us once the door was shut permanently.

So be it.

"Are there any more surprises you want to tell me about?" I asked my sire.

"Isn't that enough?" He looked disappointed that I did not display more fear.

"Quite," I admitted.

"Oh, there *is* one surprise I'd mention," he said. "Now that we know what Eleanor is capable of, it seems that the risen vampires have a choice of stealing a human body to inhabit or resurrecting their own, complete with the ability to assume the evil form that Satan personally selected for them when he made them Sluagh."

"You mean Eleanor could just as easily have come back as herself and been able to shape-shift into a snake at will instead of stealing that other young woman's body?" The horror was almost beyond my comprehension.

"My, but you do catch on fast. That is exactly what I mean." Reedrek stretched and I could hear tendons and ligaments creaking. "That was a satisfying long winter's nap," he said. "I'm feeling peckish. A taste of the voodoo blood would hit the spot right now." He held up his hands and waved his claws. "Fee, fi, foe, fum. I smell the blood of a vampire Englishman," he said, and began to make his way through the field of debris toward me.

I tried again to wrench myself free, but it was no use. I could only brace myself for the clamp of his daggerlike fangs on my neck.

Jack

As I careened into Savannah proper, I could see red and blue police and firefighters' lights everywhere. Connie and Seth would be out there somewhere helping with the rescue efforts. For lots of reasons I was glad to see that there didn't seem to be that much structural damage—miraculous when I thought about how hard the ground had shaken. Still, I figured there were people who were trapped in elevators or who had suffered heart attacks or gotten hit on the head by falling objects all over the city.

Traffic lights were out here and there, but I wouldn't have stopped at them anyway, so what did I care? Small groups of people stood on street corners and in the squares in their nightclothes. They stopped talking to stare at me as I raced by, taking the corners on two wheels.

I couldn't believe I still hadn't gotten around to getting a new battery for that damned cell phone. It hadn't been able to hold a charge since the first time Connie accidentally zapped me. When would I ever learn? At least the mansion wasn't far from where William was. I could run in, tell Mel to get a move on with her spell-casting, and be at William's side in no time flat.

I screeched to a stop in the driveway and jumped out of the 'Vette just in time to see a dark form peering into William's mansion through the panes of glass to one side of the front door. I sneaked up behind him, grabbed him by the shoulder, and whirled him around to face me.

"Well if it ain't Mr. Black Jack McShane, the very feller who sent me to hell," he drawled, using the nickname that folks used to call me way back in the old days. The bad old days.

"Yancy the muleskinner, you dirty bastard." I was mighty glad that William and I had opened communication on my way over here. It would have taken precious seconds for me to figure out what Yancy was doing here and get over the shock of it if I hadn't already known I might be running into the revived undead. It was shocking enough even with the warning.

I shook him and dirt—either from the underworld or from his grave—fogged the air around us. "The last time I saw you, you were burning on the same cross you tried to light on fire in that black congregation's churchyard," I said. "That scheme backfired on you, didn't it, you filthy Klansman?"

During the Reconstruction, William and I stayed fat and sassy on the blood of Ku Klux Klansmen and other evildoers. It was real satisfying to dispatch those KKK sons of bitches to hell.

We'd heard rumors of a cross-burning one night and thought we'd attend. The humans were easy pickings. It was a mite hard for them to run in those long robes. Yancy, the only vampire in the bunch, gave us a little more trouble.

He'd come for the pickings as well, but he was intent on preying on the black folks trying to protect their little clapboard church. Bad idea. He put up a good fight, but William and I tore him apart like a wishbone and threw him on the pyre of his own making.

"I'm back," Yancy said. "Somebody opened the gate down in hell and it was Katie, bar the door. I decided to come on up and give my favorite killers a little taste of their own medicine. Right after I have a taste of that little black filly I just saw run up the stairs in yonder."

The thought of him touching Melaphia threw me into a rage. "That's not going to happen," I told him, and unsheathed my fangs. "I killed you before, and I'll kill you again."

"I figured you'd be too yellow to take me on without William Thorne."

"You figured wrong."

"Y'all double-teamed me last time. It warn't a fair fight a'tall."

"It's one against one this time. Is that fair enough for you?"

"That sounds more like it, but I got me a little secret weapon."

"Bring it on."

Yancy's head and torso started to stretch, and I had to step back for a second to collect my wits. The mule driver had been called "muleskinner" for the way he mercilessly whipped the animals that pulled barges down by the docks. Now he was changing right in front of me, much like the twins and Seth shifted into their canine forms. But Yancy wasn't turning into a dog or wolf. He was turning into a . . . mule man?

I remembered what Eleanor had said about the special, tailor-made punishments reserved just for fallen vampires in hell. Appropriately enough, Yancy was now morphing into one of the same creatures he'd deviled while he was on earth.

Damnation. How many other moldy oldy vamps were crossing the great divide even as I watched this hideous transformation? And what kind of shapes would *they* take? I could be fighting a magic mule one minute and some other form of shape-shifting vamp demon the next. Satan only knew what William and me were going to have to face in the days ahead.

I heard the body parts popping as his arms changed into legs. Short, slick hair sprouted all over him as his clothing ripped away and his hands and feet hardened into hooves. All I could do was stare. It would have been comical had not the animal pulled back his lips to reveal a set of mulesized fangs.

"I reckon it's you what might complain it's not a fair fight this time," he drawled. "Since now I got me the power of a mule."

I tried to keep the image of Francis the talking mule out of my head. This was serious business. Not to mention gross. Yancy, standing upright, towered over me. He struck out with a sharp hoof and I threw myself backward. I managed to dodge the blow but landed in the ornamental shrubs that lined the front of the house. If I survived this assault, I was going to have a hellacious time picking the thorns out of my backside.

I was able to scramble to my feet and into the grass before he had a chance to regroup. He was having difficulty maneuvering down the steps on his rear hooves, his back to the door. How the hell was I going to kill a—a bloodsucking mule? I had no doubt my fangs could penetrate his hide, but it was going to be awfully tricky getting within biting distance. Having my skull cracked open by flying hooves wouldn't kill me, but it would stun me enough for him to do the job with his fangs.

I began to sense another's presence. I glanced toward the windows and saw Deylaud's pale face staring back at me. He held something up for me to see. It was the crossbow William kept hanging on the wall in the downstairs den, loaded up with a stake as big as a baseball bat. I had to work my way over to the door again, as close to Deylaud as I could get.

I nodded slightly to signal Deylaud that I saw. Yancy the talking vampire mule was down on the lawn with me now, so I had lost my brief advantage. I got into a crouch and feinted sideways toward the street. He started to go that way but righted himself again when he realized it was a fake. He was faster than he should have been. A *lot* faster.

"You and Thorne should'a minded your own bidness," the mule said, its yellowed teeth almost as long as its fangs.

"The welfare of the humans in Savannah, black *and* white, *is* our business," I told him. I tried to maneuver myself around so that my back was to the front door, but he blocked me.

"Well, ain't that sweet?" Yancy-mule said, his voice dripping sarcasm. "Let's just see if you can protect the folks behind that door—black *and* white—from the likes of *me.*"

He came for me and I sprang upward, somersaulting over his head and onto his back. Taken by surprise, he hesitated a moment, just long enough for me to grab his mane with both hands and sink my fangs into his neck. He made a hideous noise, somewhere between a scream and a mule's bray, and bucked furiously. I felt like a bronco buster in a rodeo, locking my knees on to the mule's flanks, holding tight to its mane. Only I needed to stay on for a helluva lot longer than eight seconds to wear him down, if that was even possible.

As I pulled harder on his mane, he brayed louder and bucked more furiously, sending me tumbling off him and onto my back at his feet. I hit the ground rolling and his right hoof grazed my cheek, opening up a gaping wound. I sprang to my feet, spitting out a chunk of his flesh the size of a baseball. My blood was flowing but his was spurting—I'd opened up an artery. Time would tell if his healing power would close the wound before it weakened him. Too bad time was something I didn't have.

We circled each other again, and I was finally positioned with my back to the door. I backed up a step and threw a glance behind me. Through the pane, I saw Deylaud nod.

The mule man charged me and reared. At the same time, Deylaud threw open the door and tossed me the crossbow. The mule's hooves were high over my head, pawing at the air before starting their downward arc.

I put the crossbow against my shoulder, aimed for where I thought its heart was, and pulled the trigger.

It was a good thing the shot was at close range. The mule's hide—not to mention its muscular rib cage—was tough. But the stake pierced it with an awful squishing sound. I staggered backward, unsure if the shot had pierced the heart and still in danger from the flailing hooves even if it had.

The mule man froze in the air on its back hooves like some ass-ugly carousel horse. Then it started to list to its left. In its death throes it morphed back into Yancy the vampire Klansman and I saw the evil in his demonic eyes.

"Fuck you, McShane," he said.

"Go to hell, Yancy," I said. "Again."

Speaking of hell—as he turned to dust I couldn't help but wonder just what happened to vampires who were killed for the *third* time. Whatever it was, Yancy was about to find out. I hoped it was nasty.

"Are you okay, Jack?" Deylaud came out to check on me. He was panting, and I remembered how sick he'd been just a few days ago.

"Thanks to you, pal." I handed him the crossbow and staggered into the house. Melaphia, Renee, and Reyha were hugging each other in the foyer. They'd seen the whole thing, and they were terrified.

"Jack, was that what I think it was?" Melaphia asked. She allowed Renee out from behind her skirt now that the vampire was dead again.

"Yes, they're coming. Mel, are your spells ready to close the portal to the underworld? William needs you to work your mojo like right *now*."

"I—I'm not sure! I've just made a start. I'm not even sure I have everything I need."

"You're going to have to try your best," I told her. "That's all we can ask. But the portal's wide open and demons like that mule-man are finding their way out. There's no time to lose."

Melaphia drew herself up. "Deylaud, get my bag." Deylaud ran up the stairs to do her bidding. "Jack, do you know exactly where the opening to the underworld is? I think I need to get as close to it as possible."

I briefly explained to Melaphia what I'd heard through William as she took the bag from Deylaud. "I'm guessing the epicenter has to be underneath the hospital if it was strong enough to break through the granite and open that steel box," I said. "That's also where they performed the ritual, so I think it's our best bet."

"Let's go, then," Melaphia said.

Renee pulled on her mother's skirts. "Mama, I want to help Uncle William. Can I come, too?"

I started to suggest locking Renee in the vault with Reyha to guard her, but to my surprise, Melaphia said, "Yes, honey. Mama would like that."

I realized that after what had happened to Renee a couple of weeks before, I didn't blame Melaphia for not wanting to let her little girl out of her sight. In fact, as Mel, Renee, Deylaud, and Reyha grabbed their coats from the hall tree and put them on, I was kind of glad that all four of them were coming along, for the same reason: I didn't want to let any of them out of my sight.

"Let's go through the tunnels," I said. "We'll get there faster."

We ran through the tunnels, Deylaud carrying Renee on his back, as fast as we could go, prepared to pop up to the surface through the nearest outlet if an aftershock started. None of us relished being buried alive. To complete my turning, William had buried me undead on the battlefield the night he made me into a blood drinker, so I knew from experience being put into the earth before your time was no fun.

We pulled up short when we got to the place where the earth had caved in. I looked up and saw starlight through the hole in the pavement. "Listen!" I said, and they were all silent. Deylaud and Reyha just looked at each other and shrugged. Their canine hearing was acute, but not half as good as mine. I could barely hear William's voice.

"He's just beyond that pile of dirt," I whispered. "I'm going to climb over it, come down on the other side, and try to get William out. Mel, are you ready?

"Yes. I think so."

"Get started, then."

She nodded and began giving instructions to the others on what they should do to help her. Then she held hands with Renee and they both began to chant. I climbed the small mountain that separated me from William and Reedrek.

As I got to the top and looked over, I saw William trapped under the rubble and Reedrek moving toward him fangs first.

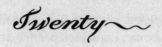

Twenty

William

I had braced myself for the killing bite, but then dirt and rocks started falling on my head. Reedrek straightened from his crouch and looked up, just in time to be flattened by the powerful body of Jack McShane.

Jack had jumped onto Reedrek from atop the mound of dirt that covered me. My sire was an old and powerful blood drinker, but his time underground without feeding had weakened him. Still, he was able to throw Jack off and stagger to his feet. Jack charged him again, flipped him over, and pinned his arms behind his back.

Jack was reaching for the chain that had bound the steel coffin when another earthquake began. I say another earthquake because this one was almost as strong as the first tremor. I knew somehow that it was not merely an aftershock.

I shut my eyes to keep out the dust and dirt. The awful roar was all I could hear. When the shaking stopped, I opened my eyes and instead of Reedrek looming before me, I saw Jack peering at me earnestly with his wide blue eyes.

"Where's Reedrek?" I asked.

"He got away. With all the dust, I didn't even see which way he ran. We'll worry about him later. Look, some of the soil and rocks have shifted off you. Let me see if I can get you out."

As Jack began to move stones and chunks of pavement off me, Deylaud joined him. "Thank the gods," he said when he saw me.

"Are Melaphia and Renee and Reyha alright?" Jack asked him.

"Yes, they're fine." Deylaud started helping Jack dig me out. He was not as strong as my offspring, but he was stronger than a human being. "They're still where you left us, just over this mound of dirt."

"Did Melaphia cause that quake just now?" I asked.

"Yes," Deylaud said. "Renee seems to be able to feel the portal and she doesn't think it's completely closed. Mel and Renee are going to try again. That's why we have to get William out right away. They're about to recast the spell and he could be buried again."

"I think I can get you, William," Jack said. He and Deylaud each grasped me under one arm and heaved. With the larger stones and chunks of asphalt gone, I felt myself coming free of the trap. The two of them helped me over and around the debris to where Melaphia, Renee, and Reyha waited. Melaphia had set out her candles and herbs.

Melaphia gasped when she saw my wound. "You

need blood," she said. "Jack, you have to take him home right now to feed."

"I can feed him right here," Jack said.

"No," I said. "The sun is almost up."

"What about you and Renee?" Jack asked Melaphia. "If the portal is open . . ."

"My sister and I will guard them with our lives," Deylaud said. "You can have no doubt of this."

Indeed, Deylaud and Reyha were fearsome creatures in dog form, especially when provoked. They had killed at my bidding more than once, and they would not hesitate to do so again. They could rip the throat from a vampire almost as easily as Jack or I could.

"I'll sneak back through the tunnels as soon as I get you home and safe in the vault," Jack said. "I'll make sure they all get home."

"The tunnels may have caved in by then," I said. "I want us all to stay together until the portal is closed."

Renee stalked up to me, a stern look on her young face. "Uncle William, you must *go*. I can feel the portal in my blood. I'll know when it's closed. If me and Mama can make the ground shake one more time, it'll be over."

I began to protest, but Jack had already picked me up in his arms and was moving quickly in the direction of home. "Wait," I said. "We should not travel through the tunnels in case of a cave-in when the next tremor starts. We have enough time to get home before sunup by the street level."

Jack nodded and carried me up to the surface, which was no more difficult than walking up on the mound of debris to the sidewalk. Melaphia and the others were in little danger of being buried as the place where they stood was open to the sky.

We surfaced behind the hospital. It was relatively quiet, but we could see a hive of activity at the end of the block near the massive building's main entrance. Police and emergency workers were evacuating patients on stretchers and in wheelchairs. Jack, with me still in his arms, had turned toward home when he literally ran into Connie Jones. She was cordoning off the gash in the earth with a makeshift barricade, winding yellow police tape around traffic cones so no one would fall into the open pit.

"How badly are you injured, William?" she asked.

"He'll be okay as long as I get him home before daylight," Jack answered for me. "But I've got to get going. I'll talk to you later."

She nodded and turned back to her task. But she pulled up short, as did Jack and I, as we all sensed the presence of more blood drinkers.

Reedrek, flanked by Damien and Eleanor, appeared out of the darkness. I saw Jack glance surreptitiously downward through the opening in the earth and back at me. *They can't see Melaphia and them from here,* he projected. I only hoped they wouldn't sense them.

"Nice try," Damien said. "But the portal's still open. Demons are jumping into the bodies of mortals even as we speak. Either that, or they're slithering up from hell in their own bodies and dragging their individual curses with them."

"I suspect your witch and her whelp must be around here somewhere. Come out, come out, wherever you are!" Reedrek sang. "Olly, olly oxen free!"

Jack set me on my feet gently. "The sun's almost

up, guys. Why don't we all go to our corners and come back out fighting again tomorrow night."

"Yes," I said. "Let's table our differences until we have more time to . . . chat."

"What fun would that be?" Eleanor asked. "I don't want to chat. I smell fresh blood right now." She eyed my wound and licked her lips.

"I agree with Eleanor. Why wait? I believe we should press our advantage, don't you agree, Reedrek?" Damien said with a smirk.

"By all means, my boy," Reedrek said. "By all means."

Something wasn't right here. I could tell that the other vampires' bravado was false. In fact, I could smell their fear. Then I looked at Connie and I realized why.

Jack

Connie appeared to be on the verge of panic. She was taking it all in, looking from one vampire to another, trying to make sense of what was going on and what she was feeling from us blood drinkers. She looked as if she couldn't interpret the vampire vibes her newly hyped-up senses were absorbing. Brand-new instincts were kicking in, and she didn't know what to do with them.

Sweat broke out on her brow despite the cold, and she shifted back and forth on the balls of her feet as if she was getting ready to pounce on somebody. I just hoped it wouldn't be me or William.

"What—what's happening to me?" she asked, and a visible shiver ran from her head down to her feet.

"I'm glad you asked me that, darling," Eleanor said. Despite her snarky tone, I could tell that she was almost as nervous as Connie. "There was one little deal the Council had to make with Satan before he would let me and the other double-deads out of the underworld."

"Unfortunately for all of us, we have to activate the Slayer," Reedrek said, not taking his eyes off Connie. "I wish it were not so, but there it is."

"I said, *What's happening to me?*" Connie repeated.

I looked at the woman I loved. Her eyes seemed to be changing shape. She blinked and put her fingertips to her lips. My God, she was growing fangs.

I wanted to go to her and get between her and the evil vamps, but something stopped me. An instinctive fear. A certainty that I was in the presence of a creature whose job it was to kill me.

"But she'll want to kill all of us," William said, trying to appeal to what might be left of his sire's sanity, I figured. If so, he was wasting his time.

"It can't be helped," Reedrek said philosophically. "A deal is a deal. Damien, will you do the honors?"

From somewhere within the folds of his long leather coat, Damien produced a sword. It was the exact twin of the sword I saw in the underworld. *Oh, shit.*

"That's my sword—" William began.

"Not anymore it's not," Eleanor said.

"You never knew the origin of this sword or its value," Damien said. "Your old friend Lalee could have told you, if you'd only thought to ask her while you had the opportunity. If you had, she would have told you that this is the sword that sets the Slayer on her path. This is one of only two steel blades in the universe that can kill a vampire more quickly than a wooden stake to the heart."

I wanted to know how William had come by the sword, but that question would have to wait until another time. I looked at my sire and saw that he was dumbfounded. William was almost never at a loss—or at least he never let it show if he was. But his usual command was slipping. He was weakening by the moment, and I didn't like how this confrontation was going down. I needed to think of something fast.

"The sword came into my possession by chance," William said.

"Nothing happens just by chance, William," Damien said. "I would have thought you were old enough and smart enough to have figured that out by now." Damien heaved the sword by the hilt, sending it flying end over end. I lunged, trying to grab it in flight, ready to lose a hand if I had to. I couldn't let Connie touch that sword.

I felt the sword cut into my fingers, but I couldn't catch it. I couldn't even slow it down; the thing had a mind of its own, and it was sailing right to Connie. I changed direction and headed toward her, convinced the sword was going to cut her in two.

Impossibly, she caught it by the hilt. When she touched it, her body convulsed like she'd grabbed a live electrical wire. Behind her a transformer blew, backlighting Connie in an eerie blue-green glow and showering her with sparks. I could barely see the whites of her eyes now. They weren't human eyes anymore, and I could see the tiny fangs when she opened her mouth.

To smile.

That was the worst part, that smile. She knew who and what she was now. She could feel it; hell, we could all feel it. She was the goddess destroyer of vampires. She was the Slayer.

I remembered what Travis had said about how Connie would be like an animal when she first turned, but I refused to believe it. My Connie was still in this creature somewhere, and if anyone could reach her and reason with her, I could.

"Connie," I said, approaching her slowly. I reached out my hand to her. Unfortunately, it was the injured hand, the one dripping blood.

She put her delicate nose in the air and sniffed as an animal would have, and the gesture horrified me on a primal level. "I smell the blood of the blood drinker," she said in someone else's voice. She came at me with the sword and I dodged away.

"What are you doing?" William asked me, alarm in his voice. "Don't go near her!"

From the corner of my eye, I saw Reedrek and Damien run away like the cowards they were. But Eleanor, she stayed and moved toward William, creeping up on him like a black widow spider.

"It's me," I told Connie. I hoped my voice was soothing despite the fact that I was terrified for all of us. I started toward her again.

"Jack!" William shouted. "Stop! You can't reason with her. Remember what Travis said!"

She lowered the sword and cocked her head to one side. "Jack? Is it you?"

Hoping to heaven she wasn't faking, I said, "Yes. Now give me the sword." I inched closer.

She looked at the sword and then at me. "Okay." She held the sword out to me and I reached for it.

She punched me in the face with her other hand, the blow coming so fast I didn't see it until it connected with my jaw. I felt myself lifted off my feet and into the air. My body hit the wall of the hospital and slid to the pavement. For a moment or two, I couldn't move or think.

And a moment or two was all it took.

Connie leaned over me and held the sword high, the maniacal smile back on her face. William started to run to me, but Eleanor caught him from behind. She jumped onto his back and threw one arm around him, clamping his neck in the crook of her arm.

"Slayer! Over here!" Eleanor screamed.

Connie whirled. I tried to raise myself up but was thrown back to the ground. My head throbbed so viciously it took a couple of seconds for me to realize that another earthquake had begun to shake the earth beneath us. I rolled on my side facing William, trying to get to my knees.

Connie seemed unaffected. She forgot me entirely and stalked toward William and Eleanor, drawing back the sword as she went.

William shook Eleanor off, and she fell to the ground hard. He squared himself as Connie charged. He blocked the blow, connecting with her forearm. Connie lost her footing, but managed to hang on to the sword. Meanwhile, Eleanor was scrambling up and away into the darkness, and I had only managed to get to my knees, although the quaking had stopped as quickly as it had begun.

Suddenly, four people came scrambling into sight from the tunnels through the opening in the street. "The portal is closed! We did it!" Melaphia yelled, but her smile of victory turned to terror as she and the others saw what was taking place on the surface.

I knew something was wrong with this picture. The timing was off. This couldn't be happening. "No, not now!" I yelled.

I was on my feet, staggering toward William, aiming to get between him and the Slayer. It wasn't Connie anymore.

The sword was on the backswing again, and this time the Slayer was pissed. I lunged, the horrified screams of Melaphia, Renee, Deylaud, and Reyha ringing in my ears.

The Slayer was too fast for me, and for William.

In a move mercifully too quick for any of us to see, she drove the sword into William's heart.

I would wonder later if time really did slow down right then, or if some primitive protective mechanism kicked in to keep my mind from shattering.

I kept on moving toward William as if in slow motion, vaguely aware that Connie had run away, disappearing into the park after Eleanor.

I reached out my hand to him and heard myself shout, "Father! No!"

He reached for me as well, and I could swear our fingertips touched just for an instant.

I yelled again, "Wait!"

But William's body was already turning to dust. I had just enough time to question why the body of my friend and father seemed to go out of focus before his form broke apart and splintered into millions of twinkling shards that scattered into the winter wind.

Twenty-one

I don't remember how we got back to William's house before sunrise. I couldn't seem to figure out a lot of things. People were sobbing, and I didn't want to think about why.

Worse than that, somewhere deep inside my mind a nagging guilt told me the reason we were all sitting here grieving was because I had done something wrong, something stupid. Whatever had happened was all my fault, and I was very, very sorry.

I was holding the pocket watch William had given me, the one he used along with the shells to get me back from the underworld. That was a favor I wouldn't be able to return.

Someone must have called Werm to come join us through what was left of the tunnels, because I heard him say, "I can't believe he's gone." Someone had been talking. I seemed to remember that Melaphia had filled Werm in on what all had happened. I had covered my ears for that part. I didn't want to hear it.

Something nudged my hand. It was Reyha's nose. It had to be daylight because she and Deylaud were in four-footed form now. She sprawled listlessly across my lap and I stroked her head mechanically.

Deylaud, whimpering, was snuggled up to Werm, who had a comforting arm around his slender shoulders. Melaphia held Renee, who had fallen into a fitful sleep.

"I can't believe this is happening," Melaphia said.

"Me neither," I murmured. Oh, gods. It was coming back to me. My body quaked, remembering the sword's blow as if I'd absorbed it myself.

"I can't accept it. I won't."

"We have to."

"What are we going to do?" she asked, her voice breaking.

How many times had William told me that if anything ever happened to him, it was my responsibility to take care of the family? Had I ever, on any of those occasions, entertained the possibility that we could be left without him? No. Not even once. What had I been thinking?

It was time for me to step up.

I eased Reyha off my lap and knelt in front of where Mel sat on the sofa. I took her hand and kissed it gently. Renee stirred and opened her eyes, so I took her little hand in mine as well. "I'll protect you," I said.

"And what if—when—the Slayer comes for you?" Melaphia asked. "What then?"

"I'll do whatever I can to stay alive until she . . . calms down. Travis said that she might reach a point where we could reason with her."

I noticed Werm was following our conversation closely, his eyes swollen from weeping. But he didn't ask any questions. He was my second now. He was going to have to grow up fast.

"You know you cannot avenge William," Melaphia said. "As much as I might want you to. Lalee has forbidden it."

"I understand. But there's another reason I can't go after her."

"Because she carries your child?"

"No," I said.

"Because we still don't know how the Slayer can be killed?"

"No, though that's true, too."

"Then why?"

"We need her help."

"With what?" Werm finally spoke up.

"The portal was open for some time," I said. "The double-dead vampire I killed here at the house made his way up from the underworld pretty quick. How many others do you reckon had the wherewithal to do the same?"

"Oh, sweet Maman," Melaphia murmured. She glanced down to make sure Renee had fallen asleep again, not that the child wouldn't eventually figure out for herself how much trouble we were all in.

Suddenly I was thinking clearly again. It was about time. I filled in Melaphia and Werm on Reedrek's rant in the tunnels and told them about the double-deads and their ability to change their appearance.

"It's our responsibility to send those mofos back to hell where they belong," I said.

"My God," Werm breathed. "There are only the two of us. How are we going to fight them all? How are we even going to *find* them?"

"There's only one thing we can do," I said. "We have to get on the good side of a vampire slayer. That's her job, right? To sniff out vampires and assassinate them."

"Yeah, but what if those vampires are . . . us?" Werm croaked.

"We'll have to figure out how to make her want to kill them more than she wants to kill us," I said.

"If you say so, Jack."

"I know you can get us through this, Jack. I have faith in you," Melaphia said, her eyes sparkling with unshed tears.

Her words meant more to me than she would ever know. I sat on the sofa between her and Werm and put an arm around each of them. "William always said Savannah was his city."

"It was," Melaphia sobbed.

I hugged them close to me. "And now it's ours."

When people say they sleep the sleep of the dead, they have no idea.

I slept dreamlessly—thank the gods—and woke with a sense of purpose. Werm was awake and feeding from the bottled blood in the refrigerator.

"You probably shouldn't open the nightclub, even if the power is back on," I said. "Why don't you lie low for a while until we get some idea of what we're facing."

"In terms of the number of double-deads, you mean?"

"Yeah. But call Seth and give him an idea of what we're up against. Tell him Connie has been activated and that he should check on her. He knows what that means."

"Done," he said, and took the back way out toward the tunnels.

I turned the corner to go upstairs and found Melaphia kneeling before her little altars.

"How long has it been since you slept?" I asked her.

She shrugged. "I had to do something. I prayed to Maman Lalee, but I don't know if it did any good. She didn't manifest."

"What'd you pray for?" I asked, even though I figured I already knew.

"I beseeched her for a favor for William. Even though she told us no one could ever come back from the underworld again, I asked if she could find it in her heart to try to get William to a better place. I can't bear to think of him suffering for eternity."

She collapsed against me and began to sob again, and I sank down to the steps with her. "I can't stand to think of it either," I said, stroking her hair. It was the thought I had been trying to suppress ever since we'd lost William. It was too painful to dwell on, so I chose not to.

"Have faith," I said. "Those two have a special relationship. Lalee will think of something."

"I hope so."

"Why are you crying, Mama?" Renee asked from the top of the stairs.

We looked up to see the little girl beaming down at us. Then Melaphia and I exchanged worried glances. Was Renee so traumatized by the sight of William's death that she had blocked it out of her mind?

"I'm just sad because I prayed to Maman Lalee to help William and I don't know if it worked."

"Of course it worked," Renee said.

"How do you know, honey?" I asked her.

"Because I saw him dancing."

Twenty-two

I went by the garage to check on any earthquake damage and explain things to the guys as best I could. They were shocked to hear about William, of course, and offered me their sympathies and vows of discretion.

I convinced Rennie to close up for a few days on account of potential demon trouble, and advised him and the irregulars to lie low until I had a handle on things. They said they understood and headed for their homes. Before Otis left I told him that later I'd fill him in on some details he'd want to take back to his Sidhe bosses.

I was checking for structural damage around the back of the building, grateful that nothing seemed to have been harmed inside or out, when I saw Huey sitting on the edge of what had been his hole. I say "what had been" because the earthquake had caused the hole to cave in, ruining all the hard work he'd put in to resurrect his Chevy Corsica.

But he didn't seem perturbed. In fact, he had himself a new friend. Or maybe I should say a closer friend.

The crow that had been perched in the tree squawking the last time I'd seen it was now perched on Huey's shoulder like some cockeyed pirate's parrot.

"Looks like you've got a feathered friend," I said.

"Yessir. She's your friend, too," Huey said.

"Come again?"

"That's what she said."

I'd heard it all now. "She said she's my friend?"

"I taught her to talk."

"Did you, now?"

"She tried for an awful long time, and finally she caught on," he said.

I was starting to believe that Huey was a regular Doctor Dolittle. Not long ago he had demonstrated his ability to speak werewolf—he could interpret their barks and whines—and now he had taught a bird to talk. At least he claimed that he had. But hearing was believing.

I bent down to get a better look at the critter, and she eyeballed me in return. "There's a pretty bird," I said. "Can the pretty bird talk?"

The crow flapped its wings indignantly. "Damn right I can. Dammit, Jack, get me out of here!"

I nearly fell over into what was left of Huey's old grave, now Huey's old mud hole. "Ginger? Is that you?"

"Hell yes," the bird said.

"How'd you get to be a bird?"

"That bitch of a boss of mine stole my body, and there's no telling what she's been doing to it. You've got to get it back for me, Jack! Get me the hell back into my body!"

"I—I will," I stammered. "I mean, I'll try. There might be a slight problem. With your body, I mean."

"Oh, geez. What?" asked the long-suffering Ginger.

"You might be a vampire."

"Don't tell me you believe in vampires."

I sighed. "A few days ago, you probably didn't believe that your boss could steal your body either."

"Okay, whatever. Just promise me you'll get me and my body back together."

"I promise."

"Good. 'Cause I look terrible in black." The Ginger bird settled down some, but didn't take her eyes off me. "Let me tell you something else. Lay off that 'pretty bird' business. And if you *ever* offer me a cracker, by God, I'm going to peck your eyes out."

My second-favorite place to go and think—other than in my car, driving fast—is the beach on Tybee Island. There's something eternal and reassuring about hearing the waves wash onto the shore over and over.

The humans had practically deserted the island, what with tsunami warnings due to the earthquakes, but when they realized the crisis had passed they would make their way back to their island paradise.

For now, the island belonged to me. Before I took on the serious thinking I had to do—that of the problem-solving variety—I let my mind wander. And I let myself grieve for my friend, my father, my William.

I thought about all the good times he and I had together, like the times we went night fishing or moonlight sailing and he told me stories of things that happened hundreds of years ago. I could have listened to him forever. I never believed that a day would come when the stories would be over.

I chose not to recall the times we'd clashed. Not tonight. Tonight was for pleasant memories.

I closed my eyes and enjoyed the salty wind on my face. When I finally opened them, I looked out into the frothy waves and thought I saw something gliding on the surface of the water. What was it? Bottlenose dolphins? Manatees? No, that couldn't be right.

It almost looked like a couple dancing on top of the water. I shook my head. *McShane, you're cracking up.* First talking birds and now merpeople. And I hadn't even had anything to drink. *That* could be remedied at least. I was going to tie one on before I went into my coffin tonight.

I saw the moonlight strike something shiny as the next wave came in. The water rolled what looked like an antique champagne bottle right up to my feet. It looked really old, like it had been battered against the sand of so many shores that it had worn down in places.

I stooped to retrieve it and saw that there was a cork in it. I removed the cork and shook out a small piece of yellowed paper so old and oxidized it almost disintegrated in my hand. I held it up to the moonlight and strained to read it, revving up my special vampire peepers.

Four words, written in an elegant hand, read, *Don't worry. I'm fine.*

"What the—"

And then I found myself on the flat of my back in

the sand, the note flying off into the wind. I tried to keep my grip on the bottle.

Connie held me down with superhuman strength, a wooden stake pressing through my shirt into the flesh right above my heart. "Hello there, lover boy. Are you ready to die?"

Would my time as head of the household last only a day? I fought to remain calm. I'd talked women into a lot of things in my long life, but no sweet talk I'd ever done had prepared me for trying to talk a vampire slayer out of staking me.

She drew the stake back and was about to bring it downward when I yelled, "You don't want to kill me!"

"Oh, yes I do," she said. "I'm itching to kill you. I *need* to kill you!" Her eyes were wild.

I could understand now what Travis had said about the slayers turning into something that wasn't human. I just hoped I'd understood him right when he said they eventually settle down, and I wondered if I could stay alive that long.

"No you don't. You need me."

She laughed, and I tried not to think about how sexy those little fangs were. Now was not the time for distractions.

"Oh, yeah? What do I need you for?" she asked sweetly. She brought the weapon to my chest again and pressed it in hard enough to draw blood.

"Do you remember that talk about portals that went on amongst us vampires last night?"

"Uh-huh." She narrowed her eyes.

Hot damn, I had her attention. "Did you understand what it meant?"

"Nope," she admitted. "What does it mean?"

"It means that the earthquake opened up a hole to hell that let a lot of nasty beasties escape into Savannah. And you need me to help you find them and kill them before they can eat any of the good citizens of our fair city."

I was pretty sure this was a bald-faced lie. She was made to root out blood drinkers, and didn't need me even a little bit, but she was a baby slayer with nobody to teach her, so she might not instinctively know what her powers were.

"Beasties?" The crazy smile disappeared. "What kind of beasties?"

"Ones with big sharp nasty teeth," I enthused. "Demons who can shape-shift into all kinds of scary monsters." I hoped to the gods that not just Connie, but Connie the cop was in there somewhere and that her natural inclination to put the welfare of the citizens first would override her need to kill little old me.

She studied me skeptically. "Demons who can change into all kinds of scary monsters, huh? That's quite a tale. How do I know you're telling the truth?"

"Well, I, uh—where's your sword?"

It was obvious she was new to all this, and she seemed genuinely confused by my question, but then she shook it off.

She was raising the stake again, when a God's-honest miracle happened. The cop radio that she wore somewhere under her jacket went off, and a dispatcher spewed some cop-speak about a crazed maniac running amok on River Street. Not your garden-variety crazed maniac, mind you, but one with four legs, a tail, and scales.

"What was that about a lizard man?" I asked. "You've got to admit it's not every day that you see something out of a Japanese horror movie menacing the tourists."

She looked at me hard, considering. "Seth can help me find these demons," she said. "And I can sniff vampires. I don't need you."

"Smell can get you and Seth only so far. I can teach you what he can't: how to think like a vampire and how to outsmart one. These demons are bloodsuckers at heart, and it takes one to know one, sweetheart."

"I don't need your help to think like a vampire. I'm half-vampire already . . . but it was a nice try."

She swung all the way back with the stake and brought it down to my heart. In a flash, I managed to move the bottle over my heart, and the stake glanced off the smooth glass.

"Hey, wait!" I said as she cursed her miss. "You haven't heard the worst part: not all of the risen un-dead will be in demon form. Some of them will look like regular folks."

"You're lying."

"No, I'm not. You remember that redheaded chick from last night? That was really Eleanor. William killed her in Europe, and she accidentally came back from the underworld with us. She could have morphed into a snake if she'd wanted to. But she stole Ginger the floozy's body to hop into when she came up from the underworld."

I was rambling but I couldn't help it. Maybe if I threw enough at her, something would stick. If it didn't I was going to be back in the underworld in a flash, suffering a torment thought up just for me. I'd probably be stuck for all eternity driving a Chevy Corsica!

"Ginger the floozy?"

I didn't think Connie's half-vampire brain was firing on all cylinders yet. I didn't know if that was good or bad, but I forged ahead. "She was one of Eleanor's whores. That was really Eleanor in Ginger's body."

Something in those scary eyes told me I was finally getting through to her. "And you can tell when one of these demons has possessed a human being?"

"Of course," I fibbed again, hoping like hell that a slayer's powers didn't include lie detecting. So far so good on that score.

Connie raised herself off me, mostly using the stake, which was against my chest again, to lift herself.

"Ow," I said. "Ow."

She hauled me up by my shirtfront as effortlessly as if I were a ragdoll, set me on my feet, and pulled me down to look at her eyeball to eyeball.

"All right. I'll let you live for now, fang boy. But when we've tracked down and destroyed all the demons, then I'm coming for you. And believe me when I tell you—you may not have had the guts to kill me when you had the chance. But I *do* have the guts to kill *you*." She shoved me so hard I landed in the surf several feet away.

That went well.

I watched her disappear into the darkness, salt water stinging the hole in my chest, which was already healing. I dug my heels into the sand and pushed myself into the ocean to float on my back and look up into the stars.

Well, just *damn*. That was so . . . *hot*.

Epilogue

A Word from the Council

Far beneath London a group of demons argued among themselves as they sat around a cauldron that belched black smoke and a foul stench.

Idly fingering the vivid but healing wound in his throat, the vampire Ulrich stood waiting for them to calm themselves. At his side stood his mate, Diana, who was trying her best not to scream.

He leaned down to whisper in her ear, "Do not worry, my dear. They won't harm us. We'll turn their bad news to our advantage."

Diana nodded, still too petrified to speak. Her most recent plan to impress the Council had failed miserably. William Cuyler Thorne, her human husband of half a millennium, had rescued the magical child she'd promised to make into a blood drinker to honor the old lords. And William had destroyed Hugo, the one they'd planned to sacrifice.

The only thing that had spared Ulrich and Diana

the full wrath of the Council was the failure of Damien, the vampire in charge of the Council's most recent scheme. By the time Diana and Ulrich had freed themselves and returned to the Council, the old lords were more interested in heaping their wrath onto Damien.

Their minion, a diminutive vampire named Mole, had just received a communiqué from Reedrek and delivered to the Council news of what had happened in Savannah. Even now Mole cowered in a corner, evidently fearing the old sires would eat the messenger.

As the Council members calmed themselves, Ulrich said in his most soothing voice, "But gentlemen, Thorne is dead. Surely that is a victory."

The eldest of the old lords, an ancient blood drinker bearing the reddest, scaliest, and most pock-marked skin, said, "The portal was closed before more than a scant few twice-killed vampires could escape." He shouted in anger, pounding the earth with his staff.

"It was supposed to have remained open until all the Sluagh made their way to the land of the living," the demon next to him said.

The unholy hubbub began again, and Ulrich cleared his throat to try to regain their attention. "If you'll pardon my directness, your lordships, it would seem a boy was sent to do a man's job."

The cowering minion gasped at Ulrich's brazenness, and Diana gaped at him in horror before taking a step to distance herself from him.

Another demon scratched himself with long pointed talons. "Do you think we are so senile as to have forgotten that you failed even more miserably than Damien did, Ulrich?"

The fiend evidently couldn't reach the right spot, because he beckoned the minion and indicated where the little vampire should scratch. Blanching in horror, Mole did as he was bidden. The demon's foot thumped the ground a few times and he sighed in relief. Diana looked as if she would swoon.

"At least I am vampire enough to come before you again," he said. "I hear Damien is in hiding for his life."

"True enough," said the first vampire. "We'll hear your proposal if you have one. And it had better be good, or you'll wish you were in hiding as well."

Ulrich nudged Diana, who was frozen in place. He urged her forward until she took a step toward the old lords. Finally she found her tongue. "S-sirs, the vampire who is in charge of Savannah now, Jack McShane, can animate the dead."

The old sires murmured among themselves. The leader said, "Do you swear this?"

"Yes," Diana said. "I have seen it. He reanimated a legion of the dead to guard us on our arrival in Savannah. And it was through his power that Eleanor was raised from the underworld. He even found his way back from there himself."

"And that was without the aid of an earthquake," Ulrich put in.

"He hadn't even intended to raise her," Diana continued. "Think of what he could accomplish if he really tried."

Ulrich nodded. "We propose to force McShane to raise selected . . . characters from the dead."

"What kind of characters?" asked a Council member

with an oozing sore in the middle of its chest. "A sorcerer of one of the old religions seems to have fixed it so that no blood drinker can ever rise again."

"No blood drinkers, perhaps, but there are plenty of others who have proven their ability to wreak havoc on humanity," Diana offered.

"Serial killers, mass murderers, terrorists. That variety of human," Ulrich added casually.

"And what makes you so sure this McShane blood drinker, this offspring of Thorne, can be influenced to resurrect these characters?" the leader asked.

Diana and Ulrich exchanged glances. They knew better than to bluff an audience of ancient and bloodthirsty master vampires.

"We believe that without his sire, he will be easily led. The loss of Thorne leaves a vacuum in his life that we will step in and fill," Ulrich said.

Diana shook her mane of golden hair, tilted her head downward, and looked up, fixing her wide blue eyes upon her audience, gestures she had practiced on men for hundreds of years. "We can be very persuasive," she purred.

"Very well," the leader said. "Go to the New World. Make haste. Do your worst."

"Yes, my lord," Diana promised, relief flooding her. Emboldened by the knowledge that she would soon be thousands of miles away from the hellhole in which she now found herself, she curtsied and added, "I give you my vow, your excellencies, I know exactly how to make Jack McShane bow to my will."

Acknowledgments

Thanks to my critique partner, author Jennifer LaBrecque, for helping make this a better book and for keeping Jack honest.

*For a sneak peek at Raven Hart's next novel in the
Savannah Vampires Chronicles read on.*

Letter from Jack

My so-called life has become a nightmare. Each
time I climb into my coffin at sunrise and the deep
death-sleep claims me, I think I'll wake up and things
will be normal again. As normal as a vampire's existence can be anyway.

In my dreams I'm in my old, ordinary life. My
maker and mentor, William Thorne, is back again
and whole. Connie, the woman I love, is a regular
human being, coping with nothing more complicated
than being a cop and the girlfriend of a vampire—as
if that wasn't tough enough. Melaphia and Renee, my
human family, are as untroubled by their own nightmares and as secure and happy as any young mother
and daughter have a right to be.

But when the moon rises and the shadows lengthen
to hide the monsters that exist on the fringe of human
consciousness, my sweet dreams of normality im-
plode under the weight of the here and now. When I
wake, the real nightmare begins.

William, my sire and the friend who had my back
for more than a hundred years, is dead, slain by the
very woman I'd give my own life for. That leaves me
alone to protect Melaphia and Renee, already tortured and traumatized by the most evil of my kind before the crowning blows of William's death and the
revelation of their most deadly secret. As the most

powerful mambos of this hemisphere, the daughters of my heart might not be as vulnerable as ordinary humans, but because they bear the priceless voodoo blood that gives vampires otherworldly powers, they are now hunted for their life force by the most evil and determined of fiends.

If that weren't enough trouble, there's a whole menagerie of monsters out to challenge the chief enforcer role I inherited from William. I have to ride herd on all things nonhuman that would otherwise be free to threaten the mortal population of Savannah, one of the most haunted places in the world. And for the first time I have to do it without William and his formidable power at my side.

Oh, and let's not forget the worst enemy of all, a council of the most evil vampires in history who are trying to harness the elemental powers of the universe to enslave peace-loving bloodsuckers like me and turn us into killing machines. Their most recent show of force produced an earthquake that briefly opened a Portal from the underworld, through which dozens of dead but reanimated vampires clawed their way topside in every demonic form imaginable. The only way I was able to convince Connie to let me live was to promise to help her track down and destroy these double-dead demons before they can wreak enough havoc to send the human world into a full-scale panic.

You see, the moment Connie murdered William, she turned into a creature that I barely recognized, part demon, part avenging angel. As a vampire slayer sworn to kill me and my kind wherever she finds us, Connie is the new favorite target for every evil blood drinker on the planet. So I have to try to protect her from them while I protect myself from her and hope to God it'll be a while before she figures out that she doesn't really need me to help her kill those demons. She's lethal enough on her own.

Oh, and incidentally, Connie's pregnant with my child but doesn't know it yet. A child that is an abomination of nature and has no right to exist, but whom I love with a ferocity that frightens me. I would do anything to insure the survival of Connie and my baby, even if it means giving them over to the care of another kind of monster altogether. Probably just as well that she hates me now, don't you think? At least that's what my rational brain tells my shattered heart.

So as you can see, reality bites. Even worse than I do.

Welcome to the new normal. Welcome to my nightmare.

Chapter One

"Hey! Watch where you're swinging that axe!" I yelled as the blade whistled through the air, grazing my cheek. "I'm trying to help you bring that demon down, you know. The least you could do is try not to lop off my head."

The demon, a nasty little number covered with slimy brown scales, ducked but not before Connie's axe connected with its shoulder. It howled in pain and outrage from the bricked-in corner of the alley we had backed it into.

"Is head-lopping one of the ways you can kill a

vampire?" Connie asked. She never took her gaze off the demon, but her eyes lit up with a deadly fervor that made me cringe because I knew it was meant for me.

"Well, yes," I admitted. "One of the few." The demon made a break for it, but I caught him in the jaw—if that hump below its mouth was a jaw—with my fist and spun him back into the corner.

Connie sighed. "I have so much to learn. So many vampires; so little time." She raised the weapon again and swung with almost as much speed and strength as I myself could muster. The demon's head left its shoulders with a spray of blood, and its body fell forward onto the pavement and turned into a pile of dirt. The smell of it mixed with the sickening-sweet stench of the nearby Dumpster and made my nose twitch with disgust.

"Another one bites the dust, uh, uh," Connie sang with a little victory dance. I watched her shimmy her shapely booty in awe, not quite sure whether I should be grossed out by her blood lust or turned on by it. I seemed to be a little of both. Maybe I'd inherited William's death wish along with all his responsibilities.

Connie turned her attention to me, noticing the trickle of blood running down my cheek. Her eyes dilated, the pupils turning into slits, the irises bloodred. She grabbed me by the neck and pulled my face next to hers so quickly it startled me. I searched her eyes for the spark that was my old Connie and didn't see it. Would it—would *she*—ever be back? Or was she lost and gone forever in the shell of this vicious, half-human killer standing in front of me now?

When she pressed her lips to my cheek, I felt myself go weak in the knees. She hadn't shown me any affection since . . . the night I tried to kill her. For her own good, of course.

I quickly realized it wasn't the hots for me that caused her to move her lovely lips along my skin, sending a shiver down my spine and a throb of desire everywhere else. As a dhampir, she was part vampire, part human, part goddess. She was savoring my blood for its flavor and its power. She was a predator now, and I was her prey of choice. She flicked out her tongue and lapped away the dribble of my blood.

"Mmm. Good to the last drop," she murmured in a throaty whisper.

Even as I glanced down to see her pull back her lips and reveal her baby fangs, I felt more yearning than terror. She was born to kill me after all, and I swear if it weren't for Mel and Renee, I would let her. As long as she made love to me one last time.

I closed my eyes, relishing the serrated rasp of those fangs across my skin, and nearly swooned. I know, I know. Kick-ass vampires with superpowers like me don't swoon. But you don't know Connie. Her hot breath burned a line from my cheek to my neck.

"Please," I heard myself beg.

"Please what?" Her tongue probed the hollow of my throat, searing my cold, dead flesh.

I bit my tongue to keep myself from murmuring "Kill me." It was tempting, but too many innocent people depended on me for their safety. I couldn't take the easy way out as much as I might want to die in Connie's arms, at the point of her fangs, and be done with it.

"Nothing," I muttered. I took hold of her shoulders and gently pushed her away from me, breaking the suction lock she had on my neck. "Remember our agreement. I help you with the demon killing and you don't eat me."

"You're going to get a nice, bloodred hicky," she teased, ignoring me.

I rubbed at the spot on my neck. It was difficult getting used to the new Connie. Before, she had been a no-nonsense woman. Oh, she had a great sense of humor and could be as playful and fun-loving as anyone, but when it came to matters of life and death—which it came to all the time because she's a cop—she was as serious as a heart attack and always in control. But the way she went about catching demons as a slayer was altogether different from the way she went about catching regular bad guys as a detective.

When she was activated as the Slayer, she'd turned wild, unpredictable, and vicious. Travis Rubio, her father and the only vampire who had faced down slayers and lived to tell the tale, said she would achieve more self-control as she matured. Right now, to her way of thinking, the only good vampire was a dead vampire. She saw those of us who refused to do harm in the same light as those who preyed on humans. I hoped that as time went on, she would develop some discrimination. I longed to be able to reason with her, to convince her to fight at our side against the evil ones. I only hoped I could keep her from killing me for that long.

And I also hoped I could keep my beloved Melaphia, the voodoo queen, from killing Connie to avenge her adoptive father's death. What was done was done. William was the first vampire that Connie had slain, and nothing could bring him back now.

William would have been the first to approve of the strategy of trying to convince Connie to come over to our side. And he would be the first to forgive her. An evil vampire named Damien, with the help of Eleanor and Reedrek, had manipulated the time and place of Connie's official switchover into Slayer mode, and William had been in the wrong place at the wrong time.

As I studied the predatory gleam in Connie's eye and the way she licked the last drop of my blood from her ruby lips, I figured my efforts to keep her from killing me had at best a fifty-fifty chance. She made a little feint toward my neck, and I dodged away.

"You're no fun," she said, thrusting out her bottom lip in that pretty pout that still drove me to distraction. "And you're not much help either. The only demons we've killed are the ones I could have identified myself because they have scales and stuff. I thought you were going to help me sniff out the ones who weren't so obvious, the ones who chose to take over human bodies."

"Oh, yeah, that," I began as if I'd forgotten our deal. "I'll be doing plenty of that. But we have to get rid of the obvious ones first so the humans won't panic." I pointed to the pile of dirt that used to be the monster. "I mean, if this guy had decided to wander into Clary's, sit down at the lunch counter, and order up a plate of humans on the half shell, it would have made the national news, and we can't have that, can we?"

"No, I guess not," Connie agreed reasonably. I

wondered if her fellow cops had noticed the change in her. Maybe she went back to acting normal when she wasn't in the presence of vampires.

"And don't forget that Saint Patrick's Day is in two days. Tourists are already flocking here from all over the country. Humans drunk on green beer and staggering around unfamiliar streets in the dark are going to be easy pickings for the demons. On the other hand, maybe you and the other cops can write off any demon sightings as the ravings of knee-walking drunk tourists. Either way, we've got to work fast."

"Is this fast enough for you?" In a move too quick for me to see, she grabbed the collar of my demin shirt and brought my face close to hers again. "Just make sure you're ready to step up when the time is right. And be fast yourself, or I'll send you back to the underworld so quick your head will spin faster than that monster's did, *loverboy*."

I winced at her sarcastic tone, but I could hardly blame her. When she found out I'd tried to kill her, she didn't take it well. Drinking Connie's blood was the most horrifying thing I'd ever had to do, but I loved her enough to let her go because it meant eternal paradise instead of enduring life as a monster like me. She didn't know my motivation, though, and she never would. She only knew I had wanted her dead, and I let her think that so she would be willing to let me go. Technically, my heart stopped beating the night William made me a vampire on a Civil War battlefield, but it truly died the night Connie stopped loving me.

The police radio on her hip squawked and distracted her enough for me to slip out of her grasp. I don't do cop-speak, but the code the dispatcher announced made Connie frown. "I'm on duty, so I've got to take the call," she said. "We'll pick this up later. Keep your cell phone on or you'll have to deal with me."

"Yes, ma'am." This whole situation might be a lot easier if I wasn't so damned turned on by authoritative women. The closer Connie came to killing me, the hotter I was for her. When she turned to walk away, the sight of her handcuffs jingling against her hip from the back of her belt gave me a thrill all the way down to my toes. Man, oh man.

It was harder to stick with *the Plan* every day that passed, and a major part of it was to keep my hands—not to mention the rest of me—off Connie Jones. Because the Plan was the only thing that might save her, the good vamps, my human family, and my unborn child. It was a good plan. Except for the fact that it depended on elements that I couldn't control as closely as I needed to.

That thought reminded me that I needed to check on the status of Seth Walker, because even though I was the man *with* the Plan, Seth was the key to its success.

Seth was the werewolf I hoped would take Connie and my baby away to safety—and as far from me as he could get them. Every time I thought about that my chest felt like someone was twisting a stake in it. I guess you could say Seth Walker was both my best friend and my worst enemy.